WK 20

Winterscroft

Anita Waller

First published in 2017 by Bloodhound Books

www.bloodhoundbooks.com

PRINT ISBN: 978-1-912175-00-0

**For Dave as we celebrate our Golden wedding anniversary,
7 January 2017.**

I often wished that I had clear,
For life, six hundred pounds a-year,
A handsome house to lodge a friend,
A river at my garden's end.
A terrace walk, and half a rood
Of land, set out to plant a wood.

'Imitation of Horace' (written 1714)

Prologue

Once upon a time there were three sisters, Rose, Violet and Lavender; a fairy-tale beginning was always there for the three girls, but it was never destined to be a fairy-tale ending.

Rose was the eldest of the three girls, born on the 16 March 1959 to doting parents, Flora and Alan Paulson. They adored the tiny girl and thought hard before naming her. Using the mother's name of Flora and the grandmother's name of Iris as an influence, they agreed on Rose and thus unwittingly started their first family tradition. Rose mirrored her name exactly. She had dark brown hair with a typical pale English complexion and huge brown eyes; she was a true beauty who charmed everyone she came into contact with.

And then early in 1962, Flora discovered she was pregnant once more. They were delighted; two children had been their decision when they married, and Flora hoped this child would be the boy she longed for. Their second child was born on 3 November 1962 and it mattered not one iota that it was another girl; they loved her just as much as they loved her big sister, Rose. They named her Violet and she was very much like Rose in appearance with her dark brown hair and big brown eyes.

Rose and Violet shared an idyllic childhood living in Castleton, Derbyshire. They lacked for nothing, they were loved and they loved each other.

However, Christmas 1972 was not a happy time. Flora spent almost the entire Christmas period ill in bed and when she finally dragged herself off to the doctors in mid-January he confirmed she was pregnant. The two girls were delighted, Flora and Alan not so much so.

The pregnancy was difficult; this came as something of a shock to Flora who had happily sailed through her first two. She convinced herself that it was a boy this time and when she went into labour on 6 August 1973 she took a pair of blue bootees into hospital with her.

When she arrived home six days later with the new baby, she swapped them for pink ones. Lavender entered their lives with gusto.

The blonde-haired beautiful whirlwind took no prisoners; everyone adored her and when she fastened her startling blue eyes on anyone they simply did as she demanded.

Rose and Violet both left home at various points to continue their education at university and Lavender was left to keep her parents young and her grandparents, Robert and Iris Paulson, on their toes in their later years.

By 1991, thirty-two-year-old Rose had become a teacher at the small primary school in Castleton. Violet, three years younger, became a translator and lived in Paris.

Lavender, the youngest, was dead.

1

24 September 1991

'Lavender, are you ready?' Rose shouted up the stairs to her younger sister, hoping she could hear and she wouldn't have to go up and get her.

Lavender picked up her bag and cast a swift glance around the bedroom. She loved living with her Mum and Dad in their half of the massive house they shared with Rose, John and the children, but today she was going into Sheffield to stay with her grandparents; a music fest was on the menu at the university and it was easier to stay overnight with them.

Her precise way of viewing life meant she liked to leave her things in order with everything in its place, especially before an extended stay in The Elms, the house her grandparents had always lived in. She checked her appearance in the mirror and picked up a brush to give her long blonde hair a final tidy before putting on the blue baseball cap to complete her outfit. She slipped on her sunglasses, hiding the azure of her eyes, and closed the door behind her.

She'd had to make decisions over the weekend, and now she felt easier in her mind. She walked down the stairs and Rose looked at her with a thoughtful expression on her face.

Lavender was a beautiful girl, her mind acknowledged, and the white jeans and blue shirt showed off her shapely figure. Even the baseball cap atop her head looked right.

'Things any clearer?'

Lavender nodded. 'Yes. I'm going to tell Matt yes, we can get engaged but we will have to wait until I've finished at uni before we think about a wedding. I don't want to lose him, Rose, and wearing his ring is my commitment to him. Don't tell Mum and Dad, though. I don't want them to know until it's official.'

Rose pulled Lavender towards her and gave her a hug. 'I won't, and I'm so pleased you've been sensible. And it's a good excuse for a party! Now come on, Nan and Grandpops are already waiting in the car.'

They walked out of the front door together. Robert Paulson was deep in conversation with John, Rose's husband. Rose went up to them and slipped her arm through her husband's.

'John, leave Grandpops alone. You're like two old washerwomen when you get together.'

Iris was waiting in the front passenger seat and smiled through the open window at her granddaughter. 'They've spent all weekend nattering. You'll be glad to see the back of us.'

Rose laughed. 'Never. Grandpops looks tired, Nan. Make him go see a doctor.'

'I will. He said yesterday he felt a bit uncomfortable but he didn't expand on it, so I don't really know what's wrong. I'll ring the surgery tomorrow. A check-up won't hurt.'

Flora and Alan both leaned into the window to kiss Iris, and she smiled at her only daughter. 'Take care of them,' she said, 'and don't take any lip from young Holly!'

Flora laughed. 'As if. Our granddaughter is one smart, beautiful cookie. Her head's never out of a book long enough to be lippy towards anyone.'

Lavender got into the back seat and took out her book. She pulled a cushion up behind her neck, stretched her long legs out on the seat and covered them with the car blanket; she settled down for the twenty-minute drive into Sheffield.

'Seatbelt,' her grandmother said.

'I can't sit like this with my seatbelt on.'

Iris shook her head in exasperation. 'Are you as argumentative as this with Matt?'

Lavender grinned. 'Que sera sera, Nan, que sera sera. Matt understands me.'

Iris couldn't help but smile. 'That's all I ever hear from you these days, que sera sera. That Doris Day should be banned from making films.'

Lavender grinned. 'I absolutely love her films, she makes me laugh.' She began to sing the words to Que Sera Sera and her Nan threw the small teddy mascot at her.

Robert got into the car still chatting with John, and put his seatbelt on before closing the door. He wound down the window. 'Thank you, Rose, sweetheart. It's been a lovely weekend.' He waved to Holly and Jacob and started the car.

Rose saw him rub his arm and grimace; she mouthed the word *doctor* to her grandmother, who nodded.

The six of them stood and waved as they watched the BMW disappear down the drive and then went back inside, Alan carrying his grandson on his shoulders.

Iris put her window up once the car began to pick up speed on the long stretch of road between Bamford and Hathersage. She reached to switch on the car radio and saw Robert wince, then rub his arm again.

They reached the end of the fast stretch and Robert didn't seem to be slowing down for the village. She glanced at him; he made a strangled sound and his head fell back. The car's speed continued to increase as his foot pressed ever more heavily on the accelerator, and she tried to move the steering wheel to go around the gradual left hand curve. His grip on it was locked and they continued in a straight line until the car smashed into the railway bridge at something over 70 miles per hour.

Robert was dead before they hit the bridge; Iris followed him by thirty seconds. Lavender lived one week.

2

March, 1997

Rose saw Matt Peterson's car turn into the driveway and followed it with her eyes as he pulled up in front of the house. He had become something of a brother to them following Lavender's death; it had hit him just as hard as it had the rest of the family.

He came into the kitchen after walking round to the rear of the house; he knew her so well, she thought with a wry smile. Cinderella Rose, always cooking and cleaning.

He handed her a huge bunch of flowers and she buried her nose in them, inhaling the fragrance.

'Thank you, these are beautiful. I'll pop them in the washing up bowl and find a vase in a bit. Coffee?'

He nodded. 'Yes, I need to talk to you.'

'Sounds serious. Scones and coffee then.'

He sat at the long kitchen table and pulled the newspaper towards him. He looked at it without reading it while Rose busied herself making the drinks and buttering scones. He didn't know what he was reading; he felt strangely nervous.

Rose looked at his face, still unchanged from the person Lavender had loved. His deep green eyes seemed cloudy today; he had worries she could tell, but Lavender had chosen well. With his regular features and dark brown hair that tended to flop forwards on to his forehead, he was a handsome young man. They would have made a spectacular couple.

She sat down and picked up her own mug. 'Okay, talk. Something wrong?'

'No, not at all. Everything's right.'

She waited.

'We're getting married, Beth and I.'

She laughed. 'Well I didn't think you were going to say anybody else, and I'm delighted. You know how fond we are of her, and it's time you asked her.'

'But...'

'Matt, Lavender's been gone over five years. I know how much you loved her, but you've moved on. We've all had to move on. We don't love her any less, never will, and I don't suppose you'll ever stop loving her, but it's a different kind of love now. Although you don't need it, you have our blessing. So, when?'

'We're going down to see Tony March today to book the church, we're hoping about four months if we can book everywhere by then. We don't want anything big; maximum about sixty people.'

'So, July possibly August? Can we help? We can have a marquee on the back lawn here if you want. Get caterers in.'

'Really? I'll tell Beth. We were thinking of one of the local hotels but that would be so much more romantic. You're a star, Rose.' He picked up a scone and took a bite. 'And these are delicious.'

'I'll pack you some up to take back with you. Where will you live?'

'There's a cottage cropped up in Castleton. Needs a lot of work. Remember old Mr. Leary who died a few weeks ago? His place. We've put in an offer so fingers crossed we'll get that. It bothered me a bit that we were leaving Mum on her own but she says she's absolutely fine with it.'

'And she will be. You're not leaving her on her own anyway, she has Tim. He's what now? Thirteen? I know he's a bit older than Holly.'

'Yeah, he's an okay kid as well, as brothers go. I think Dad dying made him grow up. You're right, I'm worrying for nothing, and thanks for being cool about this, Rose. It means a lot to me.'

'Well,' she pushed the plate of scones towards him, 'when you've decided marquee or no marquee, just let us know so John can get the garden looking its best.'

He took another scone. 'I will always love Lavender, you know that. But it's more a gentle kind of love now, one that's tucked away in my heart that I just take out occasionally and treasure. And Beth is okay with that. She knows how close we were.'

Rose placed her hand on his and they chatted for a few more minutes. As Matt stood to leave he kissed Rose on the cheek and said he would be back to confirm yea or nay for the marquee and left by the back door. Rose cradled her mug of coffee and felt sad. To lose three family members all at the same time had been hard, but the hardest one to lose had been Lavender.

She stood and reached into a high cupboard for a vase and carried it across to the flowers. She picked the bouquet up and every flower head drooped. Staring at them in horror, she quickly removed the cellophane wrapping and plunged the stems into water. Quarter of an hour earlier they had been in pristine condition; that they were now almost dead was unthinkable. She stood them in the sink and went back to the table to put the remaining scones – two, Matt had taken the rest – into a plastic box. She carried them into the pantry and spent a pleasant quarter of an hour tidying it. Once it was done to her satisfaction, she went back into the kitchen and crossed to the sink.

The flowers were completely withered and dead. She carried them out to John who was working in the garage and held them out to him.

'Think they need throwing out, love.' He laughed. 'I'll pick up some new ones for you when I go into the village. There's nothing much worth picking in the garden yet, bit early.'

'They are new,' she said. 'Matt brought them half an hour ago and they were beautiful. Their fragrance was stunning.'

He looked puzzled. 'There wasn't bleach in the water by accident or something like that, was there?'

She shook her head. 'No, they were almost dead when I put them in water.' She turned to walk away. 'I'll throw them away, but not on the compost heap. I'll put them in the bin.'

He watched as she walked towards the black wheelie bin, a look of concern on his weathered face, but he said nothing. He ran a hand through his hair that wasn't only starting to thin, it was also starting to grey. As a landscape gardener, the flowers had puzzled him. No flowers die that quickly.

That night, all six occupants of the large house shared a meal. They made sure they did this at least once a week; Rose felt that her children should know their grandparents as much as they knew their parents. She brought up the subject of Matt and Beth's wedding as they were enjoying their soup, explaining she had offered the use of the large garden to the rear and side of the house, where a marquee would be erected. The children in particular were excited by this; John and his father-in-law exchanged a glance. They knew what was coming next.

'Of course,' Rose added,' 'the gardens will have to be immaculate, so can I leave it to you two to sort that?'

Both men laughed. 'How did we know that would be said?' John asked. 'How could we possibly have guessed that?'

Rose smiled. 'So tomorrow, then?'

'When's the wedding?' John looked concerned.

'Either July or August. Matt said he would let me know when they'd got it firmly booked.'

'Loads of time then. Thank goodness for that.'

'Four months actually.' Rose laughed. 'Not loads of time. I've been thinking we could maybe lay a patio over by the rose arbour, could have some sort of live music there.'

John looked at Alan. 'Have we time to finish this meal, Alan? Will we ever get another meal? Best enjoy this one, pal, because I don't reckon we'll have much time for eating until the wedding reception.'

Holly reached across the table for a few more carrots. 'Don't worry, Daddy, Jacob will help.'

'Well, thank you, Holly. I'm sure Jacob appreciates you volunteering his services. But don't worry, I think we'll manage. We'll just get extra beer in; this could be thirsty work.'

He raised his glass of wine. 'To Matt and Bethan, and to a wonderful wedding for them.'

They all raised their glasses in acknowledgment and the discussion moved on to the following week's childcare arrangements for the two youngest members of the family. Both children went to the school where Rose was a teacher. It meant she could take them and bring them home with her;

occasionally she had an after-school meeting and that was when Alan and Flora stepped into the breach.

After arranging to collect the children on Wednesday, Flora made a note in her diary; Holly was to be collected at her normal time, but then she had to return to the school to get Jacob, who had after-school football. Rose wouldn't be home until around six o'clock, so Flora also made a note to cook for everybody that night.

Rose stacked the dishwasher and went out of the back door to join John, who was chatting to Alan and pointing out the alterations he was considering making prior to the wedding.

'It's a good job tha't in t'business, lad.' Rose smiled at her Dad's broad Yorkshire accent. Occasionally she heard some of his phrases come out of Jacob's mouth and they always made her laugh. Jacob might have been born in Derbyshire, but his roots were in Yorkshire. The large house in Sheffield where her grandparents had lived had been sold after the car accident, but that was where Alan Paulson had been born and lived until he'd met and married Flora.

With the birth of Rose, Flora and Alan had moved out to a three-bedroomed house in Hope, but when Violet had come along, they'd bought the house, Winterscroft, which they now shared with Rose, John and the children in the Blue John village of Castleton.

When Rose had tentatively suggested buying into two thirds of it, they had welcomed the idea wholeheartedly. It was much too big for the two of them – Violet was in Paris and Lavender was... gone.

It suited all of them. John's landscaping business made full use of the massive garage, and having the grandparents on board meant Rose could remain in the job she loved, teaching. In return, Alan and Flora felt safe; should anything go wrong with them, they had help on hand.

Holly and Jacob just loved living there; the arrangement was perfect for everyone.

As Wednesday came around, Flora opened her diary to check the collection times for the two children. They were an hour apart, so she decided it made sense to bring Holly home, leave her with Granddad, then take the short walk back down half an hour later to collect Jacob, rather than wait around for an hour.

She had a busy day feeding and watering John and Alan as they began to excavate the area for the new patio. They worked well together and she knew that John appreciated the extra reach that Alan offered – anything high up and Alan's 6'2" height was a bonus. She watched them working and talking, Alan's snowy white head bobbing in agreement with something John had just explained. It was hard work for them and she smiled as she remembered their faces when Rose had first suggested the notion. They had both come up with several reasons why it wasn't a good idea, reasons that Rose had clearly dismissed. They should have known better than to argue with a teacher.

Just before three o'clock, Alan came in and said they were finishing for the day. She had warned him that he would have to look after Holly for an hour – no chore in his eyes – and he quickly went upstairs for a shower. She heard John's pick-up start up with its customary growl, and knew he would be setting off to do his rounds of the current jobs his men were processing. He would be a couple of hours doing that and then they could all finally sit down to eat sometime after six.

She walked down the drive and was at the school with a couple of minutes to spare. The children erupted out of the door and she waved as she saw Holly stop and look around for her. Holly's face lit up when she spotted Flora and she ran towards her.

'Are we waiting for Jacob?'

'No, he'll be another hour at least. I'm taking you home to Granddad and coming back down in a bit.'

She gave Holly a hug and they set off for home, with Holly chatting about the Greek gods. Flora knew a lot more about Zeus than she had done previously by the time they arrived back at Winterscroft.

She made a quick cup of tea for both her and Alan, an orange juice for Holly, and watched as granddad and granddaughter went outside to the play area at the side of the kitchen window.

Holly immediately went towards the slide, had a couple of goes on that and then moved across to the swings. She saw Alan head back towards the kitchen and as he came inside she raised her eyebrows in query.

'Just going to finish off that film in the camera. There's only two or three left on it and I want to get it developed. The pictures of Winnats Pass are on it, so I'll take a couple of Holly and then tomorrow I can drop it into the camera shop.'

He picked up the camera and went back outside. Flora finished her drink, checked her watch and put on her coat. Time to get Jacob.

She watched for a minute as she heard Alan giving instructions from behind the camera to a grinning Holly who was by now on the double swing. She sniffed. There was a strange smell in the air and she briefly wondered if it was something chemical, but decided it was more like rotting meat. She set off down the drive and the smell faded.

Jacob was late getting out and it was nearly half past four before she began her second walk of the day back to

Winterscroft. As they started to go up their own drive, Jacob wrinkled his nose.

'Poo! That stinks,' the six-year-old said. 'What is it, Nan?'

'I have no idea. Let's go ask Granddad.'

'Yeah,' he concurred. 'He'll know.' He could count on his granddad knowing everything.

They reached the play area to see Holly inside the kitchen with her face pressed against the window watching Alan. He was just closing the lid of the wheelie bin.

He turned as he heard Jacob shout out to him and he waved Flora towards the kitchen.

She took hold of Jacob's hand and led him inside, gave him a glass of orange, topped up Holly's glass and sat them at the kitchen table with instructions to behave, or else. They grinned at her.

She went back outside to where her husband was still standing over by the bins.

'What's wrong?' she asked.

'Holly complained about the stink. I actually thought it were summat airborne from some business or other and told her there was nowt I could do about it. But then I wandered over here and it were stronger. I looked in here.' He pointed to the black bin.

Flora moved to lift the lid and he stopped her.

'Leave it,' he said sharply. 'Leave it till John gets back, because I dunno what to do about it. It's alive with maggots, cockroaches, earthworms and God knows what else. They're everywhere, and all that's in it as far as I can remember is the bunch of flowers Rose put in. We haven't put anything in it since. The smell once you lift the lid is bloody awful.'

He put his arm around her shoulders and led her back to the kitchen. The children were giggling and trying to hide the fact that they each had a biscuit in their mouths; she shook her head as she looked at them.

'I thought I said behave.'

'We did, Nan,' Holly said solemnly. 'The cat got them for us.'

'We don't have a cat.'

'Oh.' The two children giggled and Flora smiled. She loved these kids to bits; she couldn't tell them off.

She heard John's pick-up coming up the drive and she turned to Alan. He held up a hand.

'You stay with the monsters. I'll go see John.'

He walked across and waited for John to climb out of the truck then took him over to the bin.

The smell was even more overpowering.

'What the...?' John's eyes were beginning to water. It was foul.

'It's the bin. Now, as far as I know, the only thing in it is that bunch of flowers that Rose put in – you know, the bunch that Matt bought her. I opened it briefly and you can't even see them in the bottom. The whole bin's a bloody mass of worms, maggots and all manner of other bugs, John. I thought the two of us could deal with them, cos I'll be honest, I haven't a clue what to do.'

John looked at his father-in-law. 'Bugs?'

'Yep. I'm not normally a queasy chap, but that sight fair turned mi stomach.'

John turned and put his hand on the lid. It was hot. He slowly lifted it and then slammed it shut. It was like a horror movie. The whole interior was moving, a whirling vortex of anything that crawled, all trying to escape the confines of the bin. The smell was cloying, sickly, putrid.

He stepped away and turned to Alan. 'I reckon only fire will kill that lot, but I've no idea how we do it.'

'It'll destroy the bin.'

'That's not the problem. We can get another. How do we get fire in it? As soon as we open that lid they're going to be on the move. And if we put the fire in and slam the lid down it will put out the fire.'

Alan was quiet for a moment and then said, 'What about making a fire and standing the bin on it? If they escape out the bottom as it melts, they'll drop into the fire.'

'Okay. Let's seal this top down with duct tape so that we don't have it bouncing up and down while we're moving it, and we'll build a fire in that boggy bit down the bottom, near the pond. I'll sort it out after; make it look good again by the time of the wedding.'

Alan nodded and headed for the garage to get the duct tape. He began to seal it and left John to go and start the fire. The heat coming from the bin was starting to become pretty intense and as he stuck down the duct tape, the edges of the tape began to curl. It briefly occurred to him that they were forcing their own heat in order to escape, and then he laughed at himself. 'Reading too many Stephen Kings,' he said quietly.

He pulled the bin behind him and headed down to the pond. John had started a fire and they waited until it became really hot before manoeuvring the bin into the middle of it.

They stood and watched.

The bin began to melt at the bottom and then the sides began to bend out of shape. It sank lower and lower, the plastic spreading out and giving off a chemical smell that hurt their throats as they breathed. They had expected to see all the different creatures tumbling out as holes appeared, but that didn't happen. The duct tape curled and came off the sides, leaving it attached only to the lid. John used the hoe he had brought down with him to control the bin on the fire and flicked open the lid, now free of every piece of duct tape.

He jumped back as the lid fell open. There was nothing inside.

He looked at Alan. 'What...?'

Alan shrugged, feeling helpless. 'I don't know, John. We both saw them. There were millions of them.'

John threw the bucket of pond water onto the fire and then went to get another one. Alan remained staring into the flames, now dying down; he had no idea what had happened, but he knew what he had seen. And he knew John had seen it too.

They finished putting out the fire and walked back up to the house, unable to say anything. Neither of them could quite believe what had happened.

'I've got one of the old bins, the metal ones, in the garage. We'll use that until we can organise a new one. I'll go and get it. You go in and tell Flora we've got rid of them.' John turned to go into his garage.

He went to the back and pulled out the bin. He'd used it for various things, at various times, and now it was being returned to its original role in life. He carried it round the side of the building, past the kitchen window, and to the vacated spot left by the burnt bin. It was awkward to carry and he grinned to himself as he remembered the dustbin men of old who had manoeuvred these bins with consummate ease. They were worthy of his admiration, he thought, as he went to stand it in its designated place.

On the ground where the old bin had stood was a sprig of lavender.

3

Alan and Jacob walked down into the village on Saturday morning, the little boy frequently skipping along in front. He knew he was likely to get an ice cream out of this trip, and was eager to get down into the centre of the village.

The real purpose behind the trip was to collect Granddad's photographs from the camera shop. Holly had opted to stay with her dad and help clear away the rubbish left by the fire down near the pond. Her red wellingtons had been dug out of the bottom of a cupboard in the mud room and she had departed with John, intent on getting dirty and wet.

Jacob nodded his head solemnly when his granddad asked if he might like an ice cream, and then grinned. His plans had worked out. They went into the little teashop and ordered a tea for Alan and a dish of strawberry ice cream topped with raspberry sauce for a wide-eyed Jacob.

While Jacob went to work with his spoon, Alan took the photographs out of the bright yellow envelope and began to look through them. The ones he was particularly interested in were pictures he had taken of Winnats Pass, when the snow had covered its steep hillsides. He took a while looking through them, pleased with his amateur results. The area they lived in was noted for its spectacular beauty, but Winnats Pass was in a league of its own.

He smiled as he looked at the ones he had taken of Holly, first on the slide and then the last three on the double swing. He put all of them back into the envelope and finished his tea. The two of them walked back through the village and up to Winterscroft, deciding that when they got home they would each put on their wellies and go help to clear the area down by the pond. With the confirmation from Matt and Beth that the wedding was set for Saturday 30 August, and they would love to take Rose up on her offer of having a marquee in the garden, he knew they had to crack on and get every area ready and immaculate. Rose would accept nothing less!

Alan led Jacob into the mud room kept exclusively for wet clothes and work boots, and the little boy went over to get his wellies. He held them up and asked his granddad if they were his.

'Yes, Jacob. Holly is already wearing hers. She's down there with Daddy.' He shook his head. What on earth had possessed Rose to buy the same red wellies in different sizes for her children? Holly didn't have an issue, but Jacob invariably ended up confused.

Alan picked up a spade and the two of them began to head down the hill towards the pond area. It was starting to improve; it had been a mess after they had finished with the fire, and Rose had been none too impressed.

Holly waved when she saw them and ran up to meet them.

'Come on, Jacob, come and help. Dad says we can have an ice cream later, as soon as we finish.' Jacob took hold of her hand and followed her. A second ice cream of the day sounded good to him.

Alan moved towards John and looked at him enquiringly.

'Nothing, Alan. Absolutely nothing. Yet we both saw and gagged at the awful stink. There should be some evidence of a bin full of bugs, maggots and worms. What the bloody hell happened?'

Alan shook his head. 'No idea. Let's crack on and get it looking a'reight and we can forget about it.' They both picked up their spades and then were distracted by a sound, a tiny whimper.

Alan turned round and saw his grandchildren walking down the slight incline towards them, holding hands, marching in unison. They headed for the centre of the blackened area and then stopped. The air grew still around them and dark storm clouds gathered overhead. The first raindrops began to fall. Slowly Holly and Jacob turned to face each other, linking both hands. The atmosphere was cloying, suffocating and both men tried to cough and couldn't. It was as if they were cocooned in a woollen cloth that was preventing them from breathing. The silence was unreal; they could hear, sense and touch nothing.

Holly and Jacob stood silently for a moment, hands still interlinked, and John wanted to reach out and touch them, move them from where they were; he couldn't. It was as if a spell had been cast over the area, freezing them like statues.

Holly began to speak without moving, her eyes fixed on Jacob.

Curly worms, wiggly worms,
Lying on the grass.
Down comes the rain –

Are you taking a bath?
Children in wellie boots,
Bright shiny red.
Jump on the wiggly worms
Now they are DEAD!

Holly gave a strangled shout and fell. There was a vivid flash of lightning, then another, followed by a massive thunder crack. Jacob began to cry and knelt down by his sister. The cloying, stifling atmosphere vanished and both men immediately rushed towards her. John picked her up, aware of her unconscious state, and carried her away from the soil that was mixed in with black ash; he laid her as gently as he could, given his shaking arms, and held her across his knees and partly on the grass. The rain became torrential and he held his body over her to afford her some protection.

Her breathing was fine and he knew she had only fainted. What he didn't know was what the bloody hell had just happened. He quietly stroked her face, saying her name repeatedly and wiping away the soil that was clinging to her skin. Her eyes fluttered and opened and she stared vacantly around her.

Jacob was sobbing and Alan tried to comfort him and watch what was happening with Holly. He had heard her voice when she'd recited the poem. It wasn't Holly's voice.

Jacob clung to his grandfather, frightened and unsure about what had just happened to his sister. Why had her voice changed? Why had she fallen down?

John helped his daughter to stand, and then gently wiped away the tears that were running down her cheeks.

'Don't cry, sweetheart,' he whispered. 'It's over now.'

'What's over, Daddy?' she sobbed. 'What happened?'

'You fainted. I'm going to help you up to the house and then make you a nice sweet hot drink. You'll soon be okay.'

The four of them began the short walk back up the slope towards the house. John helped Holly as Alan held tightly to Jacob's hand. Alan couldn't resist glancing back at the dark patch of ground where the fire had been; something was very wrong down by the pond.

The rain had lessened a little by the time they reached the house, but Holly was trembling. John took her inside quickly and put a blanket around her. He laid her on the sofa and turned up the heating, while Alan got a large towel and began to dry a miserable-looking Jacob, raindrops dripping off the end of his nose.

Flora arrived with a puzzled expression on her face. She had heard Alan's call to her and sensed its urgency. She looked at her husband and he said 'Holly fainted.' She went immediately to her granddaughter and held her tightly, misguidedly drawing conclusions for the cause of the episode.

'Hush, Holly,' she said and placed a kiss on her forehead. 'It's all part of growing up. Things like this can happen to girls of your age, as you start to become a woman. Don't worry about it, it's all perfectly natural.'

John and Alan stared at each other; what they had seen down by the pond had nothing to do with puberty.

Unless puberty involved voice transfer from a dead Lavender to an alive Holly. And where the hell had the poem come from?

They went to the kitchen to make drinks and didn't know what to say. They didn't want to acknowledge what they had seen and heard, not yet.

But acknowledgement or not, the voice that had come eerily out of Holly's mouth had been Lavender's voice. Both men knew it, neither wanted to know it.

4

Rose returned from her trip to Sheffield to be told that Holly was asleep in bed; Jacob was very subdued and uncommunicative, John was pacing in and out of the downstairs rooms and her parents were closeted in their part of the large house.

When she had left that morning, everyone had known what they were doing and happily getting on with it. She stroked Jacob's head and planted a kiss on it then looked towards her husband.

'You're sure Holly's asleep?'

He nodded. 'I'm sure. She was exhausted. I've been up several times to check on her and she's out for the count, clutching on to Maximus, or whatever he's called. Rose, I need to talk to you but we need to be on our own.' He dipped his head slightly towards Jacob, and Rose acknowledged the action. She understood what he was saying.

She went up to check on her daughter and she was still asleep. Maximus the bear was slowly having the life suffocated out of him; her grip on him was relentless. Rose leaned over and kissed her; her skin felt cool, despite being under the duvet and a quilt.

She quietly left the room, convinced for the moment that they didn't need to trouble a doctor. She would see what the situation was when Holly eventually woke.

She went back downstairs and John and Jacob both turned towards her.

'She's fine. We'll see when she wakes up, but for now we don't need to worry. But later, John, I want to know what happened. This clearly isn't normal. Is Dad okay?'

'He's fine. He saw to Jacob getting back to the house because the rain was torrential, and the thunder and lightning was a bit scary for our little man. We were all wet through, so I changed Jacob, and Holly asked if she could go to bed and have a little nap. I went up ten minutes later and she'd taken off her wet clothes, put on her pjs and was fast asleep.' He moved towards his wife and held her close. 'We're all okay, Rose, we're all okay.'

She nodded. 'Okay. Till later then.'

Rose went into the kitchen and began to sort through the various packages she had acquired while in Sheffield's bustling city centre. She needed to hang the suit she had found for the wedding, as she didn't want it getting creased. She carried everything upstairs and began to put it all away. She had just put the box containing the very smart black patent shoes into her shoe cupboard when she heard a small cry coming from Holly's room.

She moved quickly down the corridor and opened the door. Holly was sitting up in bed, tears streaming down her face.

'Mummy,' she sobbed. 'A dream...'

'Hush, sweetheart,' Rose said, and pulled her daughter close. 'Dreams aren't real, you know. You'll have forgotten it by tomorrow. Just hold onto me and it will all go away.

You want to go back downstairs now? We'll be eating soon. I think Nan's doing our meal tonight.'

Holly nodded, took a huge shuddering breath and stopped crying. 'It was awful. Somebody was chasing me, trying to get in me.'

'In you?' Rose smiled. 'That wouldn't be easy, would it? Come on, let's go get you some milk, that will help calm you down.'

She helped Holly put on her dressing gown and they went to the door. Holly ran back to the bed. 'Come on, Maximus, come with me.'

She carried the bear downstairs with her and held him all night.

***

Finally, they could talk. The children were in bed and Flora and Alan had gone back to their own wing.

Rose turned to John and said, 'Talk. Tell me what happened.'

He shook his head. 'Okay, I'll tell you, but you're going to think it's crazy, I know you are.'

He began at the beginning, telling her how originally it was just the two of them, and then Alan and Jacob joined them when they got back from the village.

He paused as he remembered the sudden change in the weather. 'It was sunny all the time Holly and I were working,' he said, 'and then just as your Dad reached us it became cold and the sky went really dark. Holly walked away from me and towards Jacob and then I kind of lost track because Alan and I started to discuss what to do next. I was aware the kids were walking up the incline holding hands and I was starting to think maybe we should be heading back to the house because of the sudden change in the weather.' Again, he paused, trying to gather his thoughts into a coherent report.

'They turned around and everything went still. Silent as the grave. The kids started to walk back down towards us holding hands, but it was like... oh, I don't know what it was like, it was so damn spooky. They seemed to be keeping time as they walked and finally they stopped right in the middle of where we had that damn bonfire. By this time, neither Alan nor I could move. The atmosphere was awful. It was silent. I couldn't hear anything and I'm sure Alan was the same.'

He paused for a moment.

'Neither of us even blinked. We watched those two little kids turn to face each other; they linked both hands and then Holly began to recite a poem. I can't remember all of it but it was something about curly worms and wiggly worms and she ended it with children in red wellie boots jumping on the wiggly worms and now they were dead.'

Rose drew in a sharp breath. 'Worms? But...'

He nodded. 'I know. That bin was full almost to the brim with all manner of worms and maggots and bugs, but the only ones who knew about it were Flora and Alan, and the two of us. The children just thought we'd set the bin on fire accidentally. They knew nothing of the worms. Anyway, after this poem or whatever it was, there were two massive bolts of lightning followed by the most horrendous crash of thunder. Holly screamed and fainted, right there in the middle of the bonfire. I picked her up and carried her to the grass but that rain was ferocious. I tried to shield her with my body till she came round, because I didn't think I could carry her as a dead weight. She wasn't out for long but she was confused when she opened her eyes. We managed to get back here soaked to the skin. We called for Flora and she assumed that the issues with Holly were down to puberty, but they're not, Rose, they're not.'

Rose smiled. 'They could be, you know. That would account for the faint...'

John held up his hand. 'You're wrong. Puberty wouldn't account for the fact that the voice coming out of our eleven-year-old daughter belonged to Lavender. Lavender recited that poem, Rose, not Holly.'

For the first time in her life Rose was speechless. What the hell was John talking about? Lavender had been dead nearly six years.

'But...'

'Ask your Dad, Rose. Ask Alan.' John sounded weary. 'I knew you wouldn't be able to accept just my word, so ask your Dad. He'll tell you exactly the same. He said he was going to tell Flora tonight, so maybe tomorrow we can—'

There was a knock on their lounge door and it opened slightly.

'Can we come in?' Flora asked, her voice shaking.

'Of course,' Rose said. 'What's wrong, Mum?'

'We have something to show you.' She was clearly upset and Alan's arm was around her shoulders, supporting her.

'Come on, lass,' he said. Sit thysen down.' In that moment, his gruff Yorkshire accent enfolded them and warmed them. Rose felt comforted; and yet uneasy. Obviously, Alan had told his wife exactly what she had just had to hear; she was clearly distraught.

'Mum?' Rose reached across and touched her mother's hands. 'Can I get you anything?'

'Four brandies, Rose. We need brandy. All of us.'

Rose hesitated, and then went across to the drinks cabinet. She poured out the drinks and carried them back to the coffee table.

Alan laid a yellow photograph envelope on the table and tapped it.

'We have something to show you.'

He removed the photographs from the folder and placed them on the table. 'I finished this film off the night we burnt the bin. There were only three or four left to take, so while Flora was down at school collecting Jacob, I finished the film off with some action shots of Holly; one on the slide and two on the double swing. I got them back this morning. I was keen to see the pictures I'd taken of Winnats when we had that snow so didn't really take much notice of any of the other shots until tonight.'

He separated the three he had taken of Holly from the others and held them out to John. Rose moved closer and looked at them at the same time. John flipped through them and looked at his father-in-law with a puzzled expression on his face. Rose took the pictures from him.

He heard her say, 'Oh, my God,' and watched her hands start to shake. She was looking at the last two pictures, taken on the double swing. The first one showed Holly high in the air, but the second one showed her with the seat of the swing against her back, leaning on the chains as she prepared to jump up and allow the seat to move underneath her.

The other set of chains and the seat were in an identical position, but nobody was there holding them in place.

All four of them reached for their brandies at the same time.

5

They didn't sleep much, and just after three o'clock John got up and made tea for both of them. When he returned to the bedroom, Rose was sitting up in bed, her legs bent at the knees and her arms hugging them.

'What do we do?'

'I don't know.' He handed her a cup and she took a sip.

'It's hot,' she said, almost absent-mindedly.

'Could it be because it's made with boiling water?' He smiled at his wife, trying to ease the tension in her.

'I'm sorry,' she said, and squeezed his hand. 'I'm scared. I know it can't possibly be Lavender, she's been gone six years in September, but something's going on. What if I go and talk to Tony? Would he think I was crackers?'

'Probably, but as a vicar he'll have come across this sort of stuff before. He'll perhaps come and bless the house or something.'

She nodded and sipped at her tea. 'I can show him that photo and tell him about the other stuff with the fire; see what he thinks. I'm scared for the kids, John. They're the ones being targeted, not us.'

He shook his head. 'Actually, *they're* not. It's Holly, not Jacob. He just followed on from what his sister told him to do, he didn't pass out at the end, he wasn't on that swing and in fact, he was still in school playing football when that picture was taken. It's Holly she's targeting.'

There was a small whimper from Rose. 'So, you do think it's real? You do think Lavender is here?' and she waved her arm around the room.

'I think we need help,' was all he would admit. 'At the moment, I don't know what to think. Why now? That's the part I don't understand. Why now? What changed that would have created this? Holly approaching puberty? Does that make her vulnerable?'

Rose continued to sip at her tea, her mind whirling. 'Something else has changed. Matt is getting married. Although it wasn't public knowledge when she died, they were engaged to be married. It would have been official within a couple of weeks and she loved him to pieces, John. That's what's changed, and we're helping them with the wedding.'

'She's punishing us.' His tone was flat. 'She's fuckin' punishing us.'

Rose nodded. 'I'll have a word with Tony after the service this morning and tell him I need to see him this afternoon. I'll make sure he understands the urgency. After the service, I want you to take the children home. I'm going into the village; I need to get a couple of things.' She felt grateful in that moment for living in a tourist-led village – all the shops, without exception, opened on a Sunday; their biggest takings day of the week.

She put down her cup and slid back down the bed.

'Hold me,' she said, and John obliged.

***

The church service seemed interminable. After the final blessing, Rose ushered John and the children out as fast as she could. Alan and Flora followed quickly.

Tony March smiled at them as they approached. He liked most of his parishioners, but this family had suffered so much and yet had never lost their faith.

'Are you going for a coffee?' he asked, taking in Rose's worried expression.

'Not today, Tony,' she answered. 'I have things to do, but I would like to see you this afternoon if that's possible. It's urgent.'

And he knew it was.

'Is two o'clock any good?'

'Thank you.'

He could see tears in her eyes and briefly touched her hand. She put her arms around Holly and Jacob and the six of them left the church together.

John, Alan and Flora took the children and Rose headed off towards the village. She had shopping to do, and she needed to do it before her appointment with Tony March.

The first shop was one specialising in Blue John giftware, and as she went through the door the owner lifted a hand in acknowledgment.

'Hi, Rose. You looking for something?'

She nodded. 'I am, Pete. I want a child's crucifix with a 14″ chain. It's a gift for Holly.'

He led her over to the back counter and took out a tiny cross. It was made of silver, but inlaid with Blue John. It was exquisite.

'Oh, that's beautiful, Pete.'

She looked at the price and then asked if he had the chain. 'I want a strong one, so don't get me something flimsy. I don't want this being lost because the chain has broken.'

He showed her three chains and she chose one, paid for everything and left. As she walked past the window she saw a small freestanding crucifix, again in Blue John, and she wheeled around to go back into the shop.

After Pete had wrapped the second purchase he watched her leave the shop, a worried expression on his face. There was something not quite right about Rose, he sensed, and hoped it was nothing too serious.

He watched her cross the road and go into the bookshop, then saw her coming out five minutes later, a carrier bag clutched in her hand. She disappeared from his sight as she began the walk back up the village to Winterscroft, and he shrugged his shoulders. Whatever Rose's worries were, she would deal with them; she was strong, was Rose Broadbent.

***

Rose fed everyone but ate nothing herself. She felt sick. She didn't really know how to explain everything to Tony, and she had no idea what his reaction would be.

'I'll do the dishes,' John said as he moved to stand behind her. She was staring out of the window, deep in thought. 'Get yourself off down to see Tony. And stop worrying. He'll know what to do.'

She turned to him and smiled in acknowledgement, but her eyes were shining with unshed tears.

The sky had become overcast so she put on her coat, picked up her large handbag with the items she had bought earlier, and stepped out of the door. She shivered; it had really gone quite chilly.

Ten minutes later, she knocked on the vicarage door and Tony opened it immediately. He ushered her in and called out loudly, 'I'm busy.' There were several answering shouts from around the large house of, 'Okay', and Rose smiled. Tony and Elizabeth had instilled in their children that when Daddy was busy, he was busy, and not to be disturbed unless the house was on fire. They seemed to have a good system implemented.

'Come into the study, Rose,' he said, and opened the thick oak door.

'Sofa?' he said, 'or do we need the desk?'

'Sofa,' she said firmly. 'We don't need to write anything.'

The sofa was all-enveloping and she sank into one end of it, placing her handbag by her side. Tony sat by her and waited.

She began at the beginning, telling him of the wheelie bin contents and all the subsequent actions. She spoke of their theory around the upcoming wedding and then opened her bag. Taking out the photographs, she showed them to Tony. He looked at them for a short while, then handed them back. He still hadn't spoken, but she knew he had seen what they had all seen. Then she handed him the other items from the cavernous interior of the bag.

'I've been out and specially bought these,' she said. 'I need to protect Holly.'

She showed him the cross and chain, the crucifix and the small Bible she had bought from the bookshop.

'I bought her a small Bible,' she explained, 'so that it can go into her schoolbag at all times. The cross can be around her neck, hidden under her school shirt. I take her for PE and swimming so we can take it off for those times, but I can make sure she puts it straight back on. The crucifix is to stand by her bed.'

He stood and moved to the back of the room. He placed the stole around his shoulders and walked back to her.

'Of course I'll bless these items, Rose. I also need to come up to Winterscroft. Don't be afraid; spirits do become unsettled and Lavender's death was sudden and severe. I'll be there tomorrow when you get home from school. Can you persuade Alan and Flora to take Holly and Jacob out for an hour or so? I wouldn't want them to be frightened. Don't get me wrong, this isn't an exorcism. That would require the permission of my diocesan Bishop. This will be a blessing of your home, hopefully turning it into the refuge it always was and releasing Lavender to the peace she needs. With Jesus' help that will solve everything and we won't need to take it any further. Is that okay with you?'

She nodded. 'I'll speak with them when I get back home. I'm already feeling better about things.'

'Then tonight I'll prepare myself. I need to be mentally ready for it, as it's not something the church undertakes lightly, but occasionally we have to do it. Now come with me into the church. I need to place these on the altar.'

She followed him outside and through into the church, allowing the peace of the building to invade her thoughts.

He placed the Bible, the tiny cross and the crucifix on the altar, opened his book and blessed them. There was peace in the room and Rose felt at ease for the first time in a few days. It was the phrase *Kindly let the grace of your Holy Mysteries descend on all who are to use them* that appeared to trigger a cracking sound. Rose tried to ignore it and Tony continued with the blessing without acknowledging that anything had happened.

He wrapped all three items in his stole and handed them to Rose. 'Keep them in this until you get home; give it back to me tomorrow.'

She nodded and slipped the parcel back into her bag. 'Thank you, Tony. I feel so much better already and I appreciate you doing this for us.' She turned around and in that instant heard a second crack followed by the smashing sound of glass. They looked at each other and headed for the tiny office off the main body of the church. The office window had exploded and glass covered the tarmac outside the window.

'But...'

'I know,' Tony said. 'It's gone from the inside to the outside, so nobody has thrown a brick or any other missile. I know. I'll clean it up and get it sorted later. Let's go back to the house.'

They entered the vicarage and Tony once more called, 'Busy' before entering his study. She sat on the sofa, now more troubled than ever, and it showed on her face.

He took her hand and said a small prayer of comfort with her, then stood. 'Coffee?'

'Please. And please tell the children you're not busy now.'

'Not likely,' he said with a laugh. 'This is the only bit of peace and quiet I get.'

He poured them coffees from the ever-present percolator and they sat and talked quietly about the wedding. Beth and Matt had both been in church that morning, but had left just as quickly as Rose's family. They had gone straight to their new home, the cottage that needed so much doing to it, to carry on stripping wallpaper.

'I understand the reception is to be in a marquee at Winterscroft,' Tony said.

Rose laughed. 'You've been talking to John and Alan, haven't you? I've got them completely redesigning the back garden especially for it. They've moaned the whole time, but secretly I think they're enjoying it. It's looking good and all the roses will be in full bloom for the wedding itself. We just need sunshine. I can't organise that.'

She finished her coffee and stood. 'Thank you, Tony. You've been such a help. And leave that window, I'll send John and Alan down. If they haven't got glass big enough, they'll certainly be able to board it up until we can get glass tomorrow.'

'You're sure?' Rose nodded in reply.

'They'll be here in half an hour or so. Just make sure the children don't go near the path. What do you think caused it to shatter?'

'I've no idea. Perhaps John can shed some light on it.'

She walked across to the car and sat for a moment before starting it. The crash from the window had startled her, and she had no idea what had caused it. She drove slowly home, her mind on the blessing of the house. Lavender needed to be at rest.

John and Alan went down to the church armed with everything they might need and returned two hours later. The glass hadn't been big enough, so they'd cleared up all the shards and boarded it up.

That night, Holly came downstairs after her bath and kissed her mother.

'I'm going to bed now, Mum. I've got a book...'

Rose laughed. 'You've always got a book. Anyway, I'll come up in five minutes. I need a little chat.'

'Okay.' Mother and daughter shared a smile and Holly went to bed. When Rose walked into her room, she was immersed in Black Beauty and looked up in surprise.

'Oh,' she said. 'You made me jump. I'd forgotten you were coming.'

'I've got something for you, but you need to listen to me very carefully. This is for you to wear, always.' She handed Holly the tiny cross and chain. 'And I mean always, Holly. And if you feel that there's something happening around you that you don't understand, you take hold of it. You can take it off at school for PE and suchlike, but I'll keep it for you and put it back around your neck straight after the lesson. This is important, Holly. Are you taking it in?'

Holly's eyes were wide. She nodded and didn't speak. Rose leaned across and fastened the pretty silver necklet around her daughter's neck.

'And this,' she added, 'is to stand on your bedside table. Again, it's there to be held if you feel uncomfortable about anything. I've also bought you a small Bible. Tony March has blessed them all. The Bible will be in your school bag all the time. Don't take it out and leave it at home. Do you understand?'

'Not really,' Holly whispered, 'but I don't need to, do I?'

'Just follow what I say, Holly, that's all you need, really. Now, I'll leave you to carry on reading. Call if you need me at any time...'

'Love you, Mum.'

'And I love you too, sweetheart. Night, God bless.'

Rose smiled as she thought about the increasing use of Mum instead of Mummy. Up to about six months ago, it had always been Mummy but now things were changing, Holly was changing. She was turning into a very mature young lady.

John was sitting catching up on the Sunday newspaper. He lifted his eyes to his wife.

'Well?'

'Well, I've done what I can. Tony is coming tomorrow to bless the house. He didn't seem to think it was anything unusual, so I'm assuming he's had to do this sort of thing before. He said Lavender needs peace, needs rest, and it's probably because her death was so brutal and sudden. He's blessed the other stuff and Holly's now wearing the cross and chain. The crucifix is by her bed and this,' she waved the Bible in the air, 'is going in her school bag.'

He folded the paper and stood.

'Come and sit down. You look exhausted. Brandy?'

'Yes, please. Just a small one. What did you think about that window? What caused it?'

'No idea.' He handed her the brandy glass. 'Whatever it was cracked it from inside the office, but there was no sign of anything. Must have just been a tiny crack that chose that moment to become a bigger crack. I'm going down tomorrow to fix it properly.'

She took a sip of the drink and laid her head back.

'Is it nearly time for bed? Jacob's out for the count and Holly will be soon. I'm so tired...'

He laughed. 'Go and have a bath and get into bed. I'll bring you up a hot chocolate.'

She put the brandy glass down and stood. 'You're right. Give me half an hour before my hot choc.'

He watched her leave the room, picked up the glass and finished off her drink. Such a big drinker, his wife. Preferred hot chocolate to a Connoisseur brandy.

***

Tony felt unsettled. Rose's visit in the afternoon had been about an unexpected subject; she was clearly troubled and needed his counsel. He had the feeling he hadn't done enough, but he actually didn't know in what way he could have done more.

Should he have gone back up to Winterscroft with her? He knew he needed to prepare himself; he needed to soothe his own soul, pray, and speak to God before going up there to bless their home.

He had stayed in the church after John and Alan had finished hammering and banging at the window. All three of them hadn't been able to work out how it had happened, and it had been left with Alan to get the glass and fix it Monday morning. And so, Tony had allowed himself half an hour of peace and meditation in the church; he gave himself time to reflect on what his actions would need to be up at Winterscroft.

He checked his watch and saw it was just after six o'clock and Elizabeth would be starting to get the children ready for bed. They always ate after their brood had been despatched for the night; he enjoyed their 'couple' time.

He locked up the church but instead of turning right towards the vicarage, he walked down through the graveyard towards Lavender's grave. The family had bought the plot beneath a large oak tree and he had never seen the grave without flowers on it. He stood looking at the wording on the headstone and once again was hit by how young she had been.

In loving memory of
Lavender Paulson
6 August 1973 – 30 September 1991
A dearly loved daughter, granddaughter
and sister taken far too soon.
'The light in our world now dimmed'

His eyes couldn't leave the words; he felt transfixed by them. He saw the words Lavender Paulson and they began to shimmer. He saw other words begin to form in red – blood red. Underneath Lavender Paulson it said;

is back

He felt the pain in his chest, felt it go down his arm and then there was nothing more. He collapsed face down across the grave; his left arm came to rest on the words *is back.*

***

Elizabeth March found him an hour later. An ambulance was called but she knew it was too late. She didn't know why he had been at Lavender's grave, but it gave her a modicum of comfort to know that they knew the family well.

She had left eleven-year-old Thomas in charge at the vicarage while she went to look for Tony, and he had looked shocked at her crashing through the front door and ringing for an ambulance to go to the graveyard. She had said nothing then, other than to ask him to be a big boy and listen out for the little ones, but now she had to go back there and tell him his father was dead.

It was only later, when she was looking through Tony's diary, tears dropping onto the pages, that she saw his appointment at Winterscroft for the following day. She picked up the phone to call Rose, but it was John who answered.

She explained what had happened and heard the quick intake of breath from him.

'Tony's dead?'

'Yes, and please don't tell Rose, but his body was on Lavender's grave. I don't want her upset by the circumstances. Was the appointment for tomorrow anything urgent? I can point you...'

'No, no, Elizabeth. Leave it. You've enough on your plate. It was just wedding stuff,' he lied. 'Can we do anything to help?'

'No, thank you, John. I've had to tell Thomas tonight, but I've got to find some way of telling the three little ones tomorrow. When people start to ask, and I'm sure they will, I'll just say I found him outside the church. Is that okay? Do you know why he would have been at Lavender's grave?'

'I don't know. Was there any vandalism, graffiti?'

'No, it was as pristine as always. You all keep it beautifully clean.'

'Then I don't know. What do you want me to do about the window tomorrow? Shall I leave it until...?' He hesitated.

'No, if you've time, please do it, John. It will be one less thing for me to worry about.' She began to cry and he heard the receiver being replaced. What she hadn't been able to bring herself to tell John was that when she had found Tony, he had been clutching a sprig of lavender in his right hand, the fingers of his left hand splayed out across her name.

***

He didn't tell Rose until the following morning. She had been fast asleep when he walked into the bedroom, so he'd gone and checked on Jacob and Holly before going to bed himself.

He found it difficult to sleep; his mind was on Tony March. He felt he knew why Tony had been at Lavender's grave. He went because he needed to go.

6

John and Alan were at the church early, repairing the window. Elizabeth looked haggard. Her parents were there, sorting out taking the four children back to their home for a few days; Elizabeth's sister, Caroline, had arrived to stay with her, to help her through the difficult days ahead.

When they had finished, they walked round to the vicarage to tell her they were going and it was all secure. John handed her the key to the church and she stared at it, as if seeing it for the first time. She'd had to search for this key; it was the spare. The one used every day must still be with her husband. She began to cry and John pulled her to him. He had no words. Alan walked away, unable to deal with this outpouring; the whole village would feel the same. Tony had been a much-loved vicar of Castleton for the last ten years or so.

They left Elizabeth with Caroline, after declining a drink. Without conscious discussion, they both walked down to Lavender's grave. Adam Morton, a local police constable more used to directing tourists around the village, was standing by the side of the grave. John had privately wondered if it would be taped off as the death was unexpected, but he hoped it wouldn't be. It wasn't, and he breathed a sigh of relief.

John nodded towards the policeman. 'Adam.'

'Sorry, John, I just wanted a couple of minutes...'

'Don't let us push you away, Adam. We've been up at the vicarage sorting out a broken window and just popped down because we were here. We'll leave you in peace.' They turned and started to walk back up the graveyard towards where they had parked John's truck when they heard Adam speak.

'It seems strange. Why would he die? He was still young. And why here on your Lavender's grave? I had a lot of time for Tony March and I feel sick that he's gone. I just can't help feeling there's more to it than just a heart attack.'

They stopped and turned around.

'Was that what he died from? A heart attack?' Alan asked.

Adam shrugged. 'Seems so. But why? I've known him years. We're mates and I know for a fact he didn't have heart problems.' He shook his head and walked up to join the two men. They separated at the top of the graveyard, Adam going to the vicarage and John and Alan towards their vehicle.

There was only Flora left back at Winterscroft and she came out to meet them as soon as she heard the truck pull up on the gravel.

'Well?'

'All mended. Elizabeth is a wreck as you can imagine.' Alan shook his head. 'What a bloody mess. What the 'ell is goin' on?'

'Come on,' she said. 'Coffee's on. Come and have a drink. We've things to discuss.'

They followed her into the kitchen and she poured out three coffees. She handed them to the two men and then clasped her own against her chest.

'Tell me what's going on,' she said.

John and Alan looked at each other. Worried frowns had replaced any smiles.

'We don't know. Tony, it seems, died from a heart attack, although they'll maybe know more after the post mortem. We bumped into Adam Morton and he was just as puzzled as everybody else. He said Tony had no heart issues, so... I don't know.'

'And did he really die on Lavender's grave?' Her voice was quiet.

John nodded. 'Yes, he did.'

'But why? Why was he there?' There was anguish in Flora's tone.

'I don't know. Rose went to see him yesterday and told him about what's been happening here. She showed him the swing photograph. He took it very seriously and was supposed to be coming up here this evening to bless the house, give peace to Lavender, he said. Apparently, something like this isn't so rare, especially when it's been a brutal and early death.'

Flora choked back a sob.

'So, what happens now?'

'I have no idea. We carry on as we were, on our own, I suppose. Lavender wouldn't hurt us. She was a sweet, gentle girl; wouldn't hurt a fly. Let's put things on a back burner, help Elizabeth through the immediate problems as best we can, and then approach someone for help.'

They finished their drinks and then went outside. The area down by the pond was looking no better and they both knew it had to be tackled. They filled the wheelbarrow with assorted tools and walked down the slight incline together, neither one speaking.

John stood and surveyed the area where the fire had burnt so fiercely. They had already cleared all the burnt plastic from the bin and what was left was burnt soil and a large bare expanse that needed re-seeding.

'Alan, can you start to rake it? Get it as level as you can, and I'll take the wheelbarrow back up and get a couple of bags of topsoil out of the garage and some lawn seed. In another month, the patch will be back to how it was.'

Alan nodded and picked up the rake; John began the trek back up to the garage. He lifted the first bag onto the barrow and turned to pick up a second one. He balanced it carefully and then bent down to get a third one. As he lifted it he saw the sprig of lavender in pristine condition, despite having been under three heavy bags of topsoil. Then he smelt her.

Lavender. The air was becoming increasingly thick with its perfume, and he wheeled around, looking for her.

Nothing. Just the cloying fragrance. He moved towards the door. He needed air. John gasped as he reached the outside and leaned against the wall of the house. He had no idea what the fuck was going on, and he had even less idea how to stop it.

He felt his heart slow to a more normal rate, and he waited a couple of minutes before venturing back inside. The fragrance was still there, but very much less than it had been. He crossed to the wheelbarrow, straightened the third bag that he had just dumped on top, and wheeled it backwards out of the garage. Glad to be out in the fresh air, he walked over to his truck and picked up the lawn seed that was always carried in it and headed back down the hill towards Alan.

He was leaning on the rake, the area now level and waiting for the topsoil.

'All done,' he said. 'Will three bags be enough?' He eyed the wheelbarrow.

'Yes,' John replied. He needed time before venturing back into the garage. Three bags would have to be enough.

Alan moved to get the first bag. He sniffed. 'Bit heavy on the aftershave today, John,' he said with a grin.

He saw John's face. 'What's wrong?' Alan sniffed again. 'It's not aftershave, is it? It's—'

'Lavender.'

John sat down on the grass with a thud. 'God, Alan, I don't know what we're going to do.'

He explained what had happened in the garage and Alan listened quietly.

'Okay, t'first thing we're going to do is get this topsoil on, get t'area seeded and forget about it. That's first thing off us minds. Then we're going to be Christians.'

'We are Christians.'

'And we can pray. We'll take that little crucifix from Holly's room cos it's been blessed by Tony and we'll go in that garage and pray. God'll help us get through this. He's helped us get through worse.'

John stood and lifted the first bag from the wheelbarrow. He slashed it open and poured out the soil, then did the same with the remaining two bags. Alan raked and John began to sprinkle the lawn seed. Quarter of an hour later it was done and they stood back and looked at their work.

'That'll be grand,' Alan said. 'It'll look fine by the wedding. Come on, let's pack up and take these back up to t'garage.'

They filled the barrow with the tools and John pushed it back up the gentle incline. He wheeled it round the back of the garage and into the large lawned area at the back of the house where the marquee was to go.

'Let's go and wash,' Alan said quietly,' and get that crucifix, then I'm going to tell Flora. With her leading the church prayer group, 'appen she'll 'ave the right words.'

John nodded. 'I need to shower. I can still smell that damn stink.'

They all met in the kitchen of the Paulson wing and Flora handed them both a drink. 'Have this,' she said, 'and we'll go in the garage when we're all calm.'

John held out the small crucifix. 'Tony blessed this,' he said quietly.

She nodded. 'I know. And if we concentrate on that, maybe the three of us combined can help her find rest.'

They finished their drinks and moved into the garage, eager to do whatever needed to be done before the children arrived home from school.

Flora pulled a box towards her and placed a pristine white cloth on it. She then lit a candle and placed that on the cloth along with the crucifix and her Bible.

The three of them surrounded the makeshift altar and Flora began to speak.

'Father God, we ask that you surround this place with your angels and touch each of us with your love. Let Lavender rest now in the peace of your understanding and compassion. Give her the strength to leave us and to accept her life with us is over until we meet with her again in your heavenly place.'

She paused for a moment as the candle began to flicker. There was an eerie silence, a feeling of a cloudlike atmosphere enveloping them and she reached forward and picked up the crucifix.

'And, Father, we ask for this release for Lavender, our much-loved daughter, in Jesus' name.'

All three of them said Amen simultaneously and the door behind them opened, then slammed shut with a mighty crash. They jumped and the candle flickered once more and died. Flora looked around and grabbed hold of Alan's hand.

'Don't worry,' he whispered. 'That prayer comforted me whether Lavender has gone or not.'

'So much anger,' she murmured, 'so much anger. Did you feel it?'

'We couldn't help but feel it,' John said. 'But we've done our best in the absence of a vicar to help us.' He moved towards the door and switched on the light. The oppressive atmosphere had lifted, and Flora cleared away the items they had taken in with them. All three of them headed back to the kitchen and Flora poured three brandies.

'Medicinal purposes,' she said drily. 'We need these.'

7

John and Rose spoke later that night about the day's events. She said the children were upset by Tony's death – he had been a very popular visitor at the village school, frequently dropping in to lead assemblies, or to accompany the children on trips. Many of the children attended his Sunday School and she said it had been a very subdued atmosphere all day.

'He'll be sorely missed.' John stared at his hands.

Rose moved to sit next to him. 'What you did today was... brave. I think that's the right word. We don't know what we're dealing with and I'm not altogether convinced that Tony would have done anything more than you did. You could sense her, during the prayer?'

'Oh, yes.' His tone was grim. 'And I'll be honest, Rose; I don't think we've solved anything at all. We're not the ones she's mad at. She's just letting us know she's pissed off with somebody, and that somebody is Matt. Or, heaven forbid, Beth.'

'Maybe after the wedding—'

'Maybe it will get worse,' John said. 'I don't know what to do, Rose.'

'Well, we're five weeks away from the big day. The one person who should be told about this is Matt. Have you said anything to him?'

John shook his head. 'It sounds ridiculous. What can I say?'

'Then I'll tell him. I'll give him a ring tomorrow and ask him to come and check the garden is okay for the marquee area. We can have a chat afterwards.'

He put his arm around his wife and pulled her to him. 'I'm sorry, sweetheart, I feel as if I'm letting you down. Not protecting you in some way.'

She laughed. 'You? Let us down? You'd die first, John Broadbent.'

The door opened slowly, and Holly poked her head around it.

'Mummy,' she said, her voice a little quivery. 'Can you come upstairs a minute?'

Rose looked at John and then stood. 'Of course, sweetheart. Can't sleep?' She closed the door behind her and followed Holly up to her bedroom.

'I'm bleeding,' Holly said quietly. 'I got up to go for a wee, and I'm bleeding.'

'Okay,' Rose said quietly. 'Can you remember everything I told you about what's happening to you? Have you put on a pad?'

'Not yet, I went straight downstairs to tell you.'

'Then the first thing we need to do is put on that pad. Have you got tummy ache? Do you need a tablet?'

'It hurts a bit,' Holly said, 'but not enough to make me have a tablet.' She went to her bedside drawer and opened the new pack of pads that had been there for six months. She took one out and moved past her mother to head for the bathroom.

'You'll be okay?' Rose asked. Holly nodded and left the room.

She sat on the bed and waited for her daughter to return, her eyes resting on the crucifix on the bedside table. She moved it a little closer to the bed and shivered.

She had been sensing a link between whatever the entity was and the impending menses of her daughter. It had been obvious for some time that it wouldn't be long before Holly's periods started, and it had been the main reason for her purchase of the crucifix, the cross and chain and the Bible. She felt Holly was now vulnerable.

Holly came back to the bedroom and climbed into bed.

'I'll be okay, Mum. I just needed you to know.'

Rose leaned over and kissed her daughter. 'Sleep well, sweetheart. The pains may get worse, so if you feel you need a tablet give me a shout. Love you.' She left the room and went back downstairs.

John raised an eyebrow in query, so she told him what had happened. He was quiet for a moment.

'We need to keep a close eye on her.'

'You feel it too?'

He nodded. 'She targeted Holly at the bonfire. She spoke through her. We're woefully inept at this, you know. Let's hope today's prayers helped and she's finally moving on.'

It was around 3 am before Rose finally closed her eyes. She half expected Holly to call her, but the little girl slept soundly all night and by next morning the world looked a brighter place.

It was the last week of school before the long summer break and Rose set off with the children at eight o'clock for the walk down to school. They both enjoyed going to Breakfast Club, and every morning she dropped them off for their Cornflakes and toast before heading for her own classroom to set it up for the day ahead.

Today was going to be the start of three days of closing everything down and she had decided the children could pack everything away. They had all been sent home with instructions to bring in a carrier bag so they could take their own treasures and work home, and that's where she intended to begin. Every child's drawer would be emptied today.

These were Holly's last few days at the junior school; September would see her start her higher education. It troubled Rose that she would be away from her family, but recognised they could do nothing about it. Hopefully Lavender would have been sent away in peace by then.

Rose began by writing instructions on the blackboard, and when the children began to file in, they saw they had to gather everything from the walls that belonged to them, sort through their drawers and go to lost property to check that there was nothing there that belonged to them. They set to work with enthusiasm and soon the walls were cleared. Rose went around removing all the bits of Blu Tack and Sellotape that still clung stubbornly to the paintwork, and then they had a break out in the warm summer sunshine.

After twenty minutes, she called them back inside and they waited expectantly, unsure of which job was next. It was clear they were loving this impromptu day.

She took out a book and all the children clapped. No more jobs just yet. They appreciated the end of term practice of being read to rather than doing the reading themselves, and Mrs. Broadbent was such a good reader. She made them laugh.

'Okay, come and sit on the floor, boys and girls,' she called and they all gathered around her. She delved into her bag and took out a Dr. Seuss book. The children all cheered. They loved the way she read any of these magical books and she held it up to show them.

'If I ran the Circus? Shall we have this one?'

There was a chorus of yes pleases, and then silence descended as she began to tell the story.

By the time she had finished it was lunchtime, so she dismissed them with a word of caution; it was back to the big clean-up in the afternoon. She escorted them to the dining room before heading off to the staffroom. She was a little concerned to see Holly was looking quite pale and hadn't seemed to be taking part in the morning's activities beyond doing the bare minimum.

She ate her lunch quickly and then went out into the playground. She spotted Jacob tearing around being chased by Noah, his best friend, and waved at him. He flipped his hand at her and disappeared around the corner of the school building. She looked around and saw Holly had headed for the benches and was sitting there reading a book. Rose watched as Tamsin walked up to her; she saw Holly briefly smile and shake her head. Tamsin turned and went to join a group of girls sorting out two teams to play rounders.

Rose walked across to her daughter and stood behind her for a moment.

'Holly,' she said softly. 'Are you okay?'

Holly jumped and turned around. 'Sorry, Mum, I didn't know you were there.'

'That's okay. You're on your own. You don't want to play rounders?'

Holly shook her head. 'No, I've got tummy ache and my head feels a bit fuzzy. I'll be okay here till we go back in.'

Rose smiled at her, touched her shoulder and walked away, but not before noticing the book Holly was reading was the small Bible she had bought for her to keep in her school bag.

***

The children sat quietly at their desks waiting for their instructions. Rose glanced around, saw they were all there and clapped her hands.

'Okay, I now want you to go through your drawers and take out all the work, pictures and so on that have accumulated throughout the term, put everything into your carrier bags and hang them on your coat pegs. Does everybody understand? I will be checking all the drawers later, so if you don't do it properly the film will be cancelled.'

The entire class of eleven year olds cheered; they had hoped to watch a film, but nothing was guaranteed.

Again, Rose clapped her hands. 'Right, go empty those drawers.'

The children stood as one and moved to the bank of drawers, each drawer bearing the name of a child. There was much giggling and chatter but within five minutes all the drawers were empty and the carrier bags hung on their pegs.

Rose wheeled in the television and video stand, took a vote on Toy Story or the Lion King and popped the Lion King into the video player. There was instant quiet and once the film started she moved across to the bank of drawers to check nothing had been left in them. She found two elastic bands in Danny Allbright's drawer, a lollipop stick in Amy Walker's and a sprig of lavender in Holly's.

8

Rose waited until the children were in bed before telling John about the lavender. He didn't say anything, just stared at her.

'John?'

'I can't say anything,' he said. 'That's because I don't know what to say. Or do.'

John stood and walked across to the window, staring out across the back garden. He and Alan had spent the entire day working in it and it was looking good. The patio area, where the band would be positioned under a gazebo, looked as though it had been there for a long time, and he was very pleased with their efforts. He had been feeling good until Rose had told him about her day.

'I'm going for a little walk around the gardens,' he said, and she nodded. He clearly wanted some thinking time.

He moved to get his jacket from the mud room and remembered the letter in the pocket. He went back into the lounge and handed it to Rose. 'I met the postman halfway up the drive this morning. He gave me this from Violet and Pierre. Tell me what it says when I get back.'

She took it with a smile. She had always got on with Violet and hated her living in Paris; maybe they were coming over.

She heard the front door close and she sat down to read the letter. It was long, it was chatty and it was indeed confirmation they were coming over. They had hoped to be over for the wedding but were unable to book the time off together, so their option was to come at the weekend. She squealed in delight and reached for the phone.

'Bonjour, Pierre! Is Violet there, please?'

'Oui, ma belle Rose. Un moment, s'il vous plait.'

Violet came to the phone with laughter in her voice. 'I think Pierre has a soft spot for you. He goes all gooey eyed when you're on the phone. Are we okay coming Friday?'

Rose hesitated. 'You're fine, but do you mind if I book you into one of the guesthouses?'

'Not at all. You decorating before the wedding or something?'

'No, it's not that. I'll explain when you get here, but I think you'll be safer away from the house.'

'What? I don't understand...'

'I have things to tell you, Violet, but not over the phone. So, stop pushing.' She laughed. 'I'll give Val a ring and see if she's got an available room. How long can you stay?'

'We need to be back in Paris by a week on Saturday, so we'll stay till the Friday.'

'Brilliant. A full week with the two of you. I can't wait.'

'It will be good. We have things to tell you as well, but if you're being so secretive, then I can be too,' she said with a laugh. 'Bye, Sis.'

Rose smiled to herself as she replaced the receiver. It would be good to have them on the doorstep but she didn't want them in the house, not under the current circumstances. She hoped that their news didn't involve a move to anywhere further afield; she considered Paris to be quite far enough for her only sister to live.

She rang Val Spencer, booked Pierre and Violet in for the week and then went to look for John.

He was sitting in the rose arbour, deep in thought, but looked up with a smile at her approach. She told him what was happening and he agreed it made sense for them to spend the week with Val in Wisteria Cottage.

'We'll pay for it,' he said. 'There's no need for them to be out of pocket.'

'I've already said that to Val.'

'Great minds and all that, is it?' He put his arm around his wife and together they watched the setting sun.

'Come on,' he said. 'Let's go in. It's turning a bit cool now, and I don't like leaving the kids alone in the house when we're out here.'

***

The two days remaining of term time flashed by. The children enjoyed the change in routine, and by the end of the last day Rose felt exhausted. She had many gifts to transport home and the children had voted that they remain gift wrapped until she could share the pleasure with John. In such a small village, the children all knew John, almost as much as they knew her.

There were tears in her eyes as she said her goodbyes to them; she would see them around the village, but it wouldn't be the same as teaching them. She gave one last glance around the classroom, said hello to Myra, the cleaner, who was now about to begin the annual deep clean which happened every July, and struggled out of the gate with her parcels. She had loaded Holly and Jacob with packages and they walked the short journey home, chattering happily about the six weeks of freedom to come.

They had almost reached the imposing front door of their home when they heard the large gate at the bottom of the drive creak open, and a car engine announce the arrival of a vehicle.

The taxi pulled up at the same time as Rose and the children put their packages on the ground; they knew who was in the taxi.

Holly and Jacob ran to the car and almost dragged out the occupants.

'Aunty Violet! Uncle Pierre!'

There were smiles all round and everyone picked up packages and luggage to carry through to the kitchen.

Rose drew Violet towards her and held her. 'It's so good to see you,' she whispered.

She turned to her brother-in-law and kissed him on both cheeks. 'Bienvenue, Pierre. Good journey?'

'Very good,' he said, smiling at Rose. 'We landed in Manchester and we had pre-booked the taxi, so there was no problem.'

'Good. I thought we could all eat together and later we'll walk down to Val's with you, once the children are in bed. Val's fine with that. She says she's going to bed at eleven o'clock and if you're not there by then, you're in the shed. I think she was joking...'

Alan and Flora joined them for the meal, happy to see both of their daughters round the same table once more. Everybody missed Violet. She was the level-headed daughter, the career girl; so different to Rose in many ways, and yet so alike in many others.

She had met Pierre in Paris and they had been together ever since. Five years of marriage had seen them settle in the French capital, and Rose thought back to Violet's earlier reference of some news from them; she once more hoped it wasn't a move to somewhere distant.

With the dishes cleared away and the children in bed, the six of them sat out on the patio, enjoying their coffee. They talked of mundane things, each sister having something to impart and neither knowing where to start.

It was Alan who started to talk about Lavender and the conversation escalated. Violet and Pierre listened to what the others had to say and looked on in shocked silence.

'You mean we have a ghost?' There was almost a smile on Violet's lips.

John shook his head. 'Not in the true sense of ghost, no. We don't see anything. There's no spectral being floating around in a big white sheet. Look at this.'

He handed over the photograph showing Holly on the swing.

Pierre leaned in towards his wife and they stared at the picture together. 'Mon dieu,' Rose heard Pierre whisper.

'But...' Violet waved the photograph around. 'It's six years nearly...'

Rose nodded. 'We know. We've thought long and hard about this, believe me, and we believe the catalyst for all this activity is the wedding. Matt came to tell me they were getting married and I offered them the use of a marquee in the garden for the reception. That was the day the flowers died before they'd even been in the house half an hour.'

'And Tony March?' Violet was still looking shocked. John reached out and took her hand before speaking.

'He was found dead on Lavender's grave. We can't say with certainty there was a connection, but he was the vicar who was supposed to be officiating at the wedding. It's almost as if she's trying everything she can to stop it. It's why we've booked you into Val's. It's not good being here at the moment – and now Holly—'

'What about Holly?' Violet jumped in. 'What's wrong with Holly?'

'Nothing, other than she has now started her periods, and all along this has seemed to centre around her. The voice that came out of her mouth was definitely Lavender's voice, and I know you'll find that hard to believe, but both your Dad and I heard it. I just think she is vulnerable now.'

'I don't want to hear any more. This is ridiculous. Lavender wouldn't hurt any one of us.' Violet turned to her husband. 'Pierre...'

He pulled her close and stroked her hair. 'Okay,' he said. 'Let's change the subject for tonight. We have some news.'

Rose felt sick. She sent up a silent prayer – not too far away, please.

Violet turned to Pierre and smiled.

'Okay. We're going to have a baby.'

There was a stunned silence; Violet, career-minded Violet, pregnant? I'm never having children Violet, pregnant?

And then everyone started talking at once. Laughter, tears, it was there in abundance. Violet confirmed it was due on 30th November and that she would be coming over to England to have the baby.

'So, you'd better get this spooky stuff out the way before then, Rose, because we're coming to stay!'

No more was said about Lavender and at ten o'clock Rose and John walked down into the village with Pierre and Violet. All four of them had a cup of tea with Val, and then John and Rose walked back up to Winterscroft, arm in arm.

'They didn't want to know,' John said quietly.

'No,' his wife agreed.

'So, what do we do? Hope it all goes away?'

'I think we try and ignore it, and not mention it again when Violet and Pierre are anywhere around. Let's just enjoy our week with them. It does make me a bit wary of telling Matt, though. What if he has the same reaction?' Rose was clearly troubled.

'We have to tell him, no matter what the reaction is. If he really is the catalyst, he has to be made aware. Let's leave it until after Violet has gone back to Paris, then we'll have him up for a chat and see what he says about it all.'

***

The following day was warm with a gentle breeze, making for an extremely pleasant day. Pierre and Violet had walked up to Winterscroft after a full English breakfast courtesy of Val; they now sat on the patio sharing a pot of coffee with Alan, Flora, John and Rose.

'So, do you two have ideas on what you'd like to do?' Rose looked at them from across her coffee mug.

'Well, first of all I want to go across to the cemetery. I've bought three different little lavender plants and I want to plant them on the grave. Can I borrow a trowel, please, John?' Violet asked.

'Of course.' John stood and went into his shed, returning a minute later with the tool. 'The ground will probably be quite hard, so take care.'

Violet thanked him and slipped the trowel into the carrier bag by her side that held the plants.

'We'll do that first, and then maybe have a walk? Everybody's welcome to join us.'

The children shouted yes with great enthusiasm, and Rose stood to refill the coffee mugs.

'Do you want us all to go with you to the cemetery, or do you want time alone with Lavender? I'm easy,' Rose said. 'We can nip across the road whenever we want, you can't.'

Violet turned to Pierre. 'Alone? And come back here to round this lot up after we've finished the planting?'

'Whatever you say, chérie.'

They sat and chatted for quite a while and then Pierre and Violet set off down the drive, heading for the cemetery. The Parish Church of St. Edmund was just across the road from the large gates at the bottom of the drive, and within a couple of minutes they were standing by the graveside.

Neither of them spoke; they stood deep in shared thought of a life lost far too young.

Violet wiped away a tear and knelt down by the grave. She took the plants out of the carrier bag and then picked up the trowel. She leaned over the grave and a pain sliced through her like a knife. She cried out and Pierre dropped to her side.

'Violet?'

'A pain...' she gasped. 'Give me a minute...'

He held her, feeling scared. She remained as she was, and then smiled weakly at him. 'It's gone now. Perhaps I stretched a muscle a bit too far.'

She pushed the trowel into the earth and it went through as if the soil was butter. She pulled it out and put it in once more to dig the hole large enough for the plant. The air became still. Ethereal.

She saw Pierre shake his head as if to clear his ears and she knew he was feeling the atmospheric change too. There was no movement; the trees were motionless, no scudding clouds, just silence.

Her brain felt fogged and she blinked rapidly, trying to clear the mist that seemed to be surrounding them.

And then the soil cracked open with a sound like thunder. Violet fell forward as if a hand had hit her on the back of her head and she spread out her arms to take the brunt of the fall. She looked down and saw Lavender's face framed in the fissure created by the movement of the soil. At the same time the pain came back and Violet began to scream. She tried to pull back from the vision below her and she saw Lavender smile, a smile of derision.

She collapsed across the grave and Pierre, still fighting the atmosphere, managed to move her and lay her on her back. He looked around in desperation, praying for someone else to be in the graveyard; it was deserted. He began to run and burst into the house, yelling for them to get an ambulance.

He then turned and ran back down to be with Violet. He reached her as she started to come round, and he held her close to him. As he moved her, he could see the blood underneath her and he cried inside.

Rose and John arrived within seconds and Rose recognised what was happening without Pierre having to speak; so much blood for one tiny foetus. The ambulance was there within a few minutes and they took Violet and Pierre to the Jessop Hospital in Sheffield.

As John and Rose left the cemetery, John paused at the gate and looked back towards the grave. In red, and underneath the name Lavender, it said "is back", and he knew their prayers hadn't worked.

9

Violet came home to Winterscroft two days later, inconsolable. Their baby had been a boy and knowing that made their loss even harder.

Rose had cancelled the booking with Val, and Pierre helped her upstairs to Winterscroft's spare room. She said very little, and Pierre left her to sleep. She didn't sleep, she cried.

'Rose,' Pierre said quietly. 'I think I have to take her home as soon as she is okay to travel.'

Rose nodded. 'If that is what Violet wants to do, then that's fine by me. Sort your flights out and I'll take you to the airport. It would be safer for the two of you back home in France. Maybe you can bring her over later in the year, after this wedding is a distant memory.'

'Rose...'

'Pierre, this thing with Lavender is real. Please don't tell me you still can't accept it. You've seen first-hand what she is doing.'

Pierre shook his head. 'It was just a miscarriage, Rose, just a miscarriage. Not caused by a... a... ghost!'

Rose closed her mouth. Pierre couldn't see what was in front of his eyes, and maybe it was better that way. Maybe it would be better for all of them if they couldn't accept what was happening.

An hour later, she took a pot of coffee to the men sitting on the patio. Pierre stood.

'I'll just go and check on Violet.'

'I'll do it,' Rose said. 'I'll take her a tea and see if she's up to coming downstairs. If I need you, I'll call.'

She went upstairs carrying the tray she had already prepared, and gently pushed open the door. Violet was standing at the window, her face a picture reflecting abject misery and hurt.

Rose put down the tray and moved to take her in her arms.

'I know,' she soothed. 'I know. It hurts, and it's not a physical pain, is it? I lost a baby early on in the pregnancy, between Holly and Jacob. Only John knew, but it was a terrible time. You'll never forget this baby, but there will be another child for you.'

'It's not just that,' she sobbed. 'Losing our son is bad enough, but I saw her. Lavender. I dug into the soil to plant those damned lavenders and it opened up. I saw her face, Rose, I saw her face. She smiled. Not a nice smile. Evil.' Her breath was becoming rapid and Rose led her to the bed.

'Sit down. Take deep breaths. Does Pierre know about this?'

Violet shook her head. 'No. I didn't tell him. He was at the end of the grave so I don't think he could have seen. But I did and it will always be there. I'll never visit that damn grave again, Rose. I hope you don't mind, but I want to go home. I'm going to ask Pierre to get us a flight as soon as he can.'

Rose looked troubled. 'Whatever you think is best for you and Pierre, Violet, but I don't see nearly enough of you and now you're going home early. And in these awful circumstances. I'll take you to the airport whenever you need to go, you know I will, but—'

'Thank you. I just need the comfort of our home, I think.'

Rose poured her a cup of tea and they sat side by side on the bed.

A gentle knock on the door heralded Pierre's arrival and Rose left the bedroom to allow them privacy. She had been where they were now, and it wasn't a good place.

Ten minutes later, Pierre came downstairs and used the phone. She could hear him making the reservations and knew they would be leaving next day. Sadness overwhelmed her as she sat at the kitchen table, deep in thought.

'Do you have a minute, Rose?'

She switched on a smile for him. 'Of course, Pierre. You're leaving?'

He nodded. 'Tomorrow morning. We'll book a taxi because the flight is at nine o'clock and I don't want you driving at some ridiculous early hour. Do you have a local number for a taxi?'

She shook her head. 'No. I'm taking you. I will feel happier going with you. No arguments, Pierre.'

He walked round the table and kissed her. 'You're the best sister-in-law in the world. You know that?'

'Naturally, I know that. Now what time do we need to leave tomorrow? Five?'

'I think so. Thank you, Rose. We're going to go for a little walk down into the village now – Violet wants to get a couple of things to take back with her. I'll make sure she doesn't do too much.'

'You're a good man, Pierre. Remember, there is a future, and there will be another baby.'

'Rose, if there is another baby, we won't be anywhere near Lavender for the entire pregnancy.' And with those words she understood that Pierre now knew what they all knew.

Lavender was back.

***

Violet and Pierre sat together in the back of the car, both quiet, both unhappy and both facing a different future to the one that had been there when they had arrived in England.

Rose switched on the radio and listened to a soft Classic FM as she drove through the early morning sunrise. There were no hold-ups and she reached Manchester in plenty of time for their check-in.

She kissed them both, said she would ring later and left them to go through to the departure lounge. She went to get a coffee before heading back home; it gave her thinking time.

She was absolutely lost. She knew deep in her heart that Lavender couldn't have caused the loss of this baby, but if what Violet had said was true, Lavender had physically appeared for the first time.

Growing in strength? It was a ridiculous notion, but now there had been two deaths at that graveside. It was such a peaceful setting; a large oak tree protected it with its branches, and the whole family kept it spotlessly clean with fresh flowers at least once a week. Now it felt corrupted.

She finished her coffee and headed back to the car. The sun had gone in and she shivered. She went to the boot to take out her cardigan and then decided against it; if it was cold in the car, she could put the heating on.

There was more traffic on the road for the return journey, but in just over an hour she was driving through the gates. There was no one around so she sat in the car for a minute and just looked at this house she loved so much. It never changed. Even the front door was always stained the same colour, the wisteria and climbing roses looked the same every summer, and she knew her life was made complete by living in this huge mansion of a place.

And now she was being made to feel uncomfortable in it. The front door opened and John walked across to her.

She lowered the window and he popped his head through to kiss her.

'Everything okay? You want me to put the car away?'

She shook her head. 'No, I'll do it. I was just having a moment of feeling sorry for myself, but I'll be okay. Are the children awake?'

'Jacob is. He's talked your dad into a day of fishing, so they'll probably want a packed lunch. Holly is still in bed. She's very quiet these days. Is she okay?'

'I think she's not happy with this period business,' Rose smiled. 'There's nothing I can do about that, I'm afraid. She'll be okay when she finishes with this first one.'

He nodded. 'You're probably right. Might be a nice idea to take her shopping or something if Jacob's off out for the day. I'm going out for most of it as well, doing a complete round up of all the jobs we have on, so you two girls go and treat yourselves.'

'I'll see how she is when she gets up. I really want to get in touch with Matt at some point. I need to tell him what's been happening.'

'Invite them for a meal – but make it soon, Rose, make it soon.'

He kissed her again and opened the car door. She got out and went distractedly round to the boot to get her cardigan. Lying across it was a sprig of lavender.

She went inside and immediately rang Matt.

10

The children went to bed as soon as they had eaten their meal. Flora and Alan moved out onto the patio and gathered six chairs together as Matt and Beth brought out the cheeseboard and plates. Rose could hear them joking while she was making the coffee and hoped they would still be able to joke at the end of the night. John shimmied past her carrying a bottle of brandy, a bottle of whisky and six glasses.

He took them outside and then came back in for the coffee cups.

'Okay?' he queried.

Rose nodded. 'At the moment. This isn't going to be easy, you know. Beth didn't even know Lavender.'

'We'll manage,' he said, but Rose wasn't convinced.

She followed him out with the coffee and they all settled down, with Matt and Beth believing they would be discussing details of the wedding reception.

Instead, Rose began to speak in a halting voice. She talked for a long time; she spoke of the flowers that had died, the bin full of bugs, the voice coming from Holly's mouth, the death of Tony March and now finally Violet's miscarriage.

She went into detail, showing them the swing photograph; neither Matt nor Beth spoke.

Finally, she sat back. She had registered the shock on all their faces when she had spoken of Lavender's face in the grave; she was the only one, apart from Violet, to know of this.

'I can't believe you've not said anything before...' Matt was clearly upset.

Alan leaned across to the young man. 'We hoped, with Tony March helping us, to sort it. As Rose explained, we've tried the power of prayer, but she still isn't at rest. If everything had settled down, you didn't need to know, but now I think we've all come to the conclusion that it is this wedding that has prompted the paranormal activity that is going on, and we needed both of you to be aware.'

Beth took hold of Matt's hand and shivered. 'I told you there was something strange in our house. That smell, it's lavender. I put it down to the elderly chap who had lived there and it was probably his wife's perfume still lingering, but it isn't, is it?' Beth's voice had climbed higher as she realised what was going through her mind and out of her mouth.

Matt pulled her closer. 'Look, we'll get Gareth Bruce to come in and bless the house.' Gareth Bruce was the vicar who was temporarily standing in for Tony March, and would be marrying them. 'I'm sorry. I didn't believe you, but...'

Beth dropped her head. 'I know. It's crazy. I would never have thought in a million years this was the reason we had that smell; it comes and goes into different rooms. She's following me!'

Beth was clearly frightened. She looked around at the others. 'How are you coping? Aren't you scared? And what about Holly and Jacob?'

Flora's voice cut in. 'Jacob knows nothing, and although Holly remembers fainting down by the pond, she has no memory of the voice. We all feel she is using, or will use, Holly in some way, and yes, that's scary. But please, let's not lose sight of things here. Lavender was a lovely girl, would do anything for anyone and she loved us all. She wouldn't hurt us.'

Beth turned to the older woman. 'So, it's not classed as hurting you – your vicar dying and a miscarriage, both on her grave.'

There was silence.

Beth's apology was heartfelt. 'I'm so sorry; I shouldn't speak to you like that. I'm just so scared. I can't lose Matt, I just can't, and if our wedding is what has triggered all of this...' She broke off and began to cry.

Rose stood and drew the young girl into her arms. 'Beth, sweetheart, don't cry. You're upset because this is all new to you. I was like this when it started, but we're learning to live with it until it goes away. And you won't lose Matt. Marry him and say sod off to whatever this evil thing is, because it sure as hell isn't Lavender. At least, not the Lavender we all knew.'

***

The Tony March funeral proved to be a massive affair. Elizabeth had expected a considerable amount of mourners, but it seemed the whole village had turned out to pay their respects to their much-loved vicar.

The plot for Tony's interment was as far away from Lavender's grave as it was possible to be. The service had been a long one and everyone had followed the coffin as it was carried across the graveyard from the church.

Prayers were said around the site and slowly the coffin was lowered. All four of the March children were present and Caroline was attempting to stem tears from all of them. The youngest one, Chrissie, had no idea why she was crying; the others understood they would never see their daddy again. Thomas, in particular, felt his new role as man of the house, would be difficult. He needed his dad.

The Castle Hotel had closed its doors for the day except to residents, and welcomed in the mourners. Many stories were told of Tony's kindness and willingness to be a major player in the village and when the hotel opened up to visitors at five o'clock that evening, everyone had drifted home to remember Tony with love and sadness.

Two days later, Elizabeth moved further along the valley to a home she had rented in Hathersage. She couldn't bear to be near the place where Tony had died, couldn't stand the sight of the Paulson headstone. She felt that his death was somehow linked to Lavender; there had been no reason for him to be anywhere near that grave. She left without looking back.

***

As the wedding approached, it occurred to Rose that maybe their prayers were working. They had once again had a prayer session, this time in the lounge, and they had felt nothing. On a personal level, she prayed every night and she was sure John, Flora and Alan would be doing the same.

Two days before the wedding the marquee arrived. The garden looked magnificent and John supervised the placement of the massive tent, so that if it rained there would be shelter for everyone, even when the live music was being played. He had erected a smaller marquee over the newly paved patio area that was designated for Time Out, the local band they had booked for the reception, and he hoped he had thought of everything.

Everyone helped with the fairy lights and bunting, and Beth looked considerably happier than the last time Rose had seen her. Beth had said, with a degree of surprise, the lavender fragrance had disappeared and she no longer felt scared. The repairs and redecoration were all done, and they were so excited it was going to be their first home together.

The tables were moved into the marquee and all the chairs put in place. Rose showed Beth the dining room in Winterscroft, filled to the brim with tablecloths, cutlery, crockery and anything else that would be needed on the day.

'You forget this now, Beth. Concentrate on your dress, hair and makeup. Mum and I will see to this before the caterers get here, and then we're good to go. Just enjoy your day, sweetheart, and put all thoughts of Lavender to one side. Matt has moved on and he loves you. Never doubt that.'

'I can't thank you enough, Rose. It's going to be a beautiful day on Saturday. We need the sun to shine, but if it doesn't, it matters not one iota.'

Rose smiled. 'I'll order the sunshine. You just turn up and be beautiful.'

'She always is.' Matt's voice came from outside the patio doors, and he popped his head around. 'Are we ready to go home? I don't think we can do any more out here until Saturday morning. I'll pop up then and—'

'No, you won't,' Rose said firmly. 'We don't need you. Spend the morning with your mum and Tim. Honestly, Matt, we'll be fine. We're organised.'

'Then I'll see you in church.' He came in and took Beth's hand, then kissed Rose. 'I love you, Rose Broadbent.'

'Thank you, Matt, and I love you. Now go home. I'm busy.'

11

The sun came out.

Beth's gown, pure white silk, swished effortlessly as she held on to her father's arm, all nerves gone now. Her veil, covering her face, couldn't hide the radiance of her smile; today was their day. Her sister, Cerys, dressed in lemon, followed Beth and their father down the aisle; she had never seen Beth look so beautiful, nor her Dad so handsome.

Only Holly noticed the candle extinguishing. She whispered to her mum that it had gone out, but Rose merely put a finger to Holly's lips to remind her not to speak.

Gareth Bruce beamed at Matt and Beth as they became reunited at the front of the church. He hadn't known the couple very long but had quickly realised they were meant for each other; he was delighted to be conducting the service. He waited for Beth's veil to be taken from her face and then watched as she handed her bouquet to Cerys.

He welcomed the congregation and gave a special smile to Tim, in his official capacity as best man. He knew Matt and Tim had lost their father, and he was guessing that Tim had spent most of the morning calming Matt's nerves.

'God is love, and those who live in love live in God and God lives in them.'

His voice rang out clearly and confidently and he moved on to a short prayer before announcing the first hymn, God is Love.

Holly had been feeling a little out of sorts all morning and when she had mentioned it to Rose, her mother had explained it was probably her second period, and she should use a pad just in case. She now felt a deep ache in her stomach and she recognised it, today of all days; she didn't really rate this growing up.

She glanced up at the offending candle that had gone out and watched as it flickered back to life. She gasped and Rose looked down at her with a frown. What on earth was wrong with Holly today? Once more she touched Holly's lips with her finger.

The hymn finished and there was a clattering as everyone sat down in preparation for the main event.

'In the presence of God, Father, Son and Holy Spirit,
we have come together
to witness the marriage of Matthew and Bethan,
to pray for God's blessing on them,
to share their joy
and to celebrate their love.'

There was a huge bang as the great door at the back of the church was flung open and then slammed shut. Everyone jumped, there were a couple of shrieks, and the congregation as one, turned around to see who had come through the door so unceremoniously.

Nobody had. There were a few mutterings of the wind being to blame, and that it must have suddenly got up to gale force. They settled down once more and Gareth continued with the service.

'Marriage is a gift of God in creation
through which husband and wife may know the grace of God.
It is given
that as man and woman grow together in love and trust,
they shall be united with one another in heart, body and mind,
as Christ is united with his bride, the Church.'

Gareth looked up, suddenly feeling uneasy. He glanced around at the congregation and smiled to hide his sudden confusion, before looking back down at his book.

The noise of a hundred Bibles falling off the shelf at the back of the church caused uproar, and many of the guests stood, unsure of what was happening. They turned to look at their vicar. He was equally as nonplussed, and held up both his hands.

'Please sit down everyone and we'll continue with the service. We'll sort out our carpentry problems later,' he joked.

John, however, had seen it wasn't a carpentry problem. The shelf was just as it had been for the many years he had been a member of this church; it was just the Bibles that now lay scattered all over the floor. He vowed that before he left the church today, they would all be back on that shelf where they belonged.

Everyone settled down and Gareth waited a moment, smiling at the young couple in front of him.

'Ready?' he whispered, and they both nodded.

'The gift of marriage brings husband and wife together
in the delight and tenderness of sexual union
and joyful commitment to the end of their lives.
It is given as the foundation of family life
in which children are born and nurtured

and in which each member of the family,
in good times and in bad,
may find strength, companionship and comfort,
and grow to maturity in love.'

Beth shivered suddenly and Matt glanced at her. He had noticed a sudden drop in temperature and her arms were bare. She mouthed the word 'cold' at him and he nodded.

There were some sounds of shuffling behind them; if he had been brave enough to turn around, he would have seen many of the guests slipping on jackets that hadn't been necessary when they first arrived. Now it was icy cold.

Both candles on the altar went out and Holly gave a cry, and then slumped to the floor. Rose tried to catch her but Holly landed awkwardly, almost wedged between the seat of their pew and the back of the pew in front of them.

Val Spencer, who had been seated in the pew across the aisle from them, came to help, and between them they managed to get Holly outside and onto the bench at the side of the church porch.

'Thank you, Val,' Rose whispered. 'Go back in, don't miss the service. I'm sure she's only fainted. She wasn't very well this morning. Can you just give a thumbs up to John and my parents, they'll be worried?'

'You sure you don't need me?' Val's concern was etched on her face. 'You don't need a doctor?'

'No, it's her period, I think, and it's only her second one. Her body's still adjusting. She'll be fine, honestly. Go back and enjoy the rest of the service. We'll stay out here till everyone comes out. Besides, it's warmer out here,' she joked.

'Too right it is,' Val agreed, and left them sitting on the bench. Holly was starting to come round and Rose placed an arm around her. She kissed her and they sat quietly, enjoying the warmth of the sun.

Val went back inside, put up a thumb towards John, who nodded. She sat down as Gareth Bruce cleared his throat.

'First, I am required to ask anyone present who knows a reason why these persons may not lawfully marry, to declare it now.'

There was a shriek that grew in intensity. Beth covered her ears and Matt put his arm around her and pulled her to him. The sound continued and then was cut off abruptly. The crash of shattering glass from the small office filled the church, breaking the utter silence, and John knew he would be needed to replace the window once again.

There were cries of horror from many people in the congregation. Matt leaned towards Gareth and spoke quietly.

'No more hymns, let's get this over with and everyone outside. It's freezing and there's something not right here. Let's do it quickly, Gareth.'

Beth nodded her agreement. She felt threatened, scared – and she had been so happy.

The spoke their vows at speed, then Tim dutifully handed over both rings. He too felt unhappy, could see the tears in Beth's eyes as she raced through everything that should have been such an important part of their day.

'I give you this ring
as a sign of our marriage.
With my body I honour you,
all that I am I give to you,
and all that I have I share with you,
within the love of God,
Father, Son and Holy Spirit.'

The formalities over, Matt squeezed Beth's hand and breathed a sigh of relief. Just the register to sign and they could get out of this place that had always been a sanctuary to him.

Once again, Gareth cleared his throat. He always enjoyed the last part.

'Those whom God has joined together let no one put asunder.'

The bolt of lightning hit the floor of the aisle and travelled along it as a crack of thunder reverberated around the walls. People stood and headed for the doors, while Gareth ushered the bride and groom, Tim, Cerys and Cerys' boyfriend, Alec, towards the table behind the altar where the marriage certificate was awaiting their signatures. Cerys and Alec were their witnesses and both of them prayed it would soon be over.

'Sign it quickly,' Gareth instructed all of them. 'I don't know what's happening, but let's get out of here.'

Within five minutes, they had joined their guests milling around outside the entrance to the church, and the photographer was busy doing his job. Nobody knew what had gone wrong, just that it had, spectacularly.

An hour later, after the photographer had finished, they began to head across the road to Winterscroft's driveway. Within seconds a wind began to blow, an intense wind so fierce it blew one person into another, even making strong men stagger. They stared in horror as Beth's veil was torn from her hair. It was blown upwards, straight into the branches of the oak tree, the sentinel of Lavender's grave.

'I'll get it for you,' Matt said, and Tim stepped in front of him.

'No way, bro. I'm the tree climber. I'll get it,' and he headed for the base of the tree. He climbed to the first set of branches with a helping hand from John, but then he was on his own. He reached the branch on which it had snagged and he straddled the thick limb. He slowly shuffled along it, planning on releasing the fragile veil and dropping it down to waiting hands below, before shuffling back again. He wouldn't risk damaging the veil by dragging it back with him.

Tim reached the veil and freed it. He carefully rolled it into a ball and dropped it down to Matt. Cerys helped her anchor it back into her hair, suddenly aware that there was now no wind at all.

Tim began the slow reverse journey and froze as he heard the creak from the old branch. He remained motionless and saw Matt's upturned face.

'Don't move, Tim.' Matt ordered. 'Let's get help.'

'I'll be fine,' Tim said, a little shakily. 'I just need to get back to the main branch. It's not going to fall with my bit of a weight on it.'

This time the creak was a crack and Tim tried to move one more shuffle backwards. The next crack was louder and the branch, along with Tim, began to fall as if in slow motion. Tim banged his head on the headstone as it crashed down onto Lavender's grave.

Matt pulled him clear of the leaves and got him onto the grass. He was conscious, but a little dazed.

Rose joined Maria, Tim's mother, and they swiftly examined him. 'I'm taking him to A & E,' Maria said. 'That was a nasty bang to his head. Don't let this spoil the wedding, Rose. I'll take him in my car. If we manage to get back, we will, but if not, just enjoy the rest of the day.'

'But, Mom—' Matt said.

'Shut up, Matt,' his mother said. 'You're a married man now, go do your wedding. We'll be fine. I'll ring if there are any issues.'

They supported Tim as he went to wait for transport and then waved them off before heading up to the marquee.

It looked spectacular. The garden itself was filled with roses and they had used roses as the theme flower for the wedding. Every table had a rose centrepiece and Beth clapped her hands as she saw her wedding venue for the first time.

'How beautiful,' she breathed and turned to Matt. 'It's perfect.'

He smiled at her. He was trying very hard to hide his concern for Tim, and his anger at the fiasco that had been the wedding service. He handed her a champagne flute, then took one for himself. 'To us, and the rest of our lives together.'

She smiled. 'To us.' And they kissed.

Once everyone was seated, the caterers began to serve the meal. Gareth stood and said grace, and everyone finally settled down. The top table had been shuffled around slightly as Tim and Maria wouldn't be sharing in the wedding breakfast, but all the other tables were filled with beaming friends and relatives, the horrors of the church now forgotten.

But not by Gareth Bruce. John had promised to go back the next day to repair the broken window and Gareth decided he would have to talk to him. Something was very wrong in this family.

12

The hospital insisted Tim remain under observation for at least two hours; the lump on his head was quite impressive. Maria never left his side, remembering the sound of the bang as his head had collided with the headstone.

Maria rang Winterscroft to ask that the message be passed on to Matt; Tim was okay, but under observation, and they wouldn't be at the reception because she was taking him home after he was discharged.

Matt breathed a sigh of relief and felt easier now about the party. The music was good and everyone was up dancing in the limited space allocated for it. His first dance with Beth had been to Roberta Flack's The First Time ever I saw your Face, and his love had threatened to overwhelm him. He hoped she understood that Lavender was in his past; never forgotten, but he had a new love.

Holly felt uncomfortable. Her stomach hurt, she felt sick and she wanted to go to bed. She ate very little and was aware of a sickly cloying atmosphere in the marquee, although when she mentioned it to Jacob he looked at her as if she was mad.

'Can't smell anything,' he had said and disappeared to find Rupert, another child of around his age.

About eight o'clock she gave in and went to tell Rose how ill she felt.

'Go and get in bed, then,' Rose said. 'I'll pop up in half an hour and check you're okay.'

She trudged upstairs and into her room. The crucifix was halfway under the bed and the same sickly smell was everywhere. She gave a small cry and fell to the floor.

***

Further guests began to arrive for the evening festivities and Rose didn't go up to check on her daughter until just before nine o'clock. She was horrified to see her on the floor, her hand touching the edge of the crucifix.

She shook Holly and eventually Holly began to stir.

'Ooooh,' she moaned, her eyes still closed. 'Mum? I hurt all over.'

Rose held her tightly to her. 'I think you must have been on the floor a while, sweetheart. You'll have stiffened up. Come on, let's get you in bed.'

Holly reached for the crucifix. 'Wait,' she said. 'I need this.'

'What...?'

'There's something—'

Rose looked around. 'There's nothing here, sweetheart.'

Holly shook her head. 'You're not listening to me, Mum. Something's wrong.'

Rose helped her into her bed and kissed her forehead. Holly clutched the crucifix, keeping it in bed with her.

'Where's Maximus?' she said.

Rose looked around the room, searching for the bear.

'I can't see him. Did you take him downstairs?'

Holly shook her head. 'I don't think so.'

'I'll go look for him and bring him up later. Sleep tight, God bless,' and she kissed Holly once more.

She had a brief search downstairs for Maximus but couldn't see him; he'd better turn up, life would be hell if the bear went missing.

Rupert's parents came over to her and said they were going to take Rupert home; he was getting tired; would Rose like them to take Jacob as well?

She smiled her gratitude and went back upstairs to pack him a small bag. She crept into Holly's room and saw she was fast asleep. Maximus was lying on the floor, his back ripped open and the stuffing falling out. A sprig of lavender was stuffed into the opening. Rose stifled a scream that threatened to erupt from her and picked up the bear. Holly mustn't see this. She would have to try and repair it without Holly knowing what she was doing.

She hid the bear in the laundry basket and went downstairs to hand over both her son and his backpack of clothes.

She kissed him and watched as they set off down the drive. Although Jacob didn't seem to be targeted in any way, Rose felt it was safer for him to not be in the house tonight.

By midnight the last of the guests had gone and everything that needed to be brought inside had been. Matt and Beth had left before ten o'clock; they had booked into an airport hotel in Manchester for the night, knowing they had an early flight to the Maldives next morning.

Rose sat down with a sigh, holding tightly to a cup of tea. John had told her he wasn't going to have much to drink so that at least one person at the party was sober; she had decided to do the same.

When John joined her on the sofa, he immediately asked her what was wrong.

'Nothing,' she said. 'It's been a good day.'

'It's been a bloody awful day, starting with that debacle of a wedding service. So now do you want to tell me what's wrong?' And Rose told him.

She finished off the tale by saying that she was going to take Holly to the doctor; if there was a medical explanation for the fainting attacks she was having, that would be good. If there wasn't, that would be bad.

John pulled her to him and kissed her. 'Where's Maximus now?'

'In the laundry basket.'

He stood and went upstairs, returning a minute later holding the stuffed animal. He took out the lavender still embedded in it, crumbled it into tiny pieces and threw it in the kitchen waste.

'Come for me, Lavender,' he said, 'and leave my daughter alone.'

***

Matt and Beth stopped just outside the confines of the village in a bus lay-by and removed all the tin cans and other implements that had been tied to the car. The *just married* sign they left proudly displayed on the back window.

The hotel had pulled out all the stops and given them a beautiful room. Champagne awaited them, along with a chocolate heart that bore both their names in icing.

'You want this now?' Matt asked holding up the champagne. He hadn't had a drink all evening knowing he would be driving to the airport and champagne seemed like a good idea to him.

Beth nodded. 'I'm just going to get out of this dress and into my nightie. Thank goodness the hotel has agreed to save it for me until we come back. I'd hate to have to trail this weight to the Maldives with us.'

He pulled her to him. 'Did I tell you, Mrs. Peterson, just how beautiful you looked walking down the aisle in it? Did I?'

'Once or twice,' she grinned, and kissed him. 'I'll have a quick shower, so pour us a glass of that and we'll have our own celebration.'

She opened her suitcase and took out a white silk nightie. 'Mum made this for me,' she said. 'It's beautiful.'

His back was to her. 'Don't show me! I'll see it when you're wearing it.' There was a small pop from the champagne cork and he poured the first glass.

She closed the bathroom door behind her and he could hear her singing one of the hymns from the wedding service. He smiled and poured out the second glass.

Within five minutes she was back with him and she quite simply took his breath away. The nightie was soft, clingy and showed every curve of her. He handed her a champagne flute, then picked up his own.

'To Mr. and Mrs. Peterson,' he said. 'To a long and happy life together.'

Beth repeated the last phrase and they drank, arms entwined.

Matt put down his glass and went across to his suitcase. He opened it to take out his pyjama shorts. Across the top of his clothes was a sprig of lavender.

He found his shorts, rolled them around the sprig, then carried them into the bathroom and placed the small bundle on the vanity unit. He popped his head back around the door and smiled at his new bride.

'I'll be five minutes – don't go away.'

'As if,' she said, and saluted him with her champagne glass.

He locked the bathroom door and took out the lavender. He used the small pair of scissors from his toiletries bag and cut up the sprig onto toilet paper, hoping the sound of the shower would drown out any noise he might be making. He then screwed up the toilet paper and dropped it into the toilet. He flushed it and watched as all of it disappeared.

He had a shower and rejoined Beth to share a second glass of champagne, followed by a third before he tucked his bride into bed, already fast asleep. He breathed a sigh of relief. Matt slept very little; thoughts of Lavender invaded his mind and he knew that everything John and Rose had told him had been accurate.

He just hoped Lavender would leave them alone in the Maldives. He was sure, once there, they would be able to truly become man and wife.

***

Tim had a headache, Rose and John hardly slept, Holly had a restless night, and Matt barely closed his eyes.

Maximus the bear had tiny stitches all down his spine that Rose would have to find some explanation for, and Beth was happy. The slight twinge of unease she put down to her massive life change; it never occurred to her for one minute that Lavender was back for Matt and had had a very active day, just as active as her own had been.

She smiled in her sleep and Matt looked down on her, loving the smile.

13

The big clean-up began the next day. Rose and John got up early, but were beaten to it by Flora and Alan. The dishwasher was gently humming with a full load of glassware, and other crockery awaiting washing was being loaded on to the side.

'Morning, Mum,' Rose said and kissed her mother on the cheek. 'Couldn't sleep, then?'

'No, I couldn't. My brain was going round and round, so I decided I might as well be up and doing stuff as lying there awake. Your dad is outside scratching his head about getting that marquee down. I said I'd do bacon sandwiches all round when you two got up, so I'll make that my next job, shall I?'

'Yes, please.' Rose glanced around the kitchen. 'I remember this place when it was tidy... good night though, wasn't it?'

'Bad day,' was Flora's grim rejoinder. 'I think when this lot is cleared away and everything is back to normal, we have to sit down and talk. That church service was frightening, and not just to us. Everybody was scared, they couldn't get out fast enough. I also think Gareth wants to have a chat with all of us. He obviously suspects something is wrong.

When I went with him to the door last night he gave me a hug, then he said God's blessings on this house. It was as if he knew. When I thanked him, he said he would have a walk up to see us, and very soon. It felt a bit weird, almost like a threat of dire consequences if we didn't tell him what was wrong,' she said with a laugh.

Rose smiled. 'It's not enough we have Lavender to contend with, now we've got the local vicar. I'll put the kettle on, you start the bacon butties and we'll forget our problems for ten minutes.'

John and Alan walked through the door as she spoke.

'Morning, Dad. You okay?'

'Better now I've found out we don't have to take that blessed thing down. The people who put it up are coming at ten to take it down. Then we can sort the garden and get it back to how we like it.' He sat down at the kitchen table. 'Then we need to talk.'

Rose walked over and kissed the top of his head. 'We know. Mum and I have just said the same thing, but I don't want the children involved. Holly already suspects there's something strange going on, and I intend taking her to the doctor's this week. Surely all this fainting isn't just down to her starting her periods. I can't remember being like that.'

'No,' Flora said. 'You and Violet both sailed through it, but Lavender fainted several times when she first hit puberty. Holly is still quite young at eleven, it may simply be that.'

'And how old was—'

'Lavender? Eleven.'

Rose stared at her mother. 'Oh, my God. Surely...'

Flora took her daughter's hands in hers. 'Stop it, Rose. Stop it. Don't say or think whatever you feel right now.

Lavender is dead. Yes, she's playing stupid tricks but she can't control us.'

'She did, Mum. She made Holly recite that horrible poem after the fire, and now Holly is behaving exactly as she did. Why is she controlling Holly? I don't understand. Why does she think Holly can help her?'

John came and put his arm around his wife. 'Calm down, Rose, and pop up and check on her. She'll still be asleep I expect, but right now you need to see that she's okay.'

Rose nodded and ran upstairs. She quietly opened the door to Holly's room and stared at her daughter, her arms clasped tightly around Maximus who had been placed in bed after his operation. She was breathing lightly and easily and Rose smiled. She could see the top of the crucifix poking out from under the covers and she left it there. It clearly gave Holly comfort.

'All fine,' she announced as she walked back into the kitchen to the smell of bacon being grilled.

'Right,' Flora said. 'We'll have breakfast before we tackle anything else. Rose, make the tea. You two men sit down, there's nothing you can do until that's gone, really.' She nodded her head towards the marquee that was making the kitchen seem quite dark.

'Okay, lass.' Alan sat down and picked up the newspaper. He tried to read it but his thoughts wandered off along various paths and alleyways; he felt quite relieved when the bacon sandwich appeared and he could pretend to feel normal.

***

With the marquee now on the back of a truck and heading for Sheffield, the garden could be seen properly. John walked around with a black bag and occasionally bent down to pick up rubbish, but in the main there was very little of it. He too was avoiding being in the house and having to confront issues. He turned around and waved when he heard Holly call out from the patio doors.

'Nan says do you want a coffee, Daddy?'

'Yes, please, sweetheart. You feeling better?'

'I'm fine. I just needed a sleep, I think. Nan says two minutes.'

He acknowledged with a wave, took a last look around at the almost perfect garden and moved to walk back down the path. He shivered, aware of a change in the atmosphere. The air fell silent and somewhere in the back of his mind he recognised it as being the same feeling as the day of the worms. He shook his head but it didn't help and he had to stand still. He felt enclosed by a mist; a cloying sickly sweet smell of lavender pervaded and surrounded him.

Then he felt her. By his side, he felt her.

He heard her whisper 'It's not over yet, John. Not over yet. I am angry.'

Rose stood in the doorway and watched him. She couldn't move, couldn't go to him, and yet she knew something was wrong. She was aware of an atmosphere but couldn't get to him.

And then it was over. She saw John sink to his knees, his hands dropping on to the grass. He shook his head as if to clear it, and Rose moved towards him. She knelt down and put her arms around him.

'She spoke.' His voice was guttural. 'She spoke,' he repeated.

Rose helped him to stand; he was clearly deeply shaken and his face was grey.

'Come on,' she said. 'Let's have this coffee. Don't say anything if Holly's still in the kitchen. We'll tell Mum and Dad when she's not there.'

He nodded and followed her through the patio doors. Flora and Alan looked worried but said nothing. They had seen whatever it was that had happened play out on the lawn. Holly was sitting at the table with a glass of milk and reading her book.

John sat down and picked up his mug. His hands were trembling and Flora pushed two tablets and a glass of water towards him.

'Take them,' she said. 'They're only paracetamol. Just take them.'

He did as she said and smiled his thanks. He didn't want to talk, just sit.

They drank their coffees almost without speaking at all. Alan picked up the newspaper again and pretended to read, but nothing sank in. He was also aware that they needed to sort out the massive oak branch lying across Lavender's grave. They hadn't done anything to it the day before, being more intent on getting Tim to hospital.

'We need to ring Maria,' he said, almost absently. 'Has anybody done it?

'Yes,' Flora confirmed. 'Tim's fine, bit sore and sporting a cracker of a bruise on his right arm, a lump on his head and a tear in his trousers. Other than that, he's good. She said he wanted to come up to help clear everything away, but I said it was all under control. He's a good lad.'

Holly looked up. 'Can I go down? Take him a book, some sweets or something?'

Rose looked at John, who nodded. 'I'll check with Maria. So long as she rings me to tell me you've arrived, I don't think it will be a problem.'

Maria said it would indeed be a boost for Tim – she would put them both in the car and take them for a picnic. 'I'll drop Holly back at the end of the day some time, if that's okay,' she said. 'Tell her not to walk down – we'll get ready now, and I'll collect her.'

They waved Maria and the youngsters off and as they went back into the house the phone was ringing. Rupert's dad wanted to know if it was okay if Jacob went to the cinema with them; he would bring him home when they got back.

'So, a childless day,' Rose said. 'We need to tell you what happened outside this morning. At least, John needs to tell you. He was the target.'

John shook his head as if to clear it. 'Lavender was there. Not visibly.' He held up his hand quickly when he saw Flora jump. 'She was there because I could feel her, standing right next to me. She spoke to me. She said it wasn't over and she was angry. I couldn't move. It was that awful silence when you can't hear the birds, traffic or anything. She was insidious, if that's the right word. I'm no Browning or Keats, but that's how it felt. Then she went, and I couldn't stand up. I'd dropped to my knees and Rose was there with me. She'd seen it – and felt it? – from the doorway.'

Rose nodded. 'It was a horrible atmosphere. Like the world had stopped.'

Flora took hold of Alan's hand. 'What do we do? Where do we turn? Have we let our daughter down in some way? Can we put it right?' Then she began to cry, so many tears for her child, the youngest, the different one. So much love. Alan, shocked by the tears, stood to take her in his arms and John reached across to hold Rose's hand.

'Gareth Bruce?' he whispered.

She nodded. 'I would say so, but I don't want the children involved in any of this. We have to pick our time very carefully. I do think all four of us need to be here, and I also think Beth and Matt do too. We all need God's blessing as well as this house needing some sort of purification, so I don't think we can do anything until our honeymooners are back.'

'You're right, of course. We'll see Gareth next Sunday, see what he's got to say, but he is already guessing at things, I could tell. Seems like a good man, so I'm sure he'll be able to help.'

Alan, still holding on to Flora as if she would crumble if he let go, turned to John.

'We need to go across the road and see to the grave, get that branch removed. Take the chainsaw?'

John nodded. 'We'll finish our coffee and go across. I've the window to mend again, don't forget. Could be a busy day. It's a good job we decided to go to the evening service at church today. We'll start as the morning service finishes, then we won't disturb anyone with the racket of the chain saw. I'll squeeze the truck through the gates because we can bring the wood back here and store it in the wood shed. There's too much to wheelbarrow it here.'

Rose stood and moved to the dishwasher and began to unload it ready for the next load. She switched on the radio for background music, only to hear the newsreaders mournful tones.

She looked at the others in query.

'Somebody died? Anybody heard anything?' They all shook their heads and then heard the name Dodi Fayed.

'Oh, poor Diana, isn't that her boyfriend? She'll be devastated—'

Rose held up a hand. 'Wait...'

They all listened and then turned to each other.

'Diana? Dead?' Rose felt tears come to her eyes. 'No!'

There was silence as they took in the details of what had happened in Paris. Nobody wanted to speak and John moved into the lounge and switched the television on.

All three followed him and stared in horror at the scenes unfolding in front of them. Flora pulled Rose towards her.

'A beautiful woman, and her children still so young.'

John turned away. 'I can't watch this. I'm going to see to the grave. Coming Alan?'

Alan nodded, took one last look at the television screen and followed John outside.

Alan climbed into the passenger seat of the truck while John was collecting any tools they might need. He was beginning to feel as if there would never be an end to the stress that had been in their lives, not since the day Matt had told Rose he would be marrying Beth.

They pulled up as close to the grave as they could get. John took down the chainsaw from the truck bed and moved across to the massive branch. He sensed someone behind him and turned.

'Hi, Gareth. We're going to get this tidied up and re-stock our wood pile all at the same time, it seems. If we get finished in time I'll do the window, but if not I'll make it my first job tomorrow.'

'There's no rush, John. It's boarded up. Is everything okay at home?'

Well, I've got two ladies in floods of tears because of Diana, both my children are somewhere out in the countryside with other people and we've got this to move as well as tidy up from the wedding. Yes,' he smiled, 'we're all okay.'

'I'd like to have a chat with you sometime. Tomorrow?' Gareth wasn't smiling.

John hesitated. He didn't really know Gareth, not as well as he had known Tony March. 'Yes, I'll leave the window till tomorrow. You'll be here?'

'Definitely. And take care with this, it's some branch, isn't it?' He turned and walked away, leaving them both to stare after him.

'He's only guessing,' Alan said.

John shook his head. 'No, he knows.'

John started the chainsaw and they began to cut the branch into log-sized pieces. It took two hours of back-breaking work, but at the end of it they had restored the headstone to how it had always looked. Alan lifted the spray of flowers out of the cab and placed them in the vase.

He pressed a kiss on to his fingers and transferred it to the headstone. 'Love you, sweetheart,' he whispered, and they went back home with a truck bed full of logs.

14

John knocked at the door of the vicarage to get the keys and Gareth invited him in.

'You on your own, John?'

'Yes, Alan seems a bit under the weather. I think the last few days have sapped him of energy. I feel as if I could sleep for a week, and he's nearly twenty-five years older than me! I don't need him for this little job; it's only a pane of glass. He's calming our ladies down, who haven't stopped crying for Diana yet, and colouring a picture book with Jacob. I need the keys, that's all.'

'Come in. Want a coffee before you start?'

'That would be good, Gareth, thanks.'

They moved into the kitchen and Gareth indicated a chair at the table. He passed John a mug of coffee and sat down.

'Talk to me.'

John looked startled. 'What?'

'Talk to me. About Lavender. Tell me what happened to her. I wasn't here, and really all I know is that a very young lady died.'

'She was my sister-in-law,' John said with a sigh. 'She was beautiful, funny, and had her whole life in front of her.

She got into a car with her Nan and Granddad and he had a heart attack. The car smashed into the bridge just before you get to Hathersage. Robert was dead before it hit the bridge, Iris, her nan, died instantly and Lavender died a week later. She had just agreed to become engaged to Matt – he took it very badly. It's taken a long time for him to get over it.'

Gareth nodded thoughtfully. 'And now she's angry.'

John stared at the vicar. 'Why did you use that word?'

'Well, wouldn't you feel angry if you'd had your life taken away from you at that age?'

'Of course I would. It's just the word...'

Gareth looked at this normally quiet man sitting at his table. He was visibly shaken.

'Talk to me,' he said again, and John did.

He described what had happened a day earlier and told Gareth of Lavender's words.

He drained his mug of the coffee and Gareth took it from him and refilled it.

'Keep talking,' he said. 'I've got as much coffee as we need.'

At first John spoke hesitantly. It sounded so far-fetched, and yet everything he was saying had happened. It took a long time to tell the whole story, with Gareth occasionally asking questions and John attempting to answer him without sounding stupid.

At the end, John sat back with a sigh. 'So, you now know as much as we know. I don't mind telling you, it's scary, Gareth. Particularly for Holly. We've protected her as best we know how, and she's coping. She's become very quiet so she's obviously not comfortable with how she's feeling at the moment; luckily Jacob doesn't seem to have been targeted. At the bonfire, it was Holly who led him; he wasn't spaced out like she was, and he didn't need to recover. She did, she went straight to bed.'

'I'm going to take all of this to the Bishop. I had initially thought I would just come up to Winterscroft to give a generic sort of blessing, but that's not enough. For anything more, I have to seek my Bishop's permission, and it's not given lightly. I'm going to write down everything you've told me, get you to check it over, and make an appointment to see him. I think we need Matt and Beth here too, because he clearly is the reason all this has erupted now. She must have loved him very much.'

'She did. She gave the engagement a lot of thought because she was just starting at university. In the end, she told Rose just before she got in the car that she was going to say yes, with no marriage until after she had graduated. She was so happy...'

'Then we have to give her release, peace. I'll ring today and make that appointment, and then as soon as Beth and Matt are home we can ask Lavender to depart. I'll pop up tomorrow with my list for the Bishop and get you to check it. I know it's easy to say, John, but try not to worry, it leaves you vulnerable. And as much as you say Holly is the target, I think you need to look at your own interaction with her. She's targeting you as well, even more than Holly.'

John stood. 'Thank you, Gareth. Now, after all that coffee, I need the loo – and the keys. I'll leave you to get on with your work. I've stopped you for long enough.'

It took him under an hour to replace the windowpane and clear up the debris, but his mind was constantly aware of the proximity to Lavender's grave. He took the keys back to the vicarage and then put his tools in the truck. He walked over to the white headstone. He stood and looked at it for a while and then turned and climbed into the cab.

He was putting his faith in Gareth being able to give some peace to Lavender, but also some peace to his family. They had endured almost six months of... what? He wasn't sure. Terror? No, that was much too strong a word. Discomfort? Not strong enough. Whatever the right word was, he knew what he meant. They needed the life they had shared before Matt had turned up that day to say he was marrying Beth.

He drove home and stored the tools back in the garage. Walking round the back of the house he found most of his family having teas and coffees on the patio.

'Coffee, sweetheart?' Rose asked.

He shook his head. 'Had enough to sink a battleship,' he said. 'I've been talking to Gareth. I'll tell you everything later.'

Holly grinned. 'You mean when Jacob and I are in bed? Adult time?'

They all laughed.

'Cheeky,' her mother said. 'One more word and you'll be in bed for a month.'

They sat for quite some time enjoying the warmth of the sun and then it began to cloud over.

'It's promised rain for this afternoon so I'm going to start my rounds now,' John said. 'If it rains heavily they'll all go home and I'll get no information about what levels we're at with the jobs. And I definitely need to speak with Bob up at Stoney Middleton, because they're wanting some pretty major changes to the initial plan.'

Rose nodded. 'It's setting in for the night, but should be good again tomorrow. The gardens need it, so we can put up with half a day of rain.'

John kissed the top of his wife's head as he was about to leave and whispered, 'Gareth knows everything,' then he left. By the time he reached Stoney Middleton the rain had started.

Rose picked up her book, moved into the lounge and sat and stared into space. It seemed Gareth Bruce was involved whether that was sensible or not.

***

The sound of the car's tyres crunching on the gravel caused Rose to close her book with a snap, cross to the window and look out. Maria waved as she exited the driver door and then she saw Tim ease himself out of the passenger side, clearly still in some discomfort. She reached the front door at the same time as her visitors.

'Come in! You're very welcome. We didn't see much of you at the wedding.'

'Well,' Maria said with a smile, 'if Tarzan here hadn't gone climbing trees we would have been here all night.'

Tim grinned at Rose. 'Sorry, Mrs. Broadbent. I really didn't mean to break your tree.'

Rose laughed. 'It's not my tree, Tim, and I'm just pleased to see that it didn't break any part of you. And thank you for taking Holly off my hands yesterday. We got all the clearing up done pretty quickly because Jacob was away as well.'

Maria's dark brown eyes twinkled. 'Oh, I don't think it was any hardship for Tim. He thoroughly enjoyed his day with Holly. They get on so well and she made him laugh all day. It took his mind off his injuries, although I think they're a little more troublesome today. He's using his arm very carefully and that bruise is looking spectacular. The black eye is coming on a treat as well.'

'Well, I would say go on out to Holly, but she's come inside now it's started to rain. I'll give her a shout; she'll be up in her room reading. Please, sit down, you two. I'll make us a pot of tea, Maria. Tim, you want Coke?'

'Yes, please, Mrs. Broadbent.'

There was a thunder of footsteps coming down the stairs and Holly's excited shout of 'Mum, Mrs. Peterson's car...'

Her voice trailed away as she entered the lounge and saw their visitors.

'Hi, Holly.' Tim stood uncertainly.

Rose saw the glance pass between them and saw their obvious liking for each other. 'Holly, take Tim into the kitchen, will you? The Coke is in the fridge and Maria and I would like a pot of tea for two please. And a bun.' She turned apologetically to Maria. 'You have to have a bun. We have a million buns left over from the wedding. In fact, when you go home, you must take some with you.'

She turned to Tim and said, in her schoolteacher voice 'Have a bun. Many buns if you can manage them.' She heard Holly giggle and the two youngsters left to complete their instructions.

The two women could hear them chatting together and their frequent bouts of laughter.

'This is just what they were like all day yesterday. They got on so well.' Maria smiled as the door opened and both Holly and Tim came through carrying a plate with buns, and a tray with a teapot and cups.

Holly and Tim headed back to the kitchen, leaving Maria and Rose to sink back into the armchairs and enjoy their afternoon tea.

Maria looked slightly uncomfortable when she spoke. 'I wanted to have a word with you...'

'Oh? Problem?'

'I'm not sure. I overheard the kids talking yesterday and they were discussing Lavender.'

Rose paused with the cup halfway to her lips. 'Holly was?'

'Both of them. Holly was saying that Lavender was doing bad things and Tim was agreeing with her. He said that was why the branch broke, because it was Lavender's tree and he shouldn't have been on it. But then I heard him say that the veil was up in the tree because Lavender made it blow there. Rose, what's going on? Why, all of a sudden, does my son appear to believe in ghosts?'

'Maria, have you noticed anything at your home?'

'No, I haven't. I don't believe in such stuff.' Her brown curls moved as she shook her head to emphasise her words.

'Neither do we,' Rose said firmly. 'However, for the last six months, strange things have been happening.'

There was a brief hiatus, and then Maria spoke again. 'The smell – it was lavender, wasn't it? It was at Beth and Matt's new place. Is that what you're saying is happening? That you're smelling her fragrance?'

Rose shook her head. 'No. It's a lot more than that. Matt and Beth are aware of it, and they know everything that has happened here. We are linking it all back to the day Matt came here to tell us about the wedding. The day I offered him the use of the Winterscroft garden for the marquee.'

Maria's face turned white. 'You're seriously telling me it wasn't just some silly banter between the kids?'

'Believe me, Maria, I had no idea Tim knew anything of what's been happening here. I'm assuming Holly has told him, but we try to keep it from her. Let's have another fresh pot of tea and I'll tell you everything I know.'

She stood and went into the kitchen with the tray. Holly and Tim were sitting at the kitchen table, each engrossed in a book. They looked up as she came in.

'You've drunk that already?'

'Yes, we need a top-up. I'll do it. You two carry on. What are you reading?'

'Harry Potter and the Philosopher's Stone,' they chorused in unison.

'We bought them yesterday,' Holly explained.

Rose picked up Holly's book and saw it was for her age group.

'That's fine, Holly. Isn't it a bit young for you, Tim?'

They both laughed.

'Mum, there's murder, dark lords, prison – it's not too young for anybody, even you. I'll lend it to you when I've finished it.'

Rose shook her head and wondered how soon she would be getting requests for it to be read at school instead of Dr. Seuss. She made the tea and carried it back through to the lounge where Maria was staring out of the window.

'I'm a bit scared about what you're going to tell me,' she said.

'So are we, Maria, so are we.'

She poured out the tea and sat back down, this time on the settee. 'Come sit here,' she said and patted the space at the side of her. 'It will be easier. I have pictures to show you.'

So began a very painful hour for Maria. Rose began with the day Matt came to call and ended with the collapse of the oak branch.

'So, is Tim in danger?'

'I don't think so. I'm more concerned for Beth, to be honest. She's the one Matt has married and you know how much she loved Matt, but as I've said, Gareth Bruce is apparently on board and while I don't know the details yet, I'm sure he can help.'

'If you need me when Gareth comes, I'll be here. I don't want Tim anywhere near, though.'

'No, I agree. The children will be despatched elsewhere.'

'And you think Lavender really caused Violet's miscarriage? You think she would be that cruel, that vindictive?'

'We have to remember this isn't the Lavender we knew, the lovely girl who would do anything for anyone. This is someone who isn't at peace, at rest, and needs to be. I so hope that Gareth Bruce can do that for her.'

'Well thank you, Rose, for your honesty. None of this will be repeated, not to anybody, and certainly not to Tim.' She stood and began to move towards the door.

'I'll take him home now, but you may see him again tomorrow. He's obviously taken a shine to Holly and after the year he's had… with his dad…'

'He's welcome here anytime, Maria, you know that. You too.'

Rose and Holly waved as the car went down the drive, and Rose pulled her daughter to her. 'You like Tim?'

'He's okay,' she said, but the smile on her face confirmed that she did indeed like him.

John was wet when he finally arrived home, but he'd managed to cover every job still on the books.

'I've picked up two new ones, hopefully to start them next week,' he said. 'Both of them are neighbours of other jobs we're doing.'

'That's good,' Rose replied. 'Will we be rich?'

John laughed. 'Never in a million years, but there's half a chance we'll always be comfortable. That suit you?'

'Suits me fine,' she said, and went through to the kitchen to start the evening meal. She would tell him about Maria's visit later, and no doubt he would be telling her about Gareth. Life was certainly complicated these days.

15

Tim walked up to Winterscroft the following day and Rose wasn't surprised to see him. She didn't quite know how to handle this friendship, but saw it as a positive for Holly, who hadn't really had a good year so far. They would both be attending the same school in a few days and she liked the fact that Tim would look out for her. It was a massive thing, this move to secondary education, and she knew her sometimes insular daughter might not settle easily. It would be smoother with Tim helping her. He was two years ahead of her and knew his way around.

'Hi, Tim,' she greeted him as he walked up the drive. 'Holly and Jacob are round in the back garden. Nip through the garage, it's the easiest way.'

He thanked her and disappeared from her view. She continued to deadhead the roses, a job normally undertaken by her gardener husband, but today she needed thinking time.

She missed Lavender and the facts of her death still hurt, even after six years. Maybe she could have survived if she'd had on a seatbelt, but it was something nobody would ever know. She had been the little sister that she and Violet had adored, which was why it made no sense that her spirit would be creating such heartache now. The true essence of Lavender wasn't the side of Lavender they were now seeing.

She reached down to snip off a spent rose and jumped back as the thorn became embedded in her finger.

'Bugger,' she said under her breath. 'That hurt.' She prodded at her finger with a fingernail but knew it wasn't helping, and she went back inside to do the job properly.

The ice cube cooled her finger down and she levered the thorn partially out with a pin, then finished off the minor surgery with a pair of tweezers.

Holly came through the door to get drinks for them and saw her mother sitting at the kitchen table.

'Oh! I thought you were out front, deadheading,' she said in surprise.

Rose sucked on the now very sore finger. 'I was,' she said and burst out crying.

Holly looked at her for a moment then came around the table and awkwardly put her arms around her mother.

'Don't cry, Mummy. Please don't cry. Shall I get Nan?'

Rose shook her head and tried to smile.

'No, sweetheart, I'm fine. I hurt my finger. It's okay though.'

'And that's why you're crying?' Holly sounded dubious. 'A hurt finger?'

'Yes. Did you want drinks?'

'Yes, please. Coke for Tim, and I'm just having iced water. Jacob wants cordial. It's so hot out there.'

'Okay. Help yourself. I'm just going to get a plaster for this,' and she waved her finger around.

'So, why did you cry?' Holly was persistent as well as observant.

'Oh, just a bad day, I think. I'll be fine. No need to tell Nan or Dad.'

So, Holly followed instructions about who not to tell, and told her granddad. He was reading on the small patio outside their own lounge and Holly walked around the corner of the large house, hoping to find him.

'Mum's been crying,' she said.

Alan looked up. 'Okay, sweetheart, I'll sort it. Give me five minutes.'

She nodded and went back to join Tim and Jacob, now sitting on the lawn enjoying the drinks. Daughter duty done.

Alan found Rose sitting on the front step, a glass of water in one hand and a scrunched-up tissue in the other.

'What's up, lass?'

'Nothing, Dad. Just a bad day. Holly told you?'

'My lips are sealed.'

'It really is nothing. I was thinking about Lavender, about the way she was and how much we loved her, and I got this damn thorn in my finger. It hurt getting it out and suddenly it all felt too much, so I cried. It's as simple or as complicated as that.'

Alan put his arm around her and hugged her. 'She'll always be with us, you know.'

'I know, but not like this, like she is at the moment. For five years, I kept her locked in here,' Rose touched her heart, 'and suddenly she's out in the open again and I'm scared. I'm scared for all of us and I'm not the strong one anymore. I want her back in my heart, not killing people, hurting people.'

'She's not...'

'Dad, wake up! Tony March died on her grave! She led him there. He had no history of heart problems, so what caused his heart to stop on her grave? She did. Maybe she appeared in person and literally scared him to death, or maybe she used some other way, but we both know she killed him. Then she killed Violet's baby; he never stood a chance. Again, on her grave.'

Alan's head dropped and he looked down at his feet. 'I know tha't reight, thar't our Rose, tha't allus reight, but it in't easy to accept it.'

She smiled. His dialect broadened whenever his emotions got the better of him and she loved him for it.

'I know I'm reight, owd man. And I don't want my tears going back to Mum. Understood?'

Alan nodded and stood. 'I'll leave thee in peace, then. Shout if tha needs me.'

He walked away and her eyes filled with tears once more. As she had said, it was just one of those days.

***

Gareth Bruce had used his afternoon to write his sermon for the following week, but the one thing that kept intruding into his thoughts was Lavender Paulson. It briefly occurred to him that he might be in danger – he had married Beth and Matt – but dismissed the thought with a smile. He had seen that the Broadbent family were seriously rattled by all the happenings, but if anyone sat down and thought about it logically, as the Bishop would...

And then he remembered the wedding service and all the mayhem that had happened, the damage that had been caused and the terror on the guests' faces as they had virtually run out of his church. His sanctuary. They should have felt safe there, but on that day, they hadn't.

Young Tim could also have been killed; his head had really cracked as it hit the headstone. If that had been at a slightly different angle, he could have been Lavender's third victim.

He realised with a start that his thoughts had come full circle. He had started by thinking it maybe wasn't that serious, and ended by agreeing with himself that there had definitely been two victims who had died, and almost a third one.

He moved away from his desk and looked out of the window. He had been asked to take on the parish as a permanent move, and he had said yes. His decision was to be part of the sermon; he needed to tell his congregation that there would be stability once again. He just felt uneasy about the whole situation, just uneasy.

He put his notes into the drawer and headed for the front door. His decision about the post at Castleton meant that he could now think about moving his home to the vicarage instead of just his bed and a few bits. He missed having Lorna and the children with him, but his old parish had been in Kent and the journey backwards and forwards would have been impossible.

The relief in Lorna's voice had been obvious when he had told her his news; he hadn't told her about Lavender Paulson. The moving van would be here Wednesday and he could introduce his family to the village, but he was all too aware that he had to tell her everything. Did he do that before the move or after? If he told her before maybe she wouldn't want to come...

He felt like screaming; so many issues to be dealt with, and he was out of his depth. Then there was the appointment with the Bishop he still had to make.

He walked across to Lavender's grave and simply stood there, looking at it.

'Well, young lady, you've caused some problems.' He rested his hand on the headstone. 'Rest in peace, Lavender. The Lord bless you and keep you.'

He turned and began to walk out of the churchyard and down the steps that led into the village. He missed seeing the blood red words '*is back*' as they appeared once more, rivulets of red running down to the base of the headstone.

16

Rose and John discussed Diana's funeral, and decided to ask the children if they would like to watch it. Holly immediately said yes; she had loved the Princess and knew this would be a major event in history. She needed to see it. Rose felt the same, but her grief had threatened to overwhelm her each time she had turned the news on. New developments in the story seemed to occur every day.

The princes, Diana's children, had handled the whole situation so well, just as their training had taught them, and yet they must have been crying inside. The entire country was behind them, and Rose hoped they knew that.

Rose invited Maria and Tim up for the day; she figured if it became too much for Holly, Tim would be a comfort for her, and it was possible she would be able to comfort him. It was only nine months since he had lost his own father, and she guessed even a grand state funeral would bring back memories of the one he had so recently attended.

Maria and Tim arrived early. The cameras had been on since early morning, and Rose had switched on the television as soon as she had walked downstairs. She led their guests into the lounge and went to make tea and coffee for everyone. Flora was already there; Alan said he had a couple of jobs to do, but would join them later.

John wasn't convinced he could watch it but knew he had to show his face; Rose would never forgive him if he didn't. The gathering was a sombre one and everyone in the room at some point during that long day had tears in their eyes.

Rose produced sandwiches and fruit for lunch and everyone was quiet. There was very little to say.

With the departure of the body to Althorp, Rose finally switched off the television. There was utter silence in the room and then Holly said, 'What a beautiful lady.'

As one, they all clapped. Tim and Maria said their goodbyes and Holly and Rose waved as their car disappeared down the drive.

'That was a bad day, Mummy, but I'm glad I decided to watch it. I'm going up to my room now, if that's okay?'

'That's fine, sweetheart. I'll call you when the meal is ready.'

Rose went into the kitchen and found John taking a can of lager from the fridge.

'Want one?' he asked, waving the can at her.

'No, thanks. To be truthful, I feel like going to bed. I feel drained.'

He moved across, took her in his arms and kissed her.

She eventually pulled away and looked at him. 'Well? What was that all about?'

'Because I can. Because I love you. Because after that day, I damn well wanted to!'

She nodded. 'I know.'

She leaned against him for a moment longer and then moved to the pantry to get some potatoes.

'Chips and something for dinner,' she said. 'I've no heart for anything grander, not tonight.'

'That's fine by me. Fish fingers?'

'Fish fingers are for the kids.'

'Why should they have the best food?'

'Fish fingers it is, then.'

In the end, all six of them enjoyed fish fingers, and tried to forget a funeral that would remain in their heads till the day they died.

***

Gareth Bruce welcomed his family into the vicarage, their car arriving half an hour before the removal van. Lorna was getting used to moving; this was Gareth's third parish in as many years, but the Bishop had promised this would be a long stay. She had been a little troubled when her normally placid husband had given her a briefing of the activities around his beautiful church, but behind and beneath his words she could sense he needed her support. Their girls, three-year-old twins, Marah and Tirzah, simply took it in their stride; Mummy would always do the right thing.

Lorna wandered around the vicarage, trying to decide who should have the biggest bedroom. If the girls wanted to stay together it would make sense for them to have the one on the front of the building, but if they would agree to separate rooms they could have two of the rooms that looked out onto the back garden. Some careful persuasion was needed, she guessed.

In the end, no persuasion at all was required; Marah walked into one of the smaller bedrooms and said, 'mine, Mummy?', and Tirzah solemnly agreed with a nod of her head. For the first time her girls were separated.

They sat down that night to a salad meal. Lorna had very little energy to spare for cooking a meal; she needed to conserve it for a talk with her husband.

'So – tell me more about this... visitation, or whatever it is.'

Gareth looked at his wife for a few seconds, unsure how much to tell her, and then he began to talk. He spoke for fifteen or so minutes and she made no comment until he sat back, an exhausted expression on his face.

Lorna stood and moved to sit by him on the sofa. Taking his hand, she kissed it.

'Why didn't you tell me this before? We would have come up much earlier than this, whether it was to be permanent or not. I signed up for this, Gareth, to support and help you. I'm a bit... miffed... that you've not told me the full story until now. And what's happened to Elizabeth March? Is she okay? Did she know what was going on?'

Gareth sighed. 'I don't know. Everyone was bewildered by Tony's death. He had no health problems and his body was across Lavender's grave. Elizabeth left as soon as the funeral was out of the way, even though the Bishop told her I could be accommodated in a guest house until she felt ready to move. She definitely didn't hang about. I had two nights in Val Spencer's guesthouse, and then I moved in here. She said she was going to stay in Hathersage until Tony's affairs were sorted, but I've heard nothing since. Perhaps you...?'

His voice trailed away. He felt miserable. He hadn't even thought about Elizabeth March and her children.

'I'll find out tomorrow where she is, and ring her.' Lorna's gentle voice was the comfort he needed.

'Thank you. It's something I should have done...'

She stood. 'Come on, we're exhausted. Let's try and have a good night's sleep. It will all look better in the morning. I've not looked at your diary – what are you doing tomorrow?'

'I'm going across the road to Winterscroft. I get the Bishop's answer on the actions we can take across there tomorrow morning, so as soon as I get that I'm going to have a chat with John. You'll meet them all on Sunday when they come to church. I think you'll like Rose. She's the lady who will be teaching our two little horrors in a couple of years.'

'I'm looking forward to getting to know people, and the area. I hear nothing but good about Castleton, how spectacularly beautiful it is, so once this lot is unpacked, the girls and I will be off exploring.'

He looked around the room at the many cardboard boxes still to be unpacked, and smiled at her. 'Six months then?' he said, and switched off the light as they left the room.

***

The Bishop had agreed that action was definitely needed and had basically given Gareth carte blanche to take whatever steps were necessary to bring peace to the troubled family, and the late Lavender. He confirmed that the formal agreement was in the post, and advised Gareth to 'crack on with it' as soon as he felt able. His advice was to take a couple of days to pray and meditate before taking whatever action he decided upon, and then to do it with as many family members present as possible, excluding children.

Lorna stayed by her husband's side throughout the telephone conversation; although she would never admit it, she was scared for him. She didn't believe in ghosts, didn't even read stories of the supernatural, and yet... something was definitely out of kilter here if a Bishop was agreeing to what was virtually an exorcism.

She had a strong faith. She guessed it was about to be tested.

She was in their bedroom unpacking a box of clothes when she heard him call upstairs that he would be about half an hour. She stepped across to the window and watched as he walked across the road. He looked dejected, as if his worries were almost too much for him. It occurred to her that her husband was a different person to the one who had agreed to the temporary duties in Castleton following the untimely death of the vicar. He would recover, on that she was determined. Before he left her line of sight he acknowledged a couple of people she assumed were locals, and then he was gone.

'God bless, Gareth,' she said quietly, and went back to her unpacking.

17

Holly and Jacob were despatched to the play area, and Rose, John, Flora and Alan gathered around the kitchen table. Gareth sat at the end, Alan and Flora to his left and John and Rose to his right. He briefly led them in prayer and asked for God's guidance, then began to talk to them about what he was proposing to do.

'The Bishop obviously agreed, then?' John queried.

Gareth nodded. 'Yes. He couldn't really disagree, it was a pretty powerful presentation I made to him, and backed up with that photograph of the swing he conceded we had a problem. He's a good Bishop. Very open-minded.'

'So, when do you want to do it?' Rose asked.

'When are Beth and Matt home?'

'On Sunday, I believe.'

'Then let's go for the following Tuesday. They need to be here. It seems to me that Matt is the reason Lavender can't let go, so I think it's important that they're here. However, the Bishop has specified that no children are to be involved, so...'

Rose smiled although it didn't extend to her eyes. 'I'll ask Maria to take them both out. I'm sure she will. Tim and Holly have become really good friends and Jacob is quite happy to go wherever Holly is. I'll check with her that she is available on that day and confirm it with you.'

Flora looked troubled. 'This is all sounding very serious and scary.'

Gareth looked over the top of his glasses at her. 'It is very serious and scary. This poor child needs putting to rest, and whatever we can do to help her here is really important.'

Flora stared at him. 'She's my daughter, Gareth. If you think for one minute I don't want peace for her, you are very much mistaken. It just bothers me that it might go wrong and then we can never give her peace.'

Gareth reached out and touched her hand. 'We have five people around this table, plus two more who will be there on the day, and we all have a very deep faith. Trust in God, Flora. It's all we can do.'

They talked in generalities for a few more minutes and then Gareth left to go back to unpacking boxes. The four of them remained seated around the kitchen table, Flora pouring out cups of tea from a freshly made pot.

'I don't mind telling you all, I'm scared,' Flora admitted. 'It's like we're dabbling in the occult, but we're doing it blind. Like the Ouija boards when we were kids, when somebody would make that damn glass move and we'd all run away terrified. That's a bit how I'm feeling.'

Rose nodded. 'We're all scared, Mum. And I can't find any words to help you. That's because we all know what you mean. I could never imagine being frightened of Lavender, our beautiful Lavender, but whatever this... this entity thing is, it's not how we knew her, is it? I can't wait for this to be over, for me to feel happy again.'

Alan looked at his daughter and his wife, a frown creasing his forehead. 'I'll never let owt 'appen to you two, you know that, don't you?'

'Of course we do, Dad, but if things go wrong...'

Alan stood and carried his cup to the window. He stared out across the huge back garden and sighed. 'What on earth's happened over the last six months? Everything's changed.'

There was a massive crack of thunder and a streak of bright white lightning hit the centre of the lawn. Alan stepped back in shock and dropped his cup, spattering the wall with tea.

'Shit,' he said and held his hands to his eyes. 'That was bloody bright...'

He rubbed his eyes, suddenly aware of the silence and freezing atmosphere surrounding him. He turned and the other three were immobile at the table. He moved towards them and banged his hand down hard onto the thick oak boards.

'Oy!'

They jumped as one, and Rose let out a small cry of fear.

'Dad, are you okay?'

'I'm fine, bit dazzled by the glare but it's clearing. Sorry about the mess, I'll clean it up.'

'It's freezing,' Flora whispered. 'She's here.'

'Lavender?' Rose repeated the name. 'Lavender? Are you here?'

The cold tap turned on and John moved across to switch it off. It was icy cold to the touch. He rubbed his arms, covered in goose bumps, and turned to face them.

'Say the Lord's prayer,' he said quietly.

Instantly they felt the warmth seep back into the room and Flora began to sob.

'I can't bear this. It's like losing her all over again. She's gone, hasn't she?'

Alan nodded. 'Feel the warmth now? It was freezing until John mentioned praying. Yes, she has gone, Flora. For now. John, the lawn is smouldering… and someone needs to check on the kids.'

Alan disappeared through the patio doors to inspect the damage and John ran to the front door, heading for the play area. Rose moved to sit by her mother.

'We will be able to give her peace, we have to believe that. I just don't understand why it's happening. Why is she so mad? Did she really think Matt would spend the rest of his life brooding for her?'

Flora wiped her eyes. 'Can't let the kids see me crying. I'm sorry, Rose, I'm just feeling a bit overwhelmed.'

They heard the front door open and John came through on his own. 'They're absolutely fine. They didn't even hear that massive crack. Looks like she's able to implant that in our heads. I'll bet we're the only ones in the village who heard it and saw the lightning, and yet it looks as though we've a scorched section of grass to prove it happened.' He shook his head and walked through the patio doors to join Alan. The smoke from the lightning strike had now dissipated and Alan was just standing and looking at the shape created by the burn. It was a letter L. The smell of lavender lingered in the air and John shivered. Bloody cold.

'I'll cut the patch out,' he said, staring at the shape. 'I've some turf left over from the Hope job, so I'll use that. It'll soon blend in.'

'If she lets it,' was Alan's dry response. 'That seed we sowed down by the pond hasn't come through yet, not even any weeds growing in that area.'

John was angry. 'Then we'll sow the bloody area again. Turf it, whatever it takes.' He raised his face to the skies.

'For fuck's sake, Lavender, leave us alone!' he cried.

18

Lorna was troubled by Gareth's distance. He had returned from Winterscroft and gone directly to the study. She left him, knowing he could get a cup of tea if he wanted one. She didn't need to bother him.

However, she was bothered. He had been closeted in there for nearly four hours without food, and although the golden rule was if he was in the study he was to be left undisturbed, she was concerned.

In the end, she knocked on the door and waited. It could be something as simple as he had fallen asleep, but she had to know. He could be ill; that thought made her feel sick, and then she heard a faint, 'come in, Lorna,' and she breathed again.

She opened the door just a crack and looked inside. He was sitting on the sofa, a Bible open on his lap, a pen in his hand and a blank piece of paper on the cushion at the side of him.

She quietly closed the door behind her. 'This is bad,' she said.

He nodded.

'That house feels... possessed. I couldn't wait to get out. I honestly don't know how they're living there, but maybe they've got used to the feeling. It's in the air, a kind of malevolence.' He leaned forward, resting his elbows on his knees.

She picked up the blank piece of paper and sat by his side. 'Can I help?'

'No!' He almost shouted the word and she jumped.

'I'm sorry,' he said, and took hold of her hand. 'I need to keep you three well away from this. I'm going to spend a lot of the time between now and next Tuesday in prayer, in meditation, in going over what I have to do to give peace to this family, and to that poor girl who seems to have lost her way. So, if I go missing, don't look for me. Just trust I will be back at some point. I won't be eating much, so simple meals will do. Poached eggs or something tonight?'

Lorna nodded. She had seen him like this once before and knew he would come out the other side a different person, a better one. She stood.

'That's fine, Gareth. I wouldn't have disturbed you now if I had known your thoughts. I'll eat with the girls tonight, and feed you whenever you feel ready to eat.' She bent and kissed the top of his head and he smiled at her.

'I love you, wife.'

'And I love you, husband. Just take care,' and she left him to his thoughts.

She could hear the girls chattering together in Tirzah's bedroom, so she headed upstairs and asked if they wanted to go for a walk. They nodded enthusiastically and within five minutes they were heading along the main road, Lorna feeling pleased that they no longer had to use the double buggy. Castleton's narrow pavements were definitely not suitable for wide vehicles of any sort.

She knew no one, but several people spoke to the girls. They were always dressed alike, not because their parents felt it was right they should, but because the girls themselves insisted they wear the same clothes. Lorna had tried for a couple of months to dress them differently, but three-year olds can be so insistent, and in the end she gave in. They would be in school soon and the teachers would have the problem of guessing which twin was which, not her.

They followed a small path that led off the main road and headed upwards behind the village. When they reached the end of it they found themselves at a massive entrance to a cave, clearly a visitor attraction, called Peak Cavern.

The twins were virtually together as they spoke. 'Can we go in? Please, Mummy, can we?'

Lorna shook her head. 'Not today, sweeties, but I promise you we'll come and visit with Daddy. We're just here to find the exciting places to tell him about. Shall we go back down now, and maybe get an ice cream?'

They accepted the compromise without argument and soon were sitting on a wall with a cornet each. Lorna breathed a sigh of relief. She didn't want to be the grown-up here, as she had something of a phobia of the underground; thank goodness the girls had agreed it would be better with Daddy there.

There was a small playground and she took them for a half hour run-around before gathering them up and heading back to the vicarage.

As she opened the front door, Gareth came towards them, a smile on his face.

'I missed my ladies,' he said, and kissed all three of them. Lorna held him for a moment and then walked towards the kitchen.

'Poached eggs, girlies? Yes?'

'Yes,' they chorused as one, and disappeared upstairs to continue their game.

***

Holly was sitting on her pillow, her knees pulled up to form a book rest. She was reading Harry Potter for the second time, eager to memorise the characters' names, the strange sounding names associated with Hogwarts and the wonderful plot lines. She needed her mum to read it soon; there were things she wanted to discuss with her, just as she could discuss them with Tim. She guessed an adult would see things very differently.

It became very cold within a matter of seconds, and she pulled her duvet up around her legs, her eyes still fastened on to the page she was reading. It was then that the pages began to move, flipping faster and faster until, at the end of the book they stopped, the book left her knees and flew into the wall at the end of her bed.

She whimpered and hugged the duvet closer to her. She hardly dared look around; something was wrong, something horrible.

She turned her head and saw a figure; closed her eyes, too scared to look again. Her hand moved towards the crucifix and she grasped it firmly, swinging it around towards where she had seen the figure. She briefly opened her eyes and saw the crucifix slide through the wispy, ethereal form that was just standing there. 'Mummy,' she whispered. Then a little louder, 'Mummy!'

There was no answer.

Rose was in the kitchen preparing vegetables for the evening meal. John was sitting at the table reading his newspaper and occasionally telling his wife some snippet he had come across. They both looked at each other with fear once they did hear, 'Mummy, I need you!'

The knife fell in the sink with a clatter as Rose raced up the stairs, followed within seconds by John.

She burst into the bedroom and saw Holly cringing against the wall, the duvet covering most of her head.

'What's wrong, sweetheart, what's wrong?'

'I saw her,' she cried, and peered over the top of the duvet. Her face was white.

'Who? Who did you see, Holly?'

'Lavender. I saw her. She was by the side of my bed. She made my book pages turn on their own and then my book flew over there.' She pointed towards the wall at the end of her bed.

Rose sat on the bed and pulled her daughter into her arms. She could smell the lavender perfume all around Holly.

'Maybe it was a dream, Holly,' she said.

'I wasn't asleep. I was reading Harry Potter. She was by my side.'

Rose looked to John for support.

'What did she look like, sweetheart?' he asked.

'She had on white jeans, a blue top like a shirt and a hat like mine, like my white one, but hers was in blue.'

John looked at Rose and felt something approaching horror. He had just listened to his daughter describe Lavender as she had looked coming out of the house on the day of the accident. Holly had only been five years old on that dreadful day; he doubted she would have remembered what Lavender had worn.

'Come downstairs, sweetheart, come and have a drink. I think you must have nodded off for a moment and had a bad dream. You've heard so much about Lavender these last few weeks that you're starting to imagine her now.' She laughed in an attempt at lightening the mood.

'I saw her. She made my book pages turn really fast. I didn't dream that. And my book's somewhere over there on the floor, isn't it? You know I never throw my books around. I didn't do that, Mum.'

Mum, not Mummy. Rose felt sick. The air in Holly's room was freezing, and she helped her daughter out from under the duvet that was wrapped around her.

'Come on, it's warmer outside than it is in here.'

Holly looked at her parents, a bewildered expression on her face. How could she make them believe her?

But they did. They had believed her from the moment they had entered the bedroom. They just couldn't tell her.

She stomped downstairs, angry with them, angry with Lavender, angry. She went straight across the kitchen and out of the patio doors; she couldn't speak to them, she needed time on her own.

She shivered, still feeling the effects of the freezing cold atmosphere of her own bedroom, so she walked around the house and through into her grandparents' wing.

Alan saw her expression and stood.

'What's up, young 'un?'

'I've seen her, I've seen Lavender, and they don't believe me. She was in my bedroom, Granddad, and she made my book fly off the bed and hit the wall.'

He pulled her to him and hugged her. 'Let's go find your Nan, see what she has to say about all this.'

They didn't have to go and find Flora; she had heard their voices and came through from the kitchen.

'Alan?'

'It's our Holly, Flora. She says she's seen Lavender.'

Flora visibly cringed. 'But...'

Alan shook his head and mouthed *leave it* to her.

She nodded.

'Come and sit down, Holly,' she said gently. 'You want a drink, a biscuit or something?'

Holly shook her head. 'No, I want somebody to believe me. They didn't.'

There was a gentle knock on the connecting door and John popped his head around.

'Is...?' and stopped speaking when he realised the object of his question was having a hug with her granddad. He called through to Rose to tell her he had found Holly, and Flora waved him through.

'And tell Rose to come as well. It seems we have things to talk about,' Flora said. 'I've just made a pot of tea, come and have a drink with us.'

John nodded and went to get his wife. Her troubled face was starting to be her normal face.

By now Holly was sitting on the sofa, next to her granddad. She glared balefully at her parents. 'You don't believe me.' The accusation was blatant.

'We do,' Rose said. 'We just thought we were protecting you by trying to make you think it was a dream. Maybe it's time to talk, Holly, and not beat about the bush.'

Flora came through with a tray as Rose settled Jacob at the kitchen table with some crayons and paper. She might be forced into having 'the talk' with Holly, but there was no way she was going to have Jacob frightened.

Alan opened the conversation. 'Holly is scared, Rose. She seems to think she has seen Lavender, and this fear is real.'

John sighed, a deep long sigh. 'She has seen Lavender.'

Flora's cup wobbled in its saucer.

'See. I said I had,' Holly sobbed.

'But...' Flora carefully placed the cup and saucer on the coffee table, fearful that she might drop it.

'But how do we know? Was that going to be your question, Flora?' John's tone was grim.

'Yes, it was.'

'Tell your grandparents what Lavender was wearing when you saw her, Holly,' he said gently. 'Don't be afraid, we do believe you.'

Holly turned to Flora, while holding tightly to Alan's hand.

'She had on white jeans, a blue top like a shirt and a blue baseball cap. I couldn't see her shoes, but I saw the rest of her, and she made all the pages in my book spin through really fast, and then the book shot out of my hand and smashed into the wall. It was so scary.'

'Lavender would never hurt you,' Alan said. 'Always remember that, sweetheart.'

'I wasn't scared of her; I was scared because of what she made the book do. Books can't do what she did to it.'

'So, wasn't that the clothes Lavender was wearing when she got in the car?'

Flora nodded, misery etched into her face. 'Yes. We brought them home when she was in hospital and burnt them. So much blood... they were beyond saving.'

'Okay, Holly,' her mother interrupted. 'Remember I gave you the little cross around your neck to touch if you were troubled by anything? And the crucifix on your bedside table? Did you touch them?'

Holly nodded. 'I touched her with the crucifix but she just stood there. The book didn't stop, and she didn't disappear till you and Dad came running up the stairs. So, they don't work, do they, Mum?'

Mum. Not Mummy. She dreaded it ever changing to Mother.

Rose stood and walked towards the window, staring out at the driveway. Despite her efforts, she couldn't protect her children, and she didn't know what to do. She switched off from the muted conversation behind her, aware that all three of the adults were trying to reassure Holly, but she couldn't join in. She couldn't come up with the solicitous words of comfort that were basically lies because she believed Lavender was getting stronger despite all their efforts so far.

She needed Matt and Beth to be home so that Gareth could try whatever plans he had to lay Lavender to rest.

19

Sunday morning saw Lorna introduced to the congregation. She had taken special care with her appearance, aware that first impressions are so important. The twins had been integrated into Sunday School, and the bright sunny morning uplifted everyone. She stood by Gareth's side as the congregation left at the end of the service, although most of them moved around the side of the church heading for the church hall. Sunday morning coffee with the vicar was a tradition not given up lightly. She followed them round and was soon deep in conversation with a group of ladies who did fund-raising for the church.

'What can I do to help?' Lorna asked them.

'Well, what are you good at?' Val asked. The other six all nodded in agreement at what she had asked.

'Erm... I can bake.'

'Oh, that's good. We normally have a cake stall every Sunday morning, but since Tony... anyway, we thought we'd better suspend it till we had a definite new vicar to see whether we should carry on or not. We make about £30 a week from it.' Val opened her handbag and took out an envelope with £78.32p written on it. She handed it to Lorna.

'These are the takings from the last three weeks up to Tony dying. I've been carrying them round with me because Elizabeth did all the banking, and I didn't know if we should carry on.'

Lorna smiled. 'Then let's carry it on, see if we can't organise other things. I did all sorts of fund-raising at our last parish. Maybe we should have a meeting one night this week, thrash out some ideas. You have a chairperson?'

The ladies looked at each other. 'Well, I suppose it's Val. She talks more than us.'

Val laughed. 'Well, that's a good qualification for being a chairperson. Shall we meet in the church hall? Wednesday at seven o'clock? I can let Rose, Flora and Maria know. I think they've already left.'

Lorna tried to imagine Gareth's diary and realised he had the exorcism at Winterscroft on Tuesday. Maybe he wouldn't be up to watching the girls and putting them to bed on the Wednesday. She didn't know how he would be.

'Would you mind meeting at the vicarage instead? It's just in case Gareth has to go out or anything. I don't want to miss it just because I don't have childcare. And I'll also give Elizabeth a call and find out where the paying-in book is and check that she's okay. I'll put this in the safe until we know what we're supposed to do with it.' She waved the envelope at them.

They all agreed, continued to chat for a few minutes while washing the cups and saucers and then peace descended on the church once more.

***

Rose and Holly decided to walk to the shop before going home, and left the rest of the family to head back up to Winterscroft.

'You seem to get on really well with Tim,' Rose said.

'Huh huh.'

'You like him?'

'Sure. He's good fun and we talk a lot.' Slowly Holly was coming round from her fit of pique.

I'm pleased. He's good for you. He'll look out for you at your new school.'

She looked at her mother, a crease across her forehead. 'He's not my boyfriend, you know.'

Rose smiled at the fierce expression. 'I know, sweetheart, he's your boy friend as opposed to your boyfriend, and that's good. You're much too young to have a boyfriend.'

The frown disappeared. 'Okay, so long as you know.'

Maria stepped out of the shop door as they reached it. 'Hi,' she said. 'I'd have walked up with you if I'd known you were coming here. You okay, Holly?' she asked with a smile.

'I'm fine, thanks. Is Tim here?'

'No. He's nipped back to the church. Left his sunglasses in the pew. He should be here in a minute.'

'Let me just get my milk,' Rose said, 'and we'll walk round with you.'

Holly and Maria waited outside the shop and when Rose rejoined them, they set off to walk through the village. As they rounded the bend, they saw Tim on the opposite side of the road.

The air became still, cold as ice, the birds stopped singing and Holly, Rose and Maria stopped moving, almost stopped breathing. It seemed to them that the world had died and then, through the wraithlike fog surrounding them, they heard the faint cry of *Matt* coming from Tim's direction.

They watched as he stepped from the pavement, watched as the truck came round the bend, and watched as it hit him. The wheel had gone over him before the driver managed to stop and as he jumped down from his cab the air cleared and Maria was screaming. She ran across the road to her son, closely followed by Rose.

'Stay there, Holly,' she yelled, and ran to join Maria.

The driver was trying to get to Tim who was under the lorry, attempting to pull him out.

Maria pushed him out of the way and crawled under the lorry to cradle his head in her arms. She heard a shout that an ambulance was on the way, and then she heard Tim whisper.

'Matt. Saw Matt. And Lav...' His eyes rolled back into his head, and he was gone.

Rose reached her friend and crawled alongside her. Maria was sobbing hysterically, holding his head close to her. Rose put her arms around her as best she could, and they cried together.

And then John was there, solid and dependable as always.

'How...?'

'Val rang. She saw it happen, so I've sent Holly home. Your mum and dad will look after her. I'm here for you and Maria.'

They heard the sirens long before the ambulance arrived; the police arrived at the same time and moved the crowds away, shutting off the road and organising traffic. Maria took some persuading to leave Tim and went straight back to him once they had pulled him from under the truck.

She drew him close to her and Rose watched helplessly. She knew she had to go home and break the news to Holly, yet couldn't leave Maria and Tim.

Maria was distraught, trying to stop anyone from taking her son, but eventually he was placed in the ambulance and John and Rose took her to Winterscroft.

Rose led her into the lounge and Flora followed them in.

'Maria, I'm so sorry...'

'He's gone, Flora. Tim's dead...'

'I know, my love. Will you stay here, for now? You can't be on your own. Stay with us until Matt and Beth get back tonight.'

'Matt!' For a second she looked startled. 'That's what Tim said, what he tried to tell me in those last few seconds,' and she began to cry again.

'What did he say, Maria?' Rose gathered Maria to her. 'Tell me?'

'He said *Matt, saw Matt and Lav...*'

Rose remembered the atmosphere, the cloying stillness of the air around them, almost imprisoning them on that small section of pavement and the half-heard *Matt* that had reached them just as Tim stepped off the opposite pavement. And then the truck...

She knew that Lavender had killed again.

20

By two o'clock, Rose had made a decision.

'Pierre, I need to speak to Violet. How is she?' Rose had spoken with her sister a few days earlier and had been concerned at the unhappiness in her voice.

'Health-wise, she is good, Rose. In her head and her heart, not so good. I'll go and get her.'

'Thank you, but before you do, I need to ask you something. I'll ask Violet independently of you, but I need to hear your answer. If I sent the children to you for a couple of weeks, could you cope?'

There was no hesitation. 'Of course I could, but you will have to ask Violet, I cannot answer for her. We have both booked six weeks' compassionate leave, so...'

'Thank you,' Rose whispered. 'Can I speak to her now?'

'Of course.' She heard him place the receiver on the table and then his footsteps as they moved away. He called Violet's name, and then she heard him say, *'It's Rose.'*

'Rose? What's wrong?' She heard the anxiety in Violet's voice and felt tears trickle down her face.

'So many things, Violet, so many things. I need to put my children somewhere safe. Can I bring them to you, please? Maybe just for a couple of weeks.'

There was a moment of silence. 'But will they come here? I know Holly will be okay, but Jacob doesn't know us as well as Holly does. Will he understand? And what about school? I know you're fine about Jacob, but Holly starts at the new school in a couple of days.'

'Being off school is better than both of them being dead.' She broke down in tears.

'My God, Rose, get them on the next plane. We'd love to have them. Maybe they'll help me to feel better. What's happened to bring this on?'

'Tim is dead.'

'Tim? Matt's brother Tim? But he's only about twelve, isn't he?'

'He's thirteen. Got hit by a truck in the village after church today. Violet, he managed to say he saw Matt and Lavender. Matt is still on honeymoon, due back late tonight.'

There was a moment's pause while Violet digested the news. 'Oh, my God,' she said eventually. 'Get them here. Are you bringing them?'

'Yes. I don't want to send them by airline accompanied. I'd worry too much.'

'No, I'll send Pierre to Manchester. I'll ring you back when I know times. You need to be there, for Maria, Matt and Beth. Give me ten minutes,' and she disconnected.

As a result, Rose set off for Manchester an hour later. She had explained to Holly about Tim and the young girl had been distraught, inconsolable. She couldn't understand why her mother wanted to send her off to France, especially as she was to start at her new school in two days, and although she didn't understand her own feelings, she needed to grieve for her best friend.

Jacob just felt totally bewildered. He liked Aunty Violet and Uncle Pierre, but he thought it was time to be going back to school, or so his mum kept saying anyway.

The journey to Manchester was full of questions. John had wanted to go as well but Rose persuaded him to stay at home, to be there for Maria. The children were clearly puzzled and Holly couldn't control her tears. She was going to miss Tim so much, and when would she be able to start school? It was okay for Jacob, as his mum was his teacher; it was no longer like that for her.

Pierre was already there and waiting for them when Rose walked her two children into the departures area. She sorted their tickets out, handed them over to Pierre, kissed everybody and headed back out to her car, all within the space of half an hour. She cried most of the way home. She had never been apart from them before and hated having to do it.

As soon as she walked through the door she rang Violet, who confirmed the plane was due to land in half an hour and she would ring as soon as the children walked through her door.

'We'll keep their minds away from everything that is happening, I promise.' Violet could hear the grief in Rose's voice and just wanted to hug her.

'I know you will,' Rose said. 'Maria and I are walking round to Beth and Matt's house to be there when they arrive home. They know nothing yet.'

She tried desperately to keep busy and when Violet rang to confirm the children were with her and settled into their rooms, she breathed a huge sigh of relief.

John felt at a loss. He couldn't comfort his wife; he didn't know how. A hug simply didn't seem to be enough.

'Would you like me to go to Maria's with you?'

Rose shook her head. 'No, we'll be fine. It's going to be so hard telling them as soon as they walk through the door from their honeymoon.'

***

Maria and Rose heard the car pull up outside the cottage, then the laughter from Beth; happy laughter.

They heard the front door open, the sound of further giggles; Matt almost fell into the room as he swept his bride into his arms and carried her over the threshold.

They both saw Maria and Rose in the same instant, and Matt carefully lowered Beth to the floor.

'Mum? Rose? Is everything okay?' And he knew it wasn't.

Beth took hold of her husband's hand and turned to face him. The atmosphere inside the small lounge was tense; something had happened.

'Matt,' Maria faltered, and he crossed the room to her in three strides and pulled her to him.

'What's wrong?'

Rose spoke. 'Sit down, you two. We've something to tell you.'

Beth sat. How could everything have changed so much within one minute?

Matt looked down into his mother's face. 'Mum?'

Maria sobbed. 'It's Tim.'

'Is it the fall from that damned tree? Is he back in hospital?'

Rose intervened and led Maria to the settee. Matt followed her and sat by her side, putting his arm around her shoulders.

Maria was sobbing uncontrollably and Matt looked towards Rose. 'For God's sake, Rose...'

'It's Tim,' she said quietly. 'He died this afternoon.'

The silence in the room was broken only by the sobs from Maria. Matt seemed temporarily incapable of speech.

Eventually Beth spoke. 'No... not Tim. How? We thought he was okay...'

'It was nothing to do with the fall, Beth. He'd completely recovered from that. He stepped off the pavement on the main road and a lorry hit him.'

'What?' Matt looked outraged. 'But we're all brought up in this village knowing how bad that road is. He would never...'

Maria sighed, and leaned into her son. Her sobs had quietened a little and she spoke carefully.

'It wasn't just that, Matt. When I crawled under the lorry he was still alive, just. His last words were, he saw you and... Lavender.'

Beth stood and slammed her way into the kitchen. 'Fucking Lavender, always fucking Lavender.'

Matt stood to follow his wife, but Rose waved him back down. 'Your mum needs you, Matt. I'll go to Beth.'

Beth was leaning against the sink, taking deep breaths. 'How many more, Rose? How many more lives is she going to ruin?' she said, without turning around.

Rose walked towards her and drew her into her arms.

'Come here,' she said. 'Let me hold you. I know it's a shock, especially with it being the end of your honeymoon, but Matt is going to need you.'

Beth took a great shuddering breath and relaxed into Rose. 'Matt doesn't need me,' she mumbled.

'Of course he does. He's just lost his only brother.'

'We've just had two weeks in the Maldives, Rose; sea, sand, stunning weather, relaxed, drinks aplenty – and we still haven't made love. Bloody Lavender went with us, even if it was only in his head.'

'What?' Rose looked shocked.

'Don't say anything to him.' Tears ran down her face. 'He won't appreciate me telling you. That little show coming in was because he knew Maria would be here, we saw the light on. We thought she'd probably done something nice for us, flowers, maybe a little supper. I never expected...'

Rose's head was reeling. She was completely out of her depth. 'Did he say anything...?'

'No, just that he needed time.'

Beth shook her head as if trying to clear it. 'I don't know what to do, Rose. I feel as though I've committed bigamy. He's still married to his precious Lavender in his head.'

'Well,' Rose said gently, 'whatever has happened or not happened between you, both Maria and Matt need our support right now. Tim is dead, and in a dreadful way. I'm sure time will heal your relationship, but right now we have to be the supportive ones. Can you do it?'

Beth tore off a piece of kitchen roll and blew her nose. 'Of course. I haven't stopped loving Matt, that's not it. I just don't know what to do.'

'Then let's make some tea, and go back into them.'

21

In the end, Matt insisted Maria stay with them; he wouldn't hear of her going home, and said he should be the one to take care of her. Beth went upstairs to put bedding on their spare bed, and then Matt walked Rose back to Winterscroft.

John was waiting for her, and made her a hot chocolate. They sat on the settee without speaking for a while.

'What now?' John eventually said.

'Now we bury a lovely lad. Gareth is seeing Maria tomorrow, although I don't think that's for funeral arrangements. That could be a while, I suppose. They'll have to investigate it, but it wasn't the driver's fault, John, it really wasn't. That poor man. He'll have that for the rest of his life.'

'And Tuesday?'

'I think it's more urgent than ever, but will Matt and Beth be up to it? I don't know what to do. I've spoken with Richard about Wednesday—'

'Who?' John looked puzzled, his mind clearly not on the same wavelength as his wife's.

'Richard Hogan – my Headmaster, the man who employs me, sort of,' she said with a small smile. 'I've explained Jacob won't be back for a couple of weeks, and he's told me to go back to work when I'm ready.'

'Sorry – I'd almost forgotten there's a real world out there, with jobs and suchlike. Just saying Richard threw me. This six-week break has gone in a flash.'

'It certainly has. I'm going into Holly's school tomorrow; I've met Karen, her new Headmistress, several times, so we do know each other. I need to talk to her. And I think I need to tell her everything. I'm not sure she'll understand, but she knows I'm not a scatterbrain and she'll see my worry. She'll also know about Tim by now. I can't put Holly into any school here until we know we are all safe. We can't underestimate my sister any longer.'

***

Karen Aristocleous listened attentively as Rose spoke of their problems and what had happened over the summer. She left nothing out, but it was only when she spoke of the death of Tim and the words he had spoken at the end, that she began to believe her.

'And Holly is now in Paris with your sister?'

Rose nodded. 'I didn't know what else to do. Holly has been targeted by whatever this Lavender entity is – and believe me, Karen, I'm struggling just as much as you are in accepting that this sort of thing happens. When we spoke to our vicar, he assured us that it's a lot more common than anyone realises. He's been a help, but tomorrow will show just how much of a help. He's coming to bless the house and perform some sort of ceremony; I hesitate to say exorcism because I always believed that was to expel demons out of a person. This is laying an unhappy spirit to rest. I sound silly, don't I?'

'Not at all,' Karen said. 'And I want you to keep Holly away from all of this just as long as you need to; I can arrange extra tuition for her if she falls behind, so her education isn't the problem. Her well-being is. Please keep in touch, Rose.' She stood and held out her hand.

Rose returned the handshake and walked out of the office. Karen watched her cross the car park; she felt deeply troubled. Tim had been a popular pupil and she had the difficult job ahead of telling the other 1,000 pupils about his death. Rose's story had bothered her, but not nearly as much as the death of one of her pupils.

She sat down at her desk and continued with the job she had been doing before Rose had arrived – writing the 'welcome to school' speech for the first assembly. This was the first one in her entire career that involved explaining there had been a death.

Rose sat in the car for a few minutes and thought about the conversation she had just had with Karen Aristocleous, and wondered if she would have been so understanding if a parent had come to her with this strange story. She liked to think she would, but would she just have played along with it? Not really believed what she had been hearing? Is that what Karen had just done, or did she genuinely believe her?

She switched on the ignition and drove home deep in thought. What now? She doubted very much that the planned visit by Gareth would go ahead; surely Matt and Beth wouldn't want to take part, as they now had different issues to deal with.

She parked the car in front of the house and Flora came out to meet her.

'Everything okay?' her mother asked, and Rose nodded.

'I think so. Karen listened to everything I had to say and then said if Holly slipped behind she would provide extra support, but I think her mind was really full with Tim's death. It must be worse for her now I've come along with my tale of woe, because it puts Tim's death into a whole new sphere, doesn't it?' Rose shook her head. 'I'm feeling at a loss, Mum, not sure where to turn next. It seems we're having to tell more and more people, and I'm not altogether convinced they believe it. Maria definitely didn't, but after Tim's last words I think she does now. That just makes me feel all the more guilty.'

'Guilty?' Flora looked her daughter with concern. 'Rose, none of this is your fault. It's not anybody's fault.'

'I almost felt that I should be apologising to Karen for causing all this disruption to her school. She listened to me very patiently, didn't mock anything I was saying, but... oh, I don't know. It seemed to me I was telling her a witches and wizards story. To be fair, she didn't treat me as a silly old woman, and she was quite solicitous towards Holly, basically told me to make sure she was safe and she would help her if she needed it. I suppose I just don't like having to bring anybody else into it.'

'And Maria?' Flora queried. 'Have you heard from her?'

'No. I'm going to have a walk down there now, see if she needs anything. Heaven only knows what I'll say to her, but I need her to know if she needs anything, we're here.'

'You want me to come?'

Rose shook her head. 'No, I'll be fine. The walk might clear my head.'

Flora leaned forward and kissed her. 'Give Maria my love – and Beth and Matthew, of course. It's been a rotten end to their honeymoon.'

Rose walked slowly down the drive and just as slowly opened and closed the gates at the bottom of the drive.

The village seemed quiet, that was something that wasn't normal. Traffic, to her, appeared minimal and as she walked past the small gate that led into the churchyard, she paused.

She turned into the churchyard and walked amongst the graves until, down by the big oak tree that was now minus a branch, she stopped. The headstone was in its usual pristine condition and she looked at the inscription, as she did every time she visited the grave.

She missed Lavender, missed her every day. Her life had been a joyous one; she had been the one everyone wanted in their group, the sparkly one. The church had been full to capacity for her funeral and many of the people who came to celebrate her life had been under twenty-one.

Rose knelt down and bowed her head in prayer. She prayed silently, and she wept for the life that was wasted. The headache began to build and she reached out a trembling hand to the headstone to help her to stand. There was a flash behind her eyes and she cried aloud.

Gareth came across her still form ten minutes later and his immediate reaction was *not another one.* He felt for a pulse in Rose's neck and then began to pull her away from the grave. He laid her on the grass at the side of the path, and waved frantically at a figure at the other end of the graveyard. The woman began to walk across to him and he increased his waving. As she reached them he heard Rose moan.

'Oh my God, it's Rose,' she spluttered. 'You okay, Rose?'

Rose's response was tentative, faint. 'I will be, Joyce,' she said. 'Gareth...'

'Thanks, Joyce,' Gareth said. 'I called you because she wasn't coming round, but we'll manage now. Sorry to disturb you.'

'If you're sure – I've left flowers scattered everywhere. Just dumped them when I saw you really needed me over here.'

They watched as Joyce walked back towards her husband's grave and then Gareth helped Rose to her feet.

'Come inside the church,' he said. 'You look as though you need five minutes.'

She tried to stand. 'It's my head,' she said. 'And I feel sick. I was fine when I walked down the road...'

'Can you walk?'

Rose nodded. 'I think so. Take my arm, Gareth, I don't want to fall.'

They walked into the church with Gareth's arm around her waist; he had quickly realised her legs were like jelly and he lowered her safely onto a pew.

'I'll make some sweet tea,' he said softly. 'You sit here and don't move. And when we've had a drink, I'm going to ring John. He needs to come and collect you. Were you going somewhere or just coming here?'

She looked up guiltily. 'Oh... I was going to Maria's. I just stopped off for five minutes of prayer at Lavender's grave and then I don't really remember anything. I just know my head is pounding.'

'I'll make that tea,' he said. 'See if that helps.'

She smiled, but even that simple action hurt her head. She waited patiently for Gareth to return and gratefully took the mug of tea he offered. He handed her two tablets.

'They're only paracetamol. They might just take the edge off the headache. You haven't had any already, have you?'

'No,' she said. 'I didn't have a headache before I set off.'

'Well, I've rung Winterscroft, explained to your mum what's happened and she's going to contact John. He's somewhere in Bamford, but she's got the phone number. I said I'd hang on to you until he got here.'

She nodded in response. 'Thank you, Gareth, and thank God you found me so quickly.'

'We have to put a stop to this, Rose,' he said gently. 'Tomorrow has to go ahead, even if Matt and Beth don't feel they can be there.'

'You think this is down to Lavender? My head?'

'Don't you?'

The misery was etched into her face. 'Yes, of course I do,' she sighed. 'But I don't want to believe she's trying to hurt me.'

'She didn't cause your death,' he responded.

She looked up in surprise. 'You think she has boundaries she won't cross then? I'd rather she'd taken my life than Tim's.'

Rose felt the tears begin to trickle down her face and she reached into her pocket for a tissue. If losing Tim was hard for her, how much harder was it for Maria? And Matt and Beth? She took a sip of her tea, leaned against the back of the pew and closed her eyes.

'You're right about tomorrow, Gareth. We have to go ahead, even if Matt and Beth can't be there.' Her eyes remained closed, the headache felt less intense that way.

The door opened with a bang and John strode through.

'Rose? Oh, there you are.' He was at her side in seconds and Gareth stood up.

'I'll leave you in John's hands now, Rose. When you've finished the tea can you put the mug in the office? The Brownies are in later and I'll be in trouble if they find an empty tea mug in here.'

John shook his hand. 'Thanks, Gareth. We'll see you tomorrow?'

'Definitely, we have to try and find some way to stop this.'

John sat in the pew at the side of his wife and she opened her eyes slightly. 'I'm sorry,' she whispered. 'It's my head...'

'Finish your tea,' he said. 'Let's get you home and in bed. I think you need to sleep.'

She put her mug on the pew at the side of her and tried to stand. John quickly put his arm around her and led her towards the door. He helped her climb into the truck and then drove round to Winterscroft, thankful that Flora had opened the gates.

He helped Rose down and then stayed behind her all the way up the stairs. She lay on the bed and closed her eyes. He eased off her shoes, covered her with a blanket and closed the curtains.

'Sleep,' he said softly, and kissed her brow.

Alice Kennedy found the mug. 'Well,' she said, 'look what I've found. If we had a lady vicar, she wouldn't leave pots around for us to wash up! I'm going to tell him next time I see him.' And she took it into the small kitchen and washed it, feeling quite superior.

22

Matt and Beth made the decision not to go to Winterscroft for the blessing because they felt unable to leave Maria. She hadn't returned to her own home; she hadn't even moved out of their spare bedroom, occasionally sleeping, occasionally sitting in the small armchair and staring out of the window.

Beth took drinks and food up, but the food remained untouched. Maria was almost catatonic; everything seemed unreal to her. The death of her husband had hit her hard and she was still recovering from the shock of his heart attack; to lose her youngest son nine months later was unbearable.

Tim's last words kept playing over and over in her mind; *Matt, Matt and Lav...*

He had seen Lavender? With Matt? In her heart, she knew it was impossible, but Tim had clearly seen something. His hand had lifted in acknowledgement of someone just before he had stepped off the pavement.

She closed her eyes and allowed the medication to take her to a place where nothing hurt, where she still had her son, her sanity.

Beth stood in the bedroom doorway and looked at her new mother-in-law sleeping in the armchair, facing the window to a world that had, for her, changed forever.

This wasn't how she had imagined the start of her married life would be, and it caused Beth pain to know she would never get this time back again. They should have been cementing their love, getting to know one another properly.

Maria was so still that Beth remained a few moments longer, checking the rise and fall of her chest. There was slight movement and, satisfied that all was well for the moment, she went back downstairs to join Matt.

He was sitting at the kitchen table, just staring. Almost as still as his mother had been. Beth put her arms round him and leaned her head against the back of his head. She felt him stiffen, and abruptly moved away.

'Sorry,' she muttered, walked into the lounge and left him with his thoughts. She looked at the pile of wedding presents stacked in the corner and pulled two or three towards her.

They had decided on the flight home that they would spend Monday opening them and writing thank you letters; she now ripped the paper off the first one, from her Aunty Janice and Uncle David, and revealed a beautiful cut glass vase. She would do the job herself as he seemed to have opted out of the marriage on the day of their wedding.

'Fuck you, Lavender,' she muttered, and pulled a second gift onto her knees. The card read *Happy Wedding Day, you two guys, with lots of love from Tim xxx.*

The tears flowed freely and she couldn't open it. She placed it carefully on the floor, pulled her legs up onto the sofa and pulled a cushion towards her. Cuddling it, she drifted off into a welcome doze.

She stirred an hour later to see the cut glass vase filled with sprigs of lavender, and Matt frantically trying to remove them before she woke.

His head dropped when he realised she had seen. 'I'm just—'

'Moving them?'

He nodded, misery etched into his face.

She sat up, her face a mask of horror. 'But—'

'I don't know. I don't know how this stuff got here, Beth, I'm just trying to keep it away from you.'

She could hear the despair in his tone.

'Come here,' she said, and held out her arms. 'We'll fight her together. Don't hold back thinking you're protecting me. I love you, Matt, I'm your wife. It's time to make that a true statement.'

She stood and took him by the hand, leading him towards the stairs. At the bottom, she paused momentarily and looked back into the room. The lavender had been dumped on the carpet.

'Fuck you, Lavender,' she said for the second time in an hour, 'he's mine.'

They climbed the stairs hand in hand, and heard the crash as the cut glass vase hit the edge of the coffee table before shattering all over the carpet.

***

They cleaned up the glass, careful where they trod, occasionally smiling at each other, occasionally touching hands. Matt wrapped the vacuum cleaner cord around the handle and lifted it to put it in the pantry.

Beth looked around her, a puzzled expression on her face.

'Where's the lavender?' she said.

'I have absolutely no idea.' Matt took her in his arms and kissed her. 'And what's more, I don't care. I'm so sorry, Beth. When we got to our hotel on the first night, after we'd left the reception, I opened my case to take my toiletries into the bathroom. You had a champagne glass in your hand, that stunning nightie on... and across the top of my clothes was a sprig of lavender. That tiny thing killed any desire. I was scared for you, because through all that Lavender has done it's been obvious; it's because we've got married.'

Beth laughed. 'But we'd slept together before...'

'It's the wedding. That's always been the catalyst. Now we're together for life. Until our marriage ceremony that was never a definite to her. Now it is. And she's getting stronger, Beth. We have to be careful. She's taken Tim...' He broke off, unable to go on, and she leaned her head against his chest.

'Maybe we should go up to Winterscroft this afternoon, take part in this... whatever it is. Séance? Exorcism? Shall I go and leave you to look after Maria?'

'No!'

'But—'

'She's dangerous, Beth, you know she is. I can't let you go, and I can't go and leave you here unprotected. You and Mum are the most precious things in my life; I need to be here to look after you.'

He moved towards the kitchen. 'I'm going to make a pot of tea for Mum. Has she actually eaten anything since Sunday?'

'She's certainly had nothing since we arrived home. Take her a slice of toast. We'll see if that tempts her.' He switched on the kettle. 'And then we'll try and take our minds off all of this, and get those wedding presents opened. Luckily that vase was boxed, so at least we can replace it, then if your aunt and uncle come to visit, they need never know it got broken.'

They heard Maria's bedroom door open and expected to hear her pad along the landing towards the bathroom, but instead she came downstairs. She looked sleepy, she looked afraid, but she was downstairs.

Matt moved across to her and led her towards the armchair. 'Come and sit down. I'm just making us all a drink.'

She nodded. 'Thank you, sweetheart. I'll have a slice of toast, too, if that's all right. I need to have some strength. Whatever's happening isn't going to go away if we all weaken.'

'In the toaster now,' Beth called from the kitchen. She could hear determination in Maria's voice, even if she couldn't see her face.

'And you two, isn't it today that they're having that ceremony, or whatever it is, up at Rose's place? You need to be there, both of you. I'll be fine. I'm going to have a shower, borrow a clean nightie if I can, Beth, and settle down here, maybe watch a bit of television. I'll take advantage of your kindness and stay here tonight, but tomorrow I'm going home, and I'm not having any more of those damn tablets – I need to be awake. We have a bad time coming towards us, I know we do.'

Matt opened his mouth to protest, but Beth understood why Maria wanted to go back to her own home. She needed the familiarity, the comfort of her own surroundings, needed to be where Tim had been.

'Leave it, Matt,' she said quietly, and handed Maria the toast. 'I don't want to overface you; I can do more if you want it.'

Maria forced a smile. She didn't feel like smiling. 'Thank you, Beth. This will be enough for now.'

Matt picked up the phone. 'I'll check with Gareth. See what time he's going up there.'

23

They gathered initially in the lounge at Winterscroft. The seven people present were all nervous; no one had any idea what was likely to happen, or even if anything would happen.

Gareth had spent three days deeply meditative, and yet throughout his contemplations he'd had to deal with the death of a child; he felt under-prepared for the task ahead of him. Lorna had kept the girls away from him as much as she could, and then sent him on his way with a swift, impersonal kiss and a *God bless you* that was deeply heartfelt.

He had brought with him candles and holy water, a small leaflet detailing the words he would speak and a firm belief that God would take care of them all.

He sensed as he walked into the room that all was not good. Flora had obviously been crying and Rose was holding her in her arms.

'Mum just felt a bit overwhelmed, I think,' Rose explained. 'This is something massive, and scary, that we're going to do. It's like saying goodbye to Lavender all over again... and then, of course, there's Tim...' Her voice trailed away.

Gareth nodded and placed his bag on the coffee table. 'Can I have a glass of water, please Rose? I'll get it,' and he headed towards the kitchen.

He leaned against the sink unit and held on, his head forward. He could feel the atmosphere in the house; he couldn't say it was an evil atmosphere, it was more an expectant one. He filled a glass with water and sat at the kitchen table, leaving the two women to console each other. He took small sips, mentally preparing himself.

John and Alan appeared through the patio doors, both subdued, both aware of the monumental task facing them. John, in particular, had experienced Lavender's wrath and dreaded what the afternoon would bring.

Rose and Flora were sitting on the settee when they heard a car arrive, and knew that all the participants were now assembled. Matt had confirmed they would be there. Rose stood and went to the front door to greet them.

Beth looked just as frightened as Rose felt, and they shared a quick hug. 'Be brave, Beth,' Rose whispered. 'She can't hurt us.'

Beth smiled tremulously at the older woman. *Oh yes, she can.*

They walked into the lounge and Gareth joined them from the kitchen.

'Okay, we now need to decide where to be. Rose? Where has the strongest activity been?'

Rose thought for a second. 'I think Holly's room. It's the only place where she has actually materialised.'

There was a gasp from Beth, and Matt glared at Rose. 'When?'

'A couple of days ago. You were still on your honeymoon, and we've had other things to think about since you got back. I just never thought to tell you.' Her voice was firm, and Matt nodded that he understood.

'We do need to know though, Rose. We need to be warned if her strength is building.'

'It is.' John spoke. 'Don't be angry with Rose. Our two children are currently living in Paris because of all this, and I won't have my wife upset more than she already is.'

Matt immediately moved forward and hugged her. 'I'm sorry, Rose. My head's all over the place. She actually materialised?'

'Yes. Holly was a wreck. I have absolutely no idea why she is targeting my daughter, so until this is sorted once and for all, both the children will be staying with Violet and Pierre. Holly described what she was wearing; there was no doubt she had seen Lavender. The crucifix didn't help, so we're left with this last resort. Gareth, we're ready when you are. There are two main places, Holly's room and outside. She started outside, with the swing and the wheelie bin, then the pond area. I really don't know which to suggest.'

'Then we will concentrate on both places. Holly, for some reason, is clearly the one that is drawing this lost soul, and I suspect it's because of Holly's heightened state of vulnerability due to her age. Many prepubescent children attract poltergeists, and then as they grow out of that sudden build-up of hormones and become stabilised, the entities or whatever you choose to call them, fade away. This isn't a poltergeist we're dealing with, but it's the same situation with regard to Holly.'

No one spoke. They listened. And they knew he was right.

'So, we go to Holly's room.'

They all nodded, happy to leave the decisions with Gareth.

'Please wait down here until I call you. I need a couple of minutes to prepare and pray, and then I'll come and get you. Rose, which room is it?'

'Second on the right at the top of the stairs.' There was a noticeable tremor in Rose's voice.

'And the bathroom? I need to cleanse my hands.'

'Next door along from Holly's room.'

'Thank you.' He moved to the stairs and then looked back at them.

'Flora,' he said, 'lead them in prayer.'

She nodded and they all watched as he disappeared from view.

They looked at each other, and as one, touched hands. Flora said a very short prayer and they all followed with *amen*. The atmosphere became cooler although it was so gradual no one noticed it at first.

It was only when Gareth came to the top of the stairs to invite them to join him that they looked at each other. Everyone was cold. Rose shivered and spoke.

'Let's get on with this, let's lay her to rest properly.'

***

The room was in semi-darkness with the curtains closed and lit by only two candles. It felt crowded with all of them in there and yet it was cold, shivery cold. The two flames flickered and they stood in a circle, heads bowed, as Gareth drew them together in prayer. He blessed them all, then extended the blessing to the restless spirit who was in their presence.

Beth looked at Matt and he could see the fear in her eyes. He took hold of her hand and pulled her closer to him.

Gareth picked up the booklet from the table, handed out small cards with the responses printed on it, and paused for a moment before beginning to read.

'Lord have mercy.'

'Lord have mercy.' They spoke the familiar words automatically and in unison.

'Christ have mercy.'

'Christ have mercy.'

'Lord have mercy.'

'Lord have mercy.'

'Christ hear us.'

There was a loud crash from somewhere downstairs that caused everyone to jump. Both candles went out and Beth gave a shriek. Matt immediately reached out and pulled her to him, cradling her against his chest.

Gareth waited for them to settle down, relit the candles and they continued giving responses to his lead words. It took a long time and Flora began to feel pain in her knee from the prolonged bout of standing so still. She shuffled slightly as she tried to ease the ache and Alan looked at her carefully.

He heard Gareth begin to intone the Lord's Prayer and everyone saying the words alongside him; he closed his eyes as he had been taught from being a tiny child and felt Flora slump to the floor, rather than seeing her give way.

'Flora! Rose...' He dropped to his knees alongside his wife, relieved to see that she was conscious. 'Flora, what's wrong?'

'My knee. It feels... as though there's a knife in it.'

Gareth moved to her right side and they helped her to stand. He pulled a chair from the side of Holly's bed and they lowered her gently onto it.

He looked around at the others. 'Is anyone else feeling pain?'

They all shook their heads.

'You may. Flora is under attack, but it will go. If you feel anything like this, any of you, drop to the floor.'

Rose had moved to stand behind her mother; she placed her hands on Flora's shoulders, leaned forward and kissed the top of her head.

'Be strong, Mum,' she whispered, and Flora patted her hand. She didn't want to speak. The pain had been unbearable when she had fallen, but now she was sitting down she could cope.

Gareth began the Lord's Prayer once again; this time Alan kept his eyes open.

There was an audible sigh of relief as they all said *amen*.

'God, by your name, save me, and by your might defend my cause.' Alan spoke the words slowly. His natural reaction was to rush and get the whole thing over with, but he knew it wasn't the answer.

'God, hear my prayer; hearken to the words of my mouth,' was the fervent response of the other six.

Gareth moved on to quoting psalm 53 and he was halfway through when the cold hit him. He felt as though his blood was frozen and he was aware of his speech slowing down.

'Gareth? You okay?' John spoke as Gareth's words failed him. They heard him gasp from the intense biting cold inside him.

'Cold...' he stammered. 'Inside...'

Rose moved to the bed, pulled off the duvet and swaddled Gareth inside it.

'Gather round,' she commanded the others. 'He needs warmth.'

They linked arms and surrounded the vicar who continued to shiver violently. Flora sat on her chair and watched in silence, inwardly praying to her youngest daughter to leave Gareth alone. She was in no doubt Lavender was throwing everything at them to try and stop this blessing, this casting out.

Slowly the shivering subsided and they waited patiently for Gareth to recover enough to carry on. He felt ill. He suspected Flora felt ill. It was almost as if he had experienced an alien invasion of his body and he knew the same had happened to Flora with her knee. The pain must have been intense for her to fall to the floor.

Who would be targeted next? This entity was truly evil, and she was in the room with them.

The temperature was dropping by the second and Gareth knew he couldn't delay. He didn't want any of the others to experience what he had just felt, so he moved quickly through the psalm he had just abandoned halfway through, and then on to the small responses required after delivery of the psalm.

He felt a small degree of satisfaction as he said *the Lord be with you* and heard the familiar reply of *may He also be with you.*

'Let us pray.' They all bowed their heads, searching for the peace usually so evident with all of them when they prayed. It was hard to pray in freezing conditions.

He deliberately made the prayer a long and personal one, adding to the written prayer to build up protection for the next part of the ceremony. Cold or not, he knew the first part was the easy bit; what was to come next could potentially be an earthquake of seismic proportions. He would be speaking directly to Lavender. His mind was still having difficulties accepting the Lavender who was spoken of with such love, who had been an exemplary daughter, sister, girlfriend, with this... thing... that seemed to be plaguing them from every angle. He kept it in his mind as an entity; that was his training.

It was the smell – the lavender fragrance was everywhere. There was no denying that, and there was no denying that

Alan and John had both heard her voice come from Holly's mouth.

'Rose, how easy would it be to get five more chairs in here?'

'Very easy. We can rustle that many up from upstairs.'

'Then let's do it.'

John moved towards the door as Rose went to get the second chair that was already in the room. He turned the door knob, but the door wouldn't move. He tried again. Nothing. It was as if Super Glue had been used to seal them in, in the absence of a lock on the door.

Gareth came up behind him. 'Problem?'

John nodded. 'The door won't open. There's no lock on it...'

Gareth sprinkled the doorknob with the Holy Water, removed his stole, wrapped it around the knob and said a silent prayer, finishing with an audible, 'Go!'

He removed the stole, turned the handle and the door opened. 'One up to the good guys,' he remarked, almost under his breath – he was still angry, still very cold.

'Thank you,' John said, and moved along the corridor to get the chairs.

Eventually the only one still standing was Gareth, and he settled everyone down by placing his hand on each of their heads and giving them a short blessing.

He then stood for a moment, deep in meditative prayer. The six very scared watchers sat around in a circle, quiet, immobile.

'I command you, unclean spirit, whoever you are, along with all your minions now attacking this servant of God, by the mysteries of the incarnation, passion, resurrection, and ascension of our Lord Jesus Christ, by the descent of the Holy Spirit, by the coming of our Lord for judgment, that you tell me by some sign your name, and the day and hour of your departure.'

Rose coughed as the all-enveloping lavender perfume overwhelmed her, and somewhere in the distance she could hear all the others beginning to cough as well. Her mind felt distanced from her body and it seemed her throat was closing; the atmosphere was cloyingly thick with the stench. This lavender smell was compounded with something else, something evil that was fighting against what they were all trying to do, trying to lay their beloved to rest.

Gareth tried to continue but his mouth felt woolly; he couldn't take a deep enough breath and so he began to murmur the Lord's Prayer, over and over in his head until he felt able to speak words out loud again.

'I command you, moreover, to obey me to the letter, I who am a minister of God despite my unworthiness; nor shall you be emboldened to harm in any way this creature of God, or the bystanders, or any of their possessions.'

There was absolute silence in the room. Gareth paused and then held his arms wide.

'They shall lay their hands upon the sick and all will be well with them. May Jesus, Son of Mary, Lord and Saviour of the world, through the merits and intercession of His holy apostles, Peter and Paul, and all His saints, show you favour and mercy.'

There was a response of *amen* from everyone seated and then once more total silence, until the first book hit the wall. Everything that wasn't held down then became whipped up into a vortex of wind, sound, pressure and screams. All the books from Holly's bookstand flew around, smashing into the window, the door, and the walls. Her dressing table began to tip and crashed to the floor before anyone could get to it and as each person stood in horror the chairs were thrown around.

'Get out,' Gareth yelled at them all. 'Get out, you'll be injured.'

Rose pulled her mother towards the door, thankfully not sealed this time, and helped her onto the landing.

'Go in our bedroom, Mum, I'll go and drag Dad out, make sure the others are okay.'

She walked back into Holly's room and it was carnage. Her father was sitting on the floor holding the sheet off the bed to his head. It was red with blood. John was dragging a hysterical Beth away from Matt who looked to be dazed but conscious, sitting with his back to the wall, a chair on top of his legs.

She took Beth from John and pushed her out of the room. 'Our bedroom, Beth. Mum's in there. Look after her. I'll go and get Matt. Don't worry, he's just dazed.'

She started to go back in but John was just coming out, half carrying Alan.

'He's okay,' he said. 'Clean it and we'll have a look then. I'm going for Matt and Gareth...'

'Bathroom, Dad,' Rose said, and he followed instructions.

He groaned as he sat on the toilet seat. Rose ran water into the washbasin and reached into the cabinet for cotton wool.

'I'll clean it,' she said, 'and then we'll make the decision whether it needs stitches or not. I've got some sterile strips in so we might be okay.'

She washed the blood away gently and then pronounced herself satisfied. 'You'll live,' she said. 'I want you to take a couple of painkillers though, reckon you might have a headache later.'

'Thank you, sweetheart, now go and see how everybody else is. Did I see Matt on the floor?'

'You did. Go into our bedroom, Dad, in case Gareth still needs us. If he doesn't, we'll go downstairs.'

Walking back into Holly's room shocked her. It was destroyed. The wooden chairs would make a good bonfire, her books were scattered everywhere, furniture upended; John was helping Gareth to stand. He looked grey and definitely unsteady on his feet. Matt wasn't there, so she guessed he was with Beth.

'Is it over, Gareth?'

He shook his head. 'No, it isn't, but I don't believe we can carry on. She tried to kill, Rose. She tried to kill. I can't take any more risks with you. I need to speak with the Bishop. I need guidance before we take this any further.'

'Then let's regroup downstairs. You can't go home yet. You need a drink and time to recover.'

He nodded. 'Thank you, Rose. Is everyone all right?'

'Yes, I've cleaned Dad up – he was the worst, although I've not seen Matt. How is he?'

'All he wanted was to get to Beth. I think he's a bit groggy,' John said, 'but I'll give him a drop of brandy, see if that helps. He moved to avoid a chair and fell, then hit his head on the corner of the dressing table. He'll be fine.'

Rose nodded. 'Muster the troops, John, and bring everyone downstairs. I'll put on the kettle.'

She went into the kitchen and gasped. There was glass everywhere; it was clearly the crash they had heard earlier. The photograph of Lavender, a beautiful head and shoulders shot of her which had always hung in kitchen was smashed all over the floor. She grabbed a brush and began to sweep. She wanted no more blood to be spilt, there had been too much already. She heard John helping everybody into the lounge and then he came through to the kitchen.

'What the...?'

She pointed to the empty space on the wall. 'Lavender's picture. And it's not just broken glass; the frame is smashed and the picture ripped to shreds. John, I'm so scared.'

'Well, it's obvious from what's just happened upstairs that it's not done with yet. She fought back with everything in her power, Rose. I don't want the children anywhere near here, not just yet.'

'I totally agree. Put the kettle on, first things first. Let's get everybody calmed down. I can't send Gareth back to Lorna looking like that. He looked so ill.'

'He tried to control whatever was doing all that damage, but she's out of control, isn't she?'

Rose nodded. 'This is ridiculous. This goes against everything I believe in. Prior to this fiasco, I would have laughed at the idea of ghosts and spirits. What have we done to deserve this, John?'

'We've supported the man she loved, sweetheart, that's what we've done. We helped him marry somebody else and she still wants him. It's not over yet, not by a long way.'

24

Violet was enjoying having the children with her. Holly had been quiet, but Jacob had really taken to this unexpected holiday. They had journeyed to the Eiffel Tower, the Louvre, Notre Dame – all the usual touristy places, but they had also shared quality time with them in their apartment.

Pierre was patiently teaching Jacob to play chess and Holly was quite happy to sit and read. Her aunt had introduced her to a couple of the classics, and she was currently immersed in Little Women. Violet had given her a copy in French as well as English, and she had seen Holly comparing the two, line by line.

'You like our four girls, then, Holly?'

'Yes, I do. Will I be able to take this back home with me, Aunty Violet, please?'

'Of course, sweetheart. Both of them, they're yours.'

'When are we going home?' Holly looked troubled.

'I'm not sure. Aren't you enjoying being here?'

'Yes, I am, but I should be in my new school now. With Tim.'

Violet saw the tears begin to form and she moved swiftly to sit by her niece. She put an arm around her and drew her close.

'Don't cry, sweetheart,' she whispered. 'I know it's hard, losing your best friend. Would you like to ring your mum, have a chat with her?'

Holly shook her head. Misery was etched all the way through her.

'No, she's probably busy.'

'She won't be too busy for you, ma chérie,' Pierre called from the other side of the room. His head was bent over as he contemplated his next move on the chess board.

Inwardly, he cursed that there had been little communication from Rose, and yet he thought he understood her reasoning behind keeping away from the children. She wanted no possibility of them having any contact with Lavender.

A bloody ghost, an entity. What was he thinking? He knew it wasn't real. Ghosts were some urban myth designed to scare gullible people.

He moved a chess piece in anger and heard Jacob say checkmate.

***

Gareth walked slowly back down the lane towards the vicarage. He hoped he didn't look as bad as he felt. There would be a hefty bruise on his right arm, he was fairly sure of that; one of the chairs flying around the room had hit him with considerable force, knocking him off his feet. He had to tell Lorna the full story, make sure neither she nor the girls went anywhere near Winterscroft.

As soon as Lorna saw his face, she knew it had been bad.

'The church or a bath?'

'At this moment in time, a bath. There may be blood...'

'What? Where?'

'My arm. I feel as though I'm stuck to my shirt.'

She helped him take off his robes and sucked in her breath at the sight of the blood on his shirt sleeve.

'It's stuck to your arm. I'll have a look at what's going on before I try to peel it off. You might need to soak it off in the bath, as I don't want it to start bleeding again.'

She helped him unbutton the shirt and then tried to remove it. It slowly peeled away and she saw a gash along his upper arm. It didn't start to bleed again so she cleaned it for him, removing all the blood before he headed for the bathroom.

He hesitated at the bathroom door.

'Don't go anywhere near Winterscroft, will you, Lorna? Not you, not our girls. Nowhere near, do you understand? Not until this thing is sorted.'

'It's not sorted yet?'

He shook his head. 'Far from it. And don't go near that damn grave either.'

She heard the stress in his voice and inwardly shuddered. The bathroom door closed and she sagged against the banister. He was seriously spooked, and physically damaged, and she hadn't even asked about the family. She hoped they weren't carrying injuries as well.

She went downstairs and switched on the kettle. She would make him a drink when he got out of the bath, then put a dressing on his arm. And she would make him talk, because she wouldn't countenance him keeping it to himself. She had to know what had happened to leave him bruised and beaten. And bloody.

He came downstairs an hour later and she knew he had been praying. He looked better in his face, and he carried a clean tee shirt down with him.

'It bled a little more,' he said, 'so I figured I'd better have a dressing on it.'

She nodded. 'I've got a biggish one; it'll keep it well covered. Let me make us a cup of tea, and then I'll see to it.' She boiled the kettle for the third time and poured the water into the teapot. The large teapot. She felt this would be more than a two-mug discussion.

'Where are the girls?'

'In bed. They were both tired. It is nearly eight o'clock, Gareth.' She smiled. It was obvious time was of little relevance to him at the moment.

She poured the drinks and waited. He said nothing at first and then tried to smile at her. 'I'm sorry. I think I'm in shock to be honest. I've never seen anything like that, the terror, the violence – I don't know how we got through it without someone being seriously injured, or worse. We had a plan to start in Holly's room, and then move outside to the pond area. We didn't even get round to the second part. The first part decimated us. The room is wrecked. It will have to be completely decorated and new furniture bought before Holly can go back into it, it was that bad.'

Lorna waited. He needed to talk.

'I'll start at the beginning.' He took a deep breath and began to tell her everything. He kept nothing back; he never had, and didn't intend starting now.

For the most part she listened quietly, occasionally throwing in the odd question. It had clearly taken its toll on her husband; he looked exhausted.

He finished with his walk back down to the vicarage, after leaving the family to nurse their own wounds.

'They've stuck Alan's head back together with Steri-Strips, and I suspect all of them have taken painkillers. They all received a battering in one way or another. Flora is the one I feel for the most; Lavender was her daughter, and a beautiful girl who wouldn't hurt a fly.

This... abomination... isn't the girl any of them knew. Flora seems to be burying her head in the sand a bit. Every time anyone mentions Lavender's name she tries to interrupt, usually by saying *but...*'

Lorna nodded. 'I can understand that. It's a mum thing. She knew Lavender better than anyone, knew that she couldn't be evil, and yet this thing is. So, what happens next?'

'I'm not sure. I certainly need to talk to the Bishop. I feel awful about it all, I did everything right, Lorna, everything. It couldn't have gone more wrong. Everyone was scared witless, and that poor young lass...'

Lorna looked horrified. 'Holly wasn't there?'

'No, not Holly, the children are in Paris with Rose's sister and brother-in-law. No, I mean Beth. She's just had that lovely wedding and honeymoon, and then comes home to Tim's death and absolute mayhem today. She saw her brand-new husband lying out cold on the floor – she's in a bit of a state, as you can imagine.'

'So, they're all walking wounded? No hospital visits needed?'

'No, I think they're trying to contain it, keep it within their circle. I prayed with them before I came back down. I don't know how much good it did. You can feel it in the house, Lorna, feel a presence. I don't honestly know how they're living there.'

Lorna stood and moved to the side of her husband. 'Let me get the dressing on this cut. Your skin should be dry now, and I think you should take some painkillers too. The bruises are certainly starting to come up on this arm.' She peeled off the protective coverings from the plaster and applied it over the wound. He winced as she pressed it into place and then stood and put on his tee shirt.

'I think I will have a couple of paracetamol. I've got more aches and pains...'

She handed him the tablets she had already removed from the blister pack. 'Here, get these down you, and stop being brave.' She kissed the top of his head. 'I'm so proud of you. You're a good man, Gareth Bruce, an exceptional man.'

He swallowed the tablets. 'I'm also a scared man. There's an anniversary coming up very shortly, the anniversary of Lavender's death. It's on the 30th of this month. If she's like this now...'

***

Rose stood in the doorway of Holly's room, wondering where to start. Every chair was smashed, the dressing table was chipped in several places, the mirror completely smashed, the bookcase was demolished and her books were everywhere. The bed was unscathed apart from having no bedding on it; that was all in a heap in the middle of the floor covered with Alan's blood.

She tore a black bag off the roll and began to stuff the bedding and the duvet into it. They would load up the car and take it to the tip as soon as everything was bagged up. John could burn any wood – she could see that nothing was salvageable. There was blood smeared on the wallpaper, on the door and door jamb, on the carpet; her father had bled copiously from his head wound. Everything would have to go. She wanted no reminders of that disastrous Tuesday afternoon.

The bedding completely filled the bag; she tied the top securely and stood it on the landing. She went into the guest bedroom and brought a suitcase back with her. Holly's clothes would have to be packed away for the moment. She looked for a few seconds at the new school uniform and tears pricked her eyes. She stroked the blazer and then placed everything in the case. She had no idea when it would be safe for Holly to return and wear the navy blue clothes.

Once the suitcase had been wheeled back to the guest room, she stood in the doorway and looked around. What was left had to go; she just didn't know where to start. She heard the front door open and close and then John's shout of *Rose?*

'Up here, John,' she called back, 'surveying the wreckage.'

He ran up the stairs and stood by her side.

'That's why I'm here,' he said. 'I was going to ask Bill Carter to decorate it for us, but then had second thoughts.'

She gave a strangled laugh. 'He won't want a ghost pasting the wallpaper for him...'

'Exactly. So, I've had a word with your Dad and we're doing it. I need you to go out now and get wallpaper and stuff. White emulsion we've already got, and there's enough for two coats on the ceiling. We need new of everything else; gloss paint, paper, paste... depends what you want us to do. We're going to make a start now and clear everything out, and then get the walls stripped. I'll take everything to the tip that's not wood. Come on, sweetheart, it will be something good to welcome her home. Once it's done we'll have a day out in Sheffield and pick her some new furniture.'

She began to cry and he gathered her into his arms, then kissed the top of her head.

'Come on, this can't go on forever.'

She sniffled. 'I know, I just hate being in this house on my own. I've bagged up the bedding and put all of Holly's clothes in a suitcase in the guest bedroom, but I really didn't know what to do next. I'm looking over my shoulder all the time. I'm scared, John, scared.'

'Right, go and have a cuppa with your mum and then the two of you go and get our decorating supplies. By the time you get back here you'll feel better, this lot will be out of the house and we'll at least have started stripping the walls.'

'You're right. I'm being stupid. No more tears. I'll go and find Mum.'

As she reached the bottom of the stairs she heard the ring of the phone and went to answer it. Matt spoke briefly, telling her that Tim's funeral was to be on 26th September and he had just got back from his mum's house.

'Thank you, Matt,' she said quietly. 'I think this means Holly will have to come home. How is Maria?'

'In bits. It's as if it's suddenly become real again. I wanted her to come back with me but she said she wanted to be in her own home. I'll go down again later.'

'Then I'll go tomorrow. We're just trying to clear up the wreckage in Holly's room. I don't know what else to say, Matt...'

'None of us do, Rose, none of us do. Nothing makes sense anymore; he was thirteen, for God's sake.'

Neither of them knew, but they had finished the telephone conversation with both of them in tears.

25

The bedroom was looking pretty naked by the time Rose and Flora returned from their shopping expedition. Rose had decided on lemon as the main colour, with touches of blue to accent it.

She popped her head around the bedroom door and smiled. 'It looks enormous in here now!'

'Everything's gone to the tip that we can't burn, and all the wood is stacked up in the garage. I'll burn that next week.' John looked at her while speaking. He knew she was feeling fragile.

'Where's the bed?'

'Bed? What bed?' he said, the innocent tone not fooling her at all.

'The bed that our daughter sleeps in.'

'Oh, that bed.'

'Yes, that bed.'

Alan held up a hand. He laughed and turned to face Rose. 'Your mother and I are going to buy her a new one. I thought she might like one of those that come with a desk – she'll need a desk now she's in big school.'

'You're a star, Dad.' She walked across the room and kissed him.

'Hey, don't I get one of those?' John moved towards his wife. 'And we could use a cup of tea now the slaves are home.'

Rose tapped him on the nose. 'For that, you'll get the cup of tea, but not the kiss.'

He grinned and went back to stripping the last of the four walls. He wanted to put at least one coat of paint on the ceiling before losing the light and he renewed his efforts. Alan began to clear the floor, piling all the stripped wallpaper up before forcing it into a black bag.

'We've not done bad, lad, have we? Three hours or so and we're ready for starting it properly tomorrow. I'll be glad when they're 'ome, our kids.'

'Me too, Alan, me too. But we've things to get settled before they can come home.'

Rose opened the door with her bottom, and carried a tray of teas and a plate of biscuits carefully into the room.

'You decided on a colour, then, Rose?' her dad asked.

'Yes. We're going to paint three of the walls in a pale yellow, and on this wall,' she indicated the wall where the bed's headboard had rested, 'we're going to wallpaper it with a paper with tiny blue and lemon flowers on it. White woodwork, and it will look lovely.'

'Sounds lovely,' John said. 'And it's nice not having to rush it, even though I'm missing them both.'

'Well, don't take too long,' Rose said. 'I'm going to have to bring them home. It's Tim's funeral on the 26th, and she would never forgive us if she didn't get to say goodbye properly to him.'

'So, that gives us a week to get it finished, buy and assemble new furniture, and generally make it lovely again.'

'And fit a new carpet,' Rose added, as she walked out of the room. She'd give them slaves; time for them to find out just who the slaves were in this family.

***

Maria sat looking at the fire, her face seemingly frozen. She felt nothing; her mind was numb. The knock at the door startled her and at first she ignored it. Then she heard the letterbox move and Rose's voice called out to her.

'Maria? It's Rose. Can I come in?'

Maria stood slowly and moved into the hall. She didn't want to see anyone, least of all the sister of Lavender.

She opened the door and said, 'I'm a bit busy, Rose.'

'No, you're not.'

'Oh.' She looked nonplussed. 'Well, you'd better come in then.'

Rose followed her down the hallway and into the kitchen.

'Tea?' There was no friendliness in Maria's tone.

'Yes, please.' Rose understood the coldness emanating from her friend. 'Maria, whatever is happening isn't my fault. We're all trying desperately to put things right...'

'And how do you propose to put this right, Rose? Tim is dead. I'm burying my youngest child next week, and you think you can put that right?'

Rose slumped down onto a kitchen chair. 'Of course I can't put that right, we're just...'

Her head sank onto the table. 'I don't know what we're doing, Maria. Has Matt told you about the carry on at ours yesterday? Any one of us could have been killed and we don't know how to deal with it. Even Gareth is out of his depth.'

Maria stared at Rose. 'He's told me nothing. Just said it went well. You mean I could have lost my other son as well?'

Rose nodded. 'It was carnage, Maria. Absolute devastation. We were in Holly's room and it's now destroyed. Dad was injured the worst; there was blood everywhere from a gash on his head. Matt was knocked out for a couple of minutes, Mum collapsed because her knee gave way from the intense pain, and Gareth... he was well and truly battered by flying chairs, books and suchlike.'

Maria's face reflected the horror she was feeling.

'I knew nothing...' she stammered. 'Nothing.'

'Didn't you notice the lump on Matt's head?'

She looked miserable. 'I suppose I'm too wrapped up in myself, too much time to think at the moment. When Matt came, he had on a baseball cap; he was obviously hiding it from me. I'm sorry Rose, let's have that drink.'

Rose watched as Maria turned to switch on the kettle, wondering how this lovely woman was managing to get through each day. Two deaths inside a year would be too much for anyone to bear, and when one was her son...

They talked for an hour and Rose told her everything that had happened at Winterscroft. She left nothing out; Maria had to be as aware as the rest of them.

At the end, Maria stood and walked around the table to hug Rose.

'I'm so sorry,' she said. 'I have become so wrapped up in my own misery I forgot all of you. I forgot the pain you must be feeling. We all suffered when Lavender went. My own son was totally distraught for months, how could I not remember that? It must seem as though you're going through your loss all over again, and as for poor Beth, she didn't ask for any of this. She just chose to love Matt.'

Rose hugged her back and smiled.

'Friends again?'

'Friends again,' Maria confirmed. 'Will you help me get through next Friday?'

'Of course, that goes without saying. Is there anything I can do right now?'

'No, nothing. I've set things in motion, seeing Gareth later in the week, and I'm a bit undecided about what to do after the... funeral. I don't want anything like Tony March's wake. I just want us, the very close family, to get together and talk about Tim. Can I do that?'

'You can do what you want, Maria. Gareth can announce at the service that there will be no refreshments afterwards as the family want to grieve and remember Tim in private, and while I know all of us going back up to Winterscroft after the service would be logical because I can do the catering, I don't think it would be a good idea. What about us coming back here? I can still put a few sandwiches and buns together, just for us to have a cup of tea and remember Tim; you don't need to do anything. I can take that task from you.'

Maria remained deep in thought and then nodded. 'That's what I want. Thank you, Rose, today has been such a help to me. You're a remarkable woman, Rose Broadbent, a remarkable woman.'

Rose smiled. 'It's the teacher in me, I think. An *everything can be sorted* attitude that's inbuilt now.'

She stood and put on her coat. 'Will you be okay if I go now? I need to check on John and Dad. They're working in Holly's room.'

'No!'

Rose nodded. 'Yes, it had to be done, there was blood all over the place and the furniture needed removing so they could do everything else. I left them to it, but they might be needing some help. I'll give you a ring in the morning, so if there's anything you need me to do let me know then. And don't forget, I'll cater for the wake. Take care, Maria,' and she leaned across and kissed her. 'Everyone has your back; we're all here to support you.'

'I know, and thank you. And I'm sorry I was such a nasty cow when you arrived. I feel so much better now.'

Rose walked out of the door with a heavy heart. Maria might be sounding upbeat at the moment, but it couldn't, and wouldn't, last.

She headed up to Winterscroft, deep in thought. Talking about everything with Maria had forced her to relive the horror and her mind was troubled. If Tim was to be buried in just over a week she needed to be bringing Holly and Jacob back home by Wednesday; back into danger.

She was tempted to just 'forget' to tell Holly, but knew that would have long-term issues attached to it; Holly would never forgive her. She would have to ring her and see how she felt about coming back home for the funeral, and pray that she didn't want to.

She passed the gates to the churchyard and hesitated. Should she go to the grave? This wouldn't even have been a question six months earlier, now she wasn't sure she ever wanted to go there again. The pull to go in was strong and she hesitated, one foot on the heavy stone step, and one hand resting on the open iron gate.

Suddenly she slammed the gate closed, then leaned her head against it. She took a few deep breaths and then turned and walked away.

The good guys won that round.

26

Rose climbed the stairs wearily, and looked around the bedroom door. There was no sign of Alan; John was on the step ladder with a roller in his hand, singing along to the quietly playing radio as he painted the ceiling. She looked at him and he suddenly realised she was there. He jumped and a blob of paint fell to the floor. The carpetless floor. She smiled.

'Sorry, did I startle you?'

He nodded. 'Slightly. It's bad enough working in here, but I didn't hear you coming up the stairs...'

'Oh.' She was genuinely sorry now. Just for a moment she had felt as though she was in a normal environment. 'Has everything been okay?'

He understood what she meant. 'So far so good. This is the second coat, so tomorrow I'll paint the skirting boards and door, then we can crack on with the walls. We'll wallpaper on Friday and go shopping for the furniture on Saturday. This is harder work than gardening, so I think I chose the right career path,' he laughed.

He was glad she was back. He'd sent Alan back to Flora, aware that Alan was uncomfortable being away from his wife. She was still feeling a degree of pain in her knee and Alan had given her instructions to rest it.

That had left him alone and although nothing had happened, the atmosphere was strange. He tried to believe it was because the room was completely empty, but he knew that wasn't the reason. Lavender was the reason. He had felt her presence beside him once, and he didn't want to repeat the experience.

'Can I do anything to help?'

A cuppa would help,' he smiled. 'This is thirsty work. And five minutes with you would be good as well.'

'You going to stop and come downstairs then?'

He looked at how much ceiling was left to be painted, and nodded. 'Yes, I'll take a break. I'll just finish up to the light fitting then come down. Buns as well?'

'Might be,' she said, and walked out of the door.

She headed for the kitchen and took a box out of the pantry. It held the buns her husband was clearly craving and she placed a couple on a plate. It might be good to do a bit of baking, try to get back some normality in their lives. Maybe she could even think about going back to work. Having a supply teacher covering for her was expensive for the school and unsettling for the children. And she missed them; she missed the interaction with her pupils.

Rose switched on the kettle and took down two mugs. She popped a tea bag into each one and stood waiting for the kettle to boil.

There was a shriek of anger, followed by a cry of pain, and then silence.

She ran.

At the bottom of the stairs she stopped; John was lying there. She dropped to her knees and as she did so he moved his head slightly and groaned.

'Shit,' he whispered, 'that hurts.'

'Don't move! Just tell me what hurts.'

'My arm and my shoulder. The one underneath me.'

'I'm sending for an ambulance. We don't know what damage you've done.'

She crossed to the phone and was soon relaying the information, and receiving instructions about John's care pending the arrival of the ambulance.

She ran into the lounge and grabbed a cushion and a throw.

'John, I'm going to try and put this pillow under your head to make you feel a bit more comfortable, but if anything hurts I'll stop and you'll just have to stay as you are. Okay?'

'Okay.'

The second she tried to move his head he cried aloud and she stopped.

'We'll forget that, then. I'll get you covered up. She said to keep you warm, you might go into shock. What on earth did you do?'

His eyes were closing and she knew she needed to keep him talking.

'What did you do, John? What happened?'

His eyes flickered open briefly. 'Shoe. On stairs.'

'What? But why...?'

'Stepped on it, legs just went...'

He moaned again and she placed her finger on his lips. 'Sssh, my love, if it's hurting to talk, then don't do it. I can hear sirens so they'll be here in a minute. I need to tell Dad, they'll panic if...' The ambulance pulled up the gravel drive and swung round in front of the house. She knew she was too late to pre-warn her parents; she left John's side and opened the door.

'He's here,' she said. 'I don't know how far he's fallen, but his pain is pretty severe.'

The two men knelt down and began to speak to John, but got no response. He was unconscious.

The adjoining door burst open and Alan came through, rubbing his eyes and trying to smooth down his hair.

'What's happened, Rose? Oh my God!' He stared in horror at his son-in-law, now being prepared to have his head clamped before being stretchered into the vehicle where they could work on him with all their equipment.

Rose's face was ashen. 'He fell down the stairs, Dad. He says he stepped on a shoe, but I don't know how that could happen. The shoes I had on this morning are there,' and she pointed to the corner. 'And my slippers are on my feet. His shoes are on his feet, so...? I don't know what shoe he can mean.'

Flora limped through the door and stared aghast at the scene in front of her. 'No,' she breathed, 'she can't have done this. She can't have. Alan...?'

Alan put his arm around his wife and held her tightly to him. 'He's simply fallen down the stairs, sweetheart.'

The medics slid John carefully onto the stretcher board, and then checked him out once more before taking him out to the ambulance.

'I'm going with him,' Rose said. 'Dad, can you make sure we're all locked up tonight? I'll stay as long as John needs me.'

'Of course, sweetheart. Ring us, will you, as soon as you know anything?'

'I will.' She gave them both a kiss and went to get her coat. She saw the shoe immediately. It had obviously landed underneath John's body when he fell. It was black patent, and was one half of the pair that had been worn only once, the day of Matt and Beth's wedding. Since then they had been in their box, in the bottom of the wardrobe. She picked it up and held it out for Alan to take from her.

'That's what catapulted John downstairs. That's been in a box in my wardrobe since the evening of the wedding. They haven't been worn since. So, you were right, Mum, she did do this. Will you ring Violet, Maria and Matt or Beth, please, and fill them in. Maria, in particular, needs to know I'm not around, as she's very fragile.'

'Rose, for once in your life stop putting others first.' There was a touch of anger in Alan's voice. 'Concentrate on you two, leave everything else to us, we'll sort it.'

'I'm going in the ambulance with him, so when I want to come home I'll ring for a taxi. I know this is going to sound as paranoid as hell, but why don't you book into Val's B and B for a few days, so that you're not on your own in Winterscroft. I'm scared, Dad, really scared.'

'No!' Flora's voice was strong. 'We will not be driven out.'

The ambulance driver came to the door and said they were ready to go. 'Are you coming with us, Mrs. Broadbent?'

Rose nodded. 'I am. Dad – make the calls.' She kissed them both once more and followed the driver out of the door.

John was conscious as she climbed in and she held his hand briefly before sitting down. All the way into Sheffield he drifted in and out of consciousness and the sirens sounded for much of the way.

Once in the hospital, he was quickly whisked away from her and she sat in the waiting room. She read several magazines and then went to the water dispenser to get a drink. This was followed by a visit from someone needing John's details, and asking about medication, if any, that he was on. Then Rose was on her own once more, feeling overwhelmed by worry.

It was just after midnight when a doctor came to find her.

'He's sedated now. You can come and see him for a couple of minutes but he'll not wake up. We've given him some pretty hefty stuff so that he's not in any pain. He's got a bad break in his right arm and he's dislocated his right shoulder, which is why he couldn't move; the pain would have been too much. He's also had a nasty crack to the head which has fractured his skull, so he's going to be here for a while.'

He led her to the critical care unit and she felt as though her own heart would stop. John was hooked up to two drip feeds, his arm was strapped tightly so that it couldn't be moved and his skin was grey.

'We are hoping to operate tomorrow, but it will depend on how he is tomorrow morning. If you ring around nine o'clock we'll know more then.' He held up his hand as he saw Rose about to say she would be staying.

'No, Mrs. Broadbent, I don't advise you to stay. I advise you to go home and get a good night's sleep. There is absolutely no reason for you to be here because we will keep him sedated. He won't know anything and you will end up being ill yourself. You need to be on top form, and he doesn't need to see that you're worried, or that you look tired. Trust me, I know what I'm saying,' he said with a smile.

She nodded. 'And I understand what you're saying. Nine o'clock?'

He smiled. 'Nine o'clock, and no earlier, because we won't have reached any decisions before that, but we should have some answers by then.'

She bent and kissed John, spoke a few words to him, and walked out of the ward with tears in her eyes. She stopped by the nursing station and asked where the nearest telephone was; they obligingly rang for a taxi for her and she walked to the lifts for the long drop down to floor B, and the exit. She didn't have long to wait; within five minutes she was on her way back to Castleton. She was an emotional wreck and as the taxi pulled up outside the door, Alan and Flora came out to meet her.

'We waited for you,' her dad said. 'You're staying in our guest bedroom tonight; you're not staying on your own. No arguing, Rose.'

'Come on,' Flora said, and led her towards the door.

'Hang on, I need to pay the driver.'

'Stop fretting. Your dad will do that.'

And Alan pulled out his wallet and did as he was told.

27

Rose spoke to Maria, Violet and Matt all before eight o'clock next morning. She hadn't slept very well despite feeling safe in the guest bedroom in Alan and Flora's wing of the house.

At nine o'clock she was on the phone to the hospital. The news was good; John had suffered no setbacks during the night, his vital signs were good and they were going to take him into theatre during the morning to set his arm.

She breathed a huge sigh of relief, sat on the bottom stair and cried. She couldn't begin to imagine a life without him; they had met at school and been together ever since.

The hospital had advised her he would be out of theatre by noon or thereabouts, so she took a couple of deep breaths, stood up and walked to the corner of the hallway where she had slung the black patent shoe.

She took it upstairs and into her bedroom. Everything looked normal and she crossed to the wardrobe. The right side door was slightly open and she pulled it wide. The shoe box lid was off and only one shoe nestled inside. Tucked into the shoe was a sprig of lavender.

She gave a cry of anger, took out the shoe box and carried everything back downstairs. Alan saw her storm past their kitchen window towards the dustbins, heard the clatter as the lid was slammed in place and then saw her walk back. He left his dishwashing duties and went through to her, now sitting back on the bottom stair, crying again.

'Rose, what's happened? Is it John?'

'No, he's had a good night and they're going to operate this morning,' she sobbed. 'I've just been to check in that damn shoe box and there's a piece of lavender in it. The shoes are in the bin now. Why is she being like this, Dad? John was a wonderful brother-in-law to her, so why?'

He sat down beside her. 'I don't know, my love. I don't have any answers to this. Do you know how far John had got with t'painting?'

She nodded. 'Yes, halfway along the ceiling with the second coat. As far as the light socket. Why? I don't want you doing it, Dad.'

He hugged her. 'I'm just going to finish t'ceiling off, that's all. It needs to be done. I'll do it while you're here, so you can keep an eye on me. Make sure no shoes are left on t'stairs.'

She gave a huge shuddering sigh. 'I don't know where to turn. What do we do next?'

'What time are you going to t'hospital?'

'I'll leave about eleven.'

'Then I'll put some work clothes on and we'll go and get that ceiling finished. Your mum can finish t'breakfast dishes.'

'Mum has finished the breakfast dishes,' they heard Flora call.

'Good girl,' Alan called back. 'Did you hear everything?'

She came through the adjoining door. 'Yes, I did. Do not be in that room on your own, Alan Paulson.'

He smiled at the fiery expression on her face. 'I won't. It will only take me half an hour at t'most, so Rose will still be here.' He stood and went through to get changed. Flora took his place on the stairs.

She held her daughter's hand and squeezed it. 'Trust the hospital, sweetheart. They know what they're doing. He'll be back with us before you know it. Now, does anything need doing with the business?'

'No, I'm going to ask Tom to step up while John's not able to work. He always does when we go away, so I'm sure he won't mind. It's such a mess, isn't it, Mum? Six or seven months and it's brought us to our knees. How on earth can a dead person get into my wardrobe, take a shoe out of its box and leave it on the stairs? How?'

Flora sighed. 'I have absolutely no idea, Rose, but I do know that poltergeist activity is pretty much what we saw happen in that bedroom. They can be incredibly destructive.'

'My other worry, apart from John, is bringing the children home. When I spoke to Violet this morning, she asked me, begged me, to leave them with her. But how do I explain that to Holly when her best friend is being buried next week?'

Rose looked up as her father came back through, dressed in jeans that had seen better days, and an old sweatshirt with various shades of paint embedded in it.

'Okay, I'm going to mek a start. Half an hour should see t'ceiling done wi', and then a cup o' coffee might be welcome.'

Rose smiled. Hearing her dad speak was something she loved, and it was what she needed right at that moment.

She stood and they climbed the stairs together. The room was as John had left it, and Alan gave the paint a quick stir before pouring some into the tray. He ran the roller through it and Rose watched as he painted smoothly across the remaining area that needed to be covered.

It took Alan twenty minutes and he stood back with a satisfied expression on his face. 'That looks good. 'Appen I'll just do a bit o' glossing now.'

'Dad!'

'Look, our Rose, I don't have to climb. There's just a door and t'skirting board. It's no bother, and it's got to be done.'

'Not on your own, in this room.' The stubbornness in Rose's voice was all too evident.

'Okay. I promise not to be on my own. Either you or your mum will be with me when I'm up here.'

Rose looked at her watch. 'Okay, you have an hour and a half. I'll go and get a picnic chair or something, as we don't appear to have any chairs up here anymore, and sit and read for a bit while you get on with it.'

'Good girl.' He smiled at her. 'I'll go down with you and wash this tray and brush out while you're getting sorted, and then we'll come back up. This is a bloody nuisance, in't it?'

She nodded. 'It is, but I'll not see you in danger and on your own, Dad. Remember that, will you, when you start thinking well I could just... because you damn well can't. I mean it.'

28

Rose left for the hospital just after eleven o'clock. Flora was now ensconced in the garden chair, a book on her knee, watching her husband begin to apply the yellow emulsion to the three designated walls.

His glossing was done and he had decided only the door needed a second coat, so while he was waiting for the first coat to dry he began to bring sunshine into the room. He was clearly enjoying what he was doing, and she soon became lost in her book. She always enjoyed a good murder.

An hour later she called a halt.

'It's lunchtime, Alan.'

'But—'

'But what? We don't have a deadline for finishing this. Violet was absolutely right this morning, Rose can't bring the children back yet, whether it's Tim's funeral or not. The idea behind sending them to France was to keep them safe. They're not safe here, and tonight we have to talk with her, no matter what time she comes home.'

Alan sighed. 'I know, and I'm doing this partly to keep my mind off everything that's goin' on, and partly so young Holly has a nice room again. You're right, I'll rest for a couple of hours, do t'crossword and eat, then I'll do a bit more up here.'

***

John looked much too pale. With an outdoor job, he always had something of a tan and it frightened Rose to see him in such a state. There were intravenous tubes feeding him medication and his right arm and shoulder were encased in a pot. He was asleep.

'Is he still sedated?' she whispered to the nurse checking the IV bags.

The nurse shook her head. 'Not as such – he's asleep because of the anaesthetic. When he starts to come round the doctor will check him. If he thinks he needs to sleep for longer he will sedate him, if not we'll monitor him very closely. If he can stay alert it makes it easier to spot if anything is wrong. Try not to worry too much, Mrs. Broadbent, I'm sure he's going to be okay, it will just take time.'

Rose smiled. 'I don't care how long it takes, so long as he comes back home.'

'Are you staying?'

Rose nodded.

'Then if he shows signs of waking up, please press that bell.' The nurse pointed to the wall. 'We're in and out all the time checking on him, but sod's law says he'll wake up as we go out of the room. With you here, it's an extra pair of eyes for us.'

Rose sat in the chair by the bed and reached out to hold John's left hand. She felt tears in her eyes, and brushed them away impatiently. No tears, she didn't want John to see her cry; he had enough to concern him, without worrying about her.

She had been sitting there for over half an hour when she felt movement in his hand. The nurse had been in a couple of times, once just to look at him and once to take his blood pressure, but his finger moved when she was alone with him.

She stood and looked intently at his face, still holding his hand; nothing, no eye movements, nothing. She sat down again convinced she had imagined it because she wanted it to happen.

And this time it was a squeeze.

Once again she stood, but this time she pressed the bell.

'John? It's Rose. Can you hear me?'

Again the squeeze. Again the prickling of tears.

The nurse came through the door and Rose explained what had happened. The nurse moved to the bedside and they watched as one eye slowly opened.

'Hi, Mr. Broadbent,' the nurse said. 'You're back on the ward.' Slowly his other eye opened and he searched for Rose.

'I'm here, my love,' she said. He squeezed her hand again, and closed his eyes once more.

The nurse smiled at her. 'That's good,' she said. 'He'll do that more frequently, until he's fully awake. He knows you're here now, so he's gone back to sleep. Press the bell again when he wakes. I don't want him to be in pain. We can medicate him if he needs it.'

Then slowly, over the next ten hours John came back to her. She left him just before eleven o'clock that night, feeling satisfied that he was being taken care of by a team of experts, experts who had told her he was on the mend, but would be with them for some time.

She pulled up to the front door, locked the car and walked towards the house. Alan and Flora came out to meet her, worry etched on their faces.

'Thank goodness you're home, sweetheart,' Alan said, and led her gently through to their lounge. 'How is he?'

'He's doing well, Dad. He's in some pain, but they're giving him strong pain relief, and he was asleep when I left. He's been awake on and off all day, and he'll be in hospital for quite some time, but he's doing well for a first day.'

She sank into the armchair and allowed her parents to cosset her. It had been a long day, she was tired and she needed sleep, but most of all she needed a cup of tea that hadn't been made in a hospital.

They talked quietly until she moved to go to her own side of the house.

Alan stopped her. 'No, Rose.'

'No what?' She looked puzzled.

'You're staying with us. I won't let you be alone. Not at the moment.'

She hesitated and then nodded. 'You're right. Did you stay upstairs with Dad, Mum?'

'Too right I did, all day! The room is ready for the last wall to be wallpapered now. It looks lovely; I love that colour. We do need to talk about the children, though, Rose.'

'We don't, Mum. I've had lots of time to think today, and Violet is right. It's too dangerous to bring them back just yet. We'll get the funeral out of the way and then see about getting them home. They need to be in school.'

'Thank goodness for that. I'm glad you're being sensible about it. We can take Holly to Tim's grave when she does come home, so she can say her goodbyes there. Violet will tell her the time of the funeral and I'm sure they'll have a moment of prayer or something for him on the day itself.'

Rose kissed her parents and headed for their guest room. Sleep didn't come easily and when she did finally close her eyes it was to dream of falling down a cavernous tunnel onto glass, blood, so much blood and screams...

When she woke the next morning, she looked ill. Alan cooked breakfast and made her eat it. She felt better for the food and even better after her telephone call to the hospital. John was being moved from high dependency to a normal ward, although he would be in a side room. He needed to be quiet, they explained, and gave her the ward number.

Moving to a regular ward meant that she was only able to visit him during normal visiting hours; an improvement for John, but she felt she needed to be with him.

She also spoke with Karen Aristocleous at Holly's school; it was a courtesy call to update her on the situation with Holly, and Karen told her that the whole of Tim's fellow year pupils had requested that they go to the funeral, along with members of the football team Tim had joined.

To take her mind away from hospitals and funerals, she asked Alan to go up to Holly's room with her.

She opened the door and it was as if the room was flooded with sunshine, despite the greyness of the weather through the bedroom window.

'Oh, Dad, it's beautiful. When the wallpaper is on it will be perfect. Maybe next week I'll go into Sheffield early, get some furniture sorted and then go on to the hospital to see John.'

'Good idea. We'd like to see him, but we'll go with you. We're not leaving you here alone while we're in Sheffield. That's not going to happen, Rose.'

She nodded. 'I know. I won't argue with you. I just find the whole damn thing unbelievable, Dad. Ghosts? People coming back from the dead? I tell you, if I hadn't seen what happened with that exorcism thing...'

He could see she was getting agitated. 'Maybe it worked.'

'What? What do you mean?'

'I can't sense her anymore, and she's been ever-present in the house and outside for some time. I can't feel anything now. Was John the last fling for her? Has she given up? Can you feel her in this room? She wasn't here yesterday, and your mum and I were here all day. Maybe the real Lavender has surfaced and stopped the evil.'

Rose stood without speaking and just listened to her own heartbeat. She could feel nothing and she knew her dad was right; it was a different atmosphere. Could he possibly be reading it correctly? She hardly dared to believe.

She left Holly's room and walked along the landing to her own room. Nothing. It felt as it had always felt; a calm, serene room.

Alan stood behind her.

'See what I mean? Has she gone? Is she at peace at last?'

Rose shook her head. 'I don't know, Dad. Let's get Tim's funeral out of the way. If that runs smoothly, we can maybe believe she's given up.'

'But you don't have a sense of her?' he persisted.

'No, but that doesn't mean a thing. It only means we don't have a sense of her at this moment in time.'

His head dropped. 'I had hoped...'

She gave him a kiss on his cheek, and they left to go back downstairs. She took the wallpaper from the hall cupboard and held it up to him.

'Shall we?'

'We shall,' he said with a smile. 'We have maybe three hours before you need to go, so let's see what we can get done.'

They finished with half an hour to spare and Rose was in awe at the glowing appearance of the room. She knew Holly would love it, but more than that it took away the bad memories of the day everything in it was trashed. Holly's books were stashed in the main bedroom and a new bookcase would have to be bought; Holly need never know the real reason for the re-decoration, they could just say they took advantage of her being in France to decorate it for her.

She arrived at the hospital, parked with a degree of difficulty in the hospital's own multi-story car park, and grumbled all the way to the lifts. She then had to wait an age for one of the bank of lifts to appear. By the time she reached John's new room, she was in a bad mood, and she knew it. She took a deep breath before walking through the door. Bad moods and really ill husbands didn't go together.

His smile lit up his face when he saw her.

'Sweetheart,' was all he said, and she bent over to kiss him.

'Are you in pain?' was her first question.

'No, he grinned, 'I've got this little button here, and when you press it morphine comes into your bloodstream. It's magic. I'm quite happy, thank you.'

'I bet you are,' she laughed. 'Seriously, though, is everything okay?'

'It is. I don't think I'll be in as long as they were saying yesterday. I'll have this for a while,' he said, pointing to his arm, 'but once the pain settles down there's no reason to stay here. And nobody seems too worried about my head, so I'm not. I need to get home to get that bedroom finished, although I'll have to learn to paint with my left hand.'

'It's done. All finished. Dad did all the painting, and I helped him with the wallpaper this morning. It looks fantastic. Holly will love it.'

John looked shocked. 'Finished? It's time your dad realised he's nearly sixty-five years old. And I'm not happy him being in that room...'

'Stop worrying. We know what we're doing. You just get better and come home to us. Holly and Jacob are staying in Paris at the moment; I don't want them home until after the funeral – I'm not taking any risks.'

'Good. That makes me feel easier about being in here.' He moved slightly and winced. 'I can't see me being there, though.'

Rose laughed. 'There's not an earthly chance of you being there. And to be honest I'm hoping you're still in here. What if I break your leg as well?'

He sensed the touch of hysteria behind the joking words and knew just how worried she was. He reached across with his left hand and touched hers.

'I'll be fine. You just stay safe, Rose. Be on your guard. It's a week today, isn't it? I'm a bit confused by the days.'

'Yes. I need to see Maria. I told her I would cater, but there won't be much to do. It's just us and Maria's ever dwindling family. She doesn't want anyone else there. She wants us just to have a cup of tea and a sandwich, and talk about Tim. I'm with her on that one. She can grieve properly in front of the people she knows well, but not in front of strangers. Having said that, I think it will be a big funeral. Karen Aristocleous is allowing his fellow pupils from the same year to attend, plus a few others from his football team.'

John looked worried. 'And what if something goes wrong – all those kids, Rose. Doesn't it worry you?'

'Of course it does, but what are we supposed to do? We have to be there at the funeral. It has to be in the same graveyard as Lavender's grave because here is where Tim has always lived. Castleton is the only home he ever knew. If you think I'm not seriously scared, then you don't know me at all, John Broadbent.'

She saw him draw in a breath with pain as he tried to turn to her.

'Press your button,' she said. 'Stop being a brave little soldier. If you need pain relief, then have it.'

'My word, you're stroppy today. I thought you looked out of sorts when you came through the door.'

'Parking problems, lift problems, and too much coffee. I'm sorry, I shouldn't be like this. I miss you, John, and I don't want you to come home. Not in this battered state, anyway. You need to be able-bodied to handle everything we have thrown at us, and I mean literally thrown at us.'

He talked calmly to her and she lay against him for a while, stroking his hair. By the time visiting hours were over, she felt much better.

'Drive carefully, sweetheart, and I'll see you tomorrow,' he said.

'No, I'm coming back tonight.'

'No.'

'Yes.'

'No. I find the evenings quite tiring, so stay safe at home. Look after Alan and Flora. Are you still using their guest bedroom?'

'I am. They won't let me sleep in our half of the house, not on my own, anyway.'

His tone became serious. 'Then please stay with them, Rose. Listen to your dad. For an old 'un he's a mighty sensible feller. Leave our side of the house alone, and if you have to go into it, make sure someone goes with you. Please, Rose...'

She recognised the anguish and the worry in his voice, and nodded. 'I'll stay with Mum and Dad, don't worry. But after this funeral, I have to get the children back. They need to be in school, and so do I. Are you absolutely sure you don't want me to come back tonight?'

'Certain. Bring your mum and dad tomorrow. Stay close to them, Rose. I love you.'

'And I love you.' She leaned over to kiss him. 'I want you home, but not until you're well. Take care, my love.'

She drove home without really noticing the journey, and was quite surprised to find herself entering the open gates at the bottom of the drive.

Another day closer to the funeral, another day closer to getting Holly and Jacob back home.

29

Saturday morning was cold, but with clear blue skies and sunshine. Rose, Alan and Flora breakfasted early and set off for Sheffield to do some serious furniture shopping.

Alan was adamant he was buying the new bed, so Rose picked out a single bed instead of the planned cabin bed.

'Are you sure?' Alan queried. 'Wouldn't she prefer one of these?' He pointed to the bed a few yards away.

'Yes, she probably would, but in a couple of years it will become a pain having to climb into bed rather than just get in. I think this one, with the second slide-out bed underneath, is better for her.'

By the time they had finished their shopping Holly had a new bookcase, desk, small dressing table and wardrobe, and a very pretty bedside rug in lemon. The carpet would be delivered and fitted on Monday, with the furniture arriving Wednesday.

'Coffee? My treat...' Rose shepherded her parents towards the store's coffee shop and they all sank down gratefully into the tub chairs.

'That was good,' she grinned. 'I love spending money.'

'We know,' was her father's dry response.

'Holly will be amazed when she comes home and sees all this lot set up. Maybe we can all start to recover. I think you're right, Dad, Lavender does seem to have gone.'

'Or she's licking her wounds and getting ready for t'next round,' Alan said quietly. 'It wouldn't pay for us to underestimate anything, tha knows.'

They sipped slowly at their drinks, each lost in their own thoughts.

***

John folded the newspaper and placed it carefully on the bedside locker. He thought he might have a go at the crossword later, if he could manage to manoeuvre his arm sufficiently to balance a paper and write as well. He eased himself slowly back onto the pillow and briefly closed his eyes. His headache had lessened considerably; still there, but not of the intensity he had suffered when he was first admitted. He needed to get home and losing the headache would be a massive step in the right direction.

Slowly he drifted off to sleep, lulled by the pervading aroma of lavender. He didn't notice it, it was insidious. Gary Bailey, the doctor on duty, opened the door and moved to the bedside. He sniffed the air, wrinkling his nose at the same time. It was strange that any sort of odour other than medical should be in the room; the patient had had no visitors yet, and nurses didn't wear perfume so that smells weren't masked. He picked up the notes from the end of the bed and began to read.

'No,' John said, his eyes tightly closed. 'No, get away from me!' Gary looked towards his patient and waited. He didn't want to waken him unnecessarily, but equally he didn't want a distressed patient on his hands possibly causing further injury to the shoulder and arm. There was a long, deep sigh from the man on the bed.

'Lavender, get the fuck...' John's head was beginning to move from side to side and Dr. Bailey leaned forward to touch the undamaged arm. He shook John gently, and pulled his hand away quickly. The man was burning up. He grabbed at the notes and checked his last temperature reading – ten minutes earlier and perfectly normal. John was now seriously trying to escape his sleeping thoughts; the thrashing of his head became more violent, his words more disjointed.

'Stop, Lavender, stop. Go. Dead. Stay dead. Leave us alone!' His last words came out in full volume, and Bailey reached across to press the bell for assistance. Within seconds a nurse was there and she looked at the man who had earlier been joking with her, with shock on her face.

'What...?'

'I don't know. Let's wake him. I'll stand at the injured side. Pull up the bed sides; we don't want him throwing himself on the floor. And I want his temperature re-taking. He's red-hot.'

The smell of lavender got stronger and Lucy looked across at Gary.

'What's that smell?'

'I have no idea. It's very cloying, very flowery, but we're using nothing that would cause it.'

They secured the sides and the doctor shook John.

'John, can you hear me? John?'

John moaned and then screamed 'NO!'

The bed visibly moved and Lucy jumped back in alarm.

'Put the damn brake on,' Gary yelled, as he tried to calm his patient.

'The damn brake is on,' Lucy said quietly. She leaned across the bed side and began to stroke John's head.

'Sssh,' she intoned. 'Wake up, John, you're having a bad dream. Wake up.' She continued to stroke his head, aware of just how hot he felt. She had no idea what on earth had caused such a massive fever spike, and she looked at the doctor.

'I'm going to take his temperature,' she said, and he nodded. John was whispering, making small mewling noises as if in pain, then his hand came up as if to ward off a blow.

Lucy checked his temperature and looked puzzled.

'What is it?' Gary asked.

'Normal,' she said. 'Absolutely normal.'

'Do it again. Use a different thermometer.'

She left the room and was back very quickly. They waited for the reading to register and Lucy checked again.

'Normal.'

'Let's get a litre of saline into him. Whatever the thermometer is saying, he is burning up. And what's that bloody smell? Can we open a window, please?'

Lucy turned to do as he instructed and she heard a low moan come from the bed. His eyes were still closed but the words were still coming out of his mouth. They didn't make sense and she kept hearing the word lavender.

'That's it,' she said.

'What?' Gary Bailey looked up from the chart he had been writing on. 'What's it?'

'He keeps saying lavender, said it several times, but that's what the smell is. Is he trying to tell us he doesn't like the smell?'

'I have no idea, but I think we should bring his family in. There's maybe something from that head injury that is now showing up. I'm booking him in for a repeat scan; we need to take a closer look. Get the saline set up, that's a start, but I can't help but feel we're missing something. Ring his wife, Lucy. I'll get on to the scan department. We need to sort this.'

The bottom end of the bed began to swing around and Lucy gave a small scream.

'I said put the brake on,' the doctor said.

'Doctor Bailey, the brake is on and was on the last time you said it. I don't know how the bed is moving. I'll move it back.'

She released the brake and swung the bed back into position, then clicked on the brake. She pushed it and it didn't move. 'The brake is on,' she said coldly.

'Sorry, Lucy, I don't doubt you. But how can one of these hefty things move anyway, all on its own?'

She left and returned with the saline. Hanging it on the stand took seconds and she connected John to it.

He was still mumbling, and she heard the word 'worms' and what she thought was 'Tim.' She stroked his head again in an attempt at calming him and suddenly his eyes opened.

'Doctor!'

Bailey moved towards his patient, but as he reached the bed John's eyes closed, he gave a huge sigh and seemed to sink into the covers.

'Go and ring his wife, now,' he told Lucy, and she ran from the room.

It was pointless; Rose was just finishing her cup of coffee, along with Alan and Flora. They left the restaurant, headed towards the car park and within ten minutes were on the way to the hospital for the two o'clock visiting session.

They were early; all three of them sat outside the ward doors. Strict hospital rules about the patients' nap time between 1 and 2pm meant that the doors were locked. They chatted about the furniture they had just ordered and looked up as the door opened. Lucy saw them and instantly recognised Rose.

'Please,' she said. 'I've been calling you. Do you have a mobile phone?'

Rose shook her head. 'No, I've resisted getting one. What's wrong?'

'Just come through here. Doctor Bailey is still on the ward – in fact, he's in with John. He'll explain.'

Alan put his arm around his daughter and hugged her. 'Come on, let's go and see him.'

Lucy accompanied them to the door of John's room and Rose felt sick. Her husband was linked up to an array of machines, with two IV tubes attached to him and an oxygen mask on his face. When she had last seen him, he had almost been back to his normal self, chatty, caring and worried about her. Now he was lying in a bed, no obvious signs of life apart from the gentle beep of the machines, and she had known nothing of what was happening.

'Mrs. Broadbent? We've been trying to reach you, but we don't have a mobile number for you.'

'I don't have one...' she said faintly. 'What's happened?' She stepped towards the bed. 'John...'

'We don't know what's happened yet. He's going down for a scan in five minutes, as we need to look at his head wound again.' The doctor shook his head as if doubting his own words. 'He was asleep when I came in, so I just had a look at his chart and he began to get quite agitated. He was obviously dreaming, he wanted somebody to leave him alone, kept saying dead, go away and things like that. He was very hot, but we checked his temperature twice and it showed normal.' He hesitated.

'As at this moment I have no idea what is wrong. As a precaution, I have put him on a saline drip and an antibiotic, in case there is some infection in there we're not seeing. We should know more after the scan.'

'And he's now sedated?' Rose asked.

'No, he's lapsed into unconsciousness. I don't want to sedate him; I actually need him to come round. When he can talk, we can assess if he has had some sort of stroke, but while he's out of it, we can't. The scan will tell us more.'

'Thank you,' she whispered, and pulled a chair close to his bedside. Taking hold of his hand, she began to speak to him.

'I'm here, my love. Now would be a good time to come round.' She looked up as the door opened. A porter stood there, accompanied by Lucy.

'We're going to take John down for his scan, now,' she said. 'You can either wait here, or go and get a coffee. He'll be at least an hour.'

Rose stood and looked at her parents. 'Let's go get a drink. I'll go mad waiting in here.' She bent and kissed John and he was wheeled from the room, Lucy pushing along the drip stand and keeping pace with the porter.

They walked in silence towards the bank of lifts. Rose pressed for D floor and insisted her parents find them a table while she got the drinks. She wanted two minutes completely alone with her thoughts.

Lavender had caused this. She knew it without a shadow of a doubt; Gary Bailey's description of the words John had been using rang around her head – dead, go away, leave. She felt grief overwhelm her; had she intended the fall to kill him? Was she now going to finish him off? Why? What had John ever done to Lavender that could cause such hatred? So many questions with no answers.

She carried the tray across to Flora and Alan. Their faces were pinched; they were clearly having difficulty coming to terms with the developing situation. Alan stood to help and took the tray from her.

'Sit down, lass. What can we do? Go private? We've got the money...'

'If money had been the answer then we could have got rid of Lavender long ago, because let's face it, Mum, Dad, all of this is down to Lavender. You know it. You heard what Dr. Bailey said, the words John had used, and you could smell that bloody lavender in his room. She's not gone quiet at all; she's finishing off what she started with the fall down the stairs. She expected to kill him then, so now she's trying here.'

Alan's head dropped. 'We feel guilty enough, Rose. Don't rub it in anymore, please.'

'Why should you feel guilty, Dad? You didn't push John down the stairs, kill Tim, kill Tony, and scare Holly half to death. She did.' She could feel her voice rising, and people began to stare.

She sat down and pulled her drink towards her. She felt suddenly old; too old to cope with the stress and the problems. And she had no idea how to handle anything anymore.

She looked at her watch. Ten minutes. This was going to be a long and difficult hour. And it was clear she was going to spend it stopping her parents from feeling guilty at having given birth to Lavender.

30

They had been sitting in the side ward for half an hour when John was returned to them. He was still unconscious and Lucy said he had remained in that state all the time he had been out of his room.

Dr. Bailey came in an hour after John's return carrying the pictures of John's brain.

'There is nothing,' he said. 'There is a marked improvement from when he was brought in; no bleed, nothing. Three of us have pored over these because there is absolutely no reason for John to be in the coma that he's in.'

'Coma?' Rose lifted frightened eyes to him.

'It appears so, Mrs. Broadbent. He has simply shut down. And it's for no apparent reason.'

'But... for how long?'

'I have no idea. He could wake up in an hour, or he could wake up in four years. Or he could remain like this forever. Coma is a mystery. Every patient is different and until the patient's eyes open we know nothing. I'm so sorry; I wish I did have some answers for you.'

Rose felt numb. Life was unthinkable without John and it was becoming seriously unthinkable without the children. They had to come home now. Their chatter could be the one thing that brought him back to them. She made the decision that immediately after Tim's funeral she would fly to Paris and bring Holly and Jacob home.

They sat by the bed for hours, occasionally talking, taking it in turns to go and get something to eat, and all the time watching for signs of improvement in John.

After a promise from the nurse that she would ring if there was any significant change, they headed back to the car park, each feeling as miserable as it was possible to feel. Their morning had started off so promisingly; the new furniture chosen and bought, thoughts of bringing John home...

It was now taken as read that Rose would be staying in her parents' guest room for the foreseeable future. Flora made them all hot chocolate, although nobody wanted food. Rose carried hers through to the bedroom and finally gave in to the tears. Seeing John so lifeless had been almost like a death. So much death in her life... she couldn't let John go. She vowed to see him the next day on her own and to talk constantly to him. She would get him back. Her own voice would let him know how much he was loved, needed. He had to come back.

She slept fitfully. By six o'clock she had given in and was sitting in the kitchen drinking coffee when Flora walked through the door.

'You couldn't sleep either?' she asked, smiling at her daughter. 'What time are you going to the hospital?'

'I don't know. They didn't actually move him from the ordinary ward, so I suppose it's just normal visiting hours. I'll ring in a couple of hours and see what the situation is like. Let's just be thankful nobody rang us through the night. I was so scared, Mum, scared I'd never see him again.'

'Me too, sweetheart, but he's made it through the night. Let's hope for good news when you ring.'

Flora busied herself getting breakfast ready, holding back tears. She couldn't let Rose see just how worried she was, proved by the sleepless night she had just spent.

'Scrambled eggs okay?' she asked.

'Fine, Mum, but let me do it. You come and sit down.'

Still fighting tears, Flora shook her head. 'No, you're my guest.' She took a bowl out of the cupboard, picked up an egg and dropped it on the floor.

And the held back tears began to flow. She slid down onto the floor, holding herself and rocking as the pent-up sorrow spilled out of her.

'Mum?' Rose dropped to the floor alongside her mother and held her. 'Oh, Mum, come on. We'll get through it.' They sat together on the cold tiles, neither able to stop the outpouring of anguish.

And that was where Alan found them. He stared around the kitchen, and then moved across to get them to their feet.

'Flora? Are you hurt?'

She shook her head. 'Not physically, Alan. I think we're just a bit overwhelmed. The egg...'

'You're crying because of an egg?' He looked incredulous. 'An egg?'

He pulled them both to him. 'Come on, my ladies, this isn't like you two.' He held them tightly for a moment and then led them to the table.

'Sit down, I'll make us a fresh pot of tea and we'll start the day again, shall we?'

They both gave him a very weak smile, and he turned and walked straight through the splattered egg. The weak smiles turned to hysterical laughter, and so the day began.

***

John had been moved into the high dependency unit and Rose was with him by nine o'clock. Flora and Alan went down to church and during the service Gareth spoke of John and his need for their prayers.

As they came outside after the service, the well-wishers gathered around them, eager to support the family. Flora noticed that Maria was absent, along with Matt and Beth, so she suggested to Alan that they walk down to Maria's home, just to check that everything was as it should be.

Maria's smile of welcome was forced. She didn't really want to see anyone, but she held the door open for Alan and Flora to walk through.

'Tea? Coffee?'

'Yes, please. We didn't stay after the service, so could certainly use a drink.'

Maria walked through to the kitchen and was soon back with a loaded tray. She placed it carefully on the coffee table and began to pour.

Flora felt uncomfortable. 'Maria, are you all right?'

Maria handed her a mug of tea, the look on her face saying she was far from all right; a long, long way from all right.

'That was a crass thing to ask, particularly stupid,' Flora said gently. 'But I had to come...'

Maria nodded. 'I can't go to church.'

'What?'

'What sort of God would allow Tim to leave me, to lose his life when he had it all in front of him? Thirteen, Flora! Thirteen!'

She began to cry and Flora nodded to Alan, whispering 'go' as she pulled Maria into her arms.

Flora held her until the wracking sobs subsided, and she felt Maria collapse onto her shoulder.

'Come and sit down, Maria.' She led her to the settee, and then poured her a mug of tea.

'Here.' She handed it to Maria and sat by her side.

'Do you want to talk?' Flora waited while Maria composed herself a little.

'I'm not sure what to say,' she said finally. 'I bury my boy in five days' time, less than a year after his father. I'm scared to death that something will happen to Matt or Beth...'

'Has something happened to them?' Flora's fear was etched on her face.

'No, but they're spooked. I can see it in them. Matt, of course, is having time off work until after Tim's funeral, so at least he's with Beth all the time, but what happens when he goes back to work? When life goes back to normal? She's not going to just disappear, is she, your daughter?' There was venom in Maria's voice.

'No, she's not,' Flora said quietly. 'We thought she had, but now we have John in a coma in hospital for no obvious reason. Nothing is showing up on the scans or x-rays, and how can we say to the doctors that the reason he is in a coma is a girl called Lavender who has been dead for six years?'

Maria looked horror-struck. 'No! Not John... how could she hurt him? I thought he was in hospital because he'd fallen downstairs and hurt his shoulder, but a coma! That's something else altogether.'

Flora quietly filled her in on everything that had happened with John and Maria looked more horrified by the second.

'And why isn't Gareth helping?' she demanded. 'Okay, the first attempt went wrong, but that doesn't mean he can't try again.'

'Maria, that first "attempt" as you call it was so catastrophic I'm not sure we can go through it again, never mind Gareth. I believe Lavender was there through her own choice that day; she seems to be so strong now that she isn't confined to Winterscroft, she moves around freely. Both the nurse and the doctor at the Hallamshire spoke of a smell of lavender, although obviously they didn't know the significance. We did. She is growing, and we don't know what to do, how to stop her. If Gareth did try for another cleansing or whatever it is, she doesn't even need to turn up. She could be in the Hallamshire finishing John off, or in Paris with the children.'

'No!' Maria eyes opened wide. 'No!'

Flora nodded. 'I'm not sure if the others have thought it through as far as this, but I didn't sleep last night; my mind wouldn't let me.'

'And Friday...' Flora could hear the fear in Maria's voice.

'Yes, Friday. Listen to me, Maria. I think Friday will be okay. She has done what she set out to do, she sent Matt a very clear message. And we all lost Tim because of that message. I think she will leave you alone.'

'You know, Flora,' Maria began, 'this is why I didn't want a wake for Tim. I was scared that something else would happen, and there's going to be quite a few people there. I don't want anyone else hurt – and if I'm honest, I'm not a good mixer, I will feel more comfortable coming back to my own home with people I love.'

'And to get back to the more mundane,' Flora smiled, 'I know Rose said she would cater for you. Well, now you have me. I'm taking this off Rose's shoulders. Besides, I make better cakes. I'll be down very early Friday morning with food. You don't have to think about anything other than Tim.'

Flora stood. 'Have we cleared the air? We're all here for you, Maria. Pick up that phone anytime, and don't turn your back on God. Talk to Gareth, it's what he's there for.' She picked up her coat. 'Keep the faith, Maria, keep the faith.'

31

The churchyard was full of people all dressed in bright colours; the hearse had pulled up to the tiny gate opening onto the tarmacked path and everyone was waiting in absolute silence, preparing to greet Tim as he completed his two minute, very short, last journey.

Maria, Matt, Beth and Maria's two sisters, Sue and Eve, accompanied by their husbands, James and Bill, had walked behind the hearse and joined Rose, Flora and Alan at the gate.

The back door of the hearse lifted and Matt, Alan, James and Bill stepped forward to hoist the coffin onto their shoulders.

The crowd, as one, began to clap, and as Tim's family followed the coffin down the aisle the mourners waiting patiently inside continued the ovation. Nothing could have prepared Rose for the sight in front of her. The church was packed, even to the extent of standing mourners down the sides and at the back. She had assumed everyone outside would now be following them into the church. She was wrong; they were outside because there was no more room inside.

Maria heard, but nothing was registering. She reached for Beth's hand and together they moved on to the front pew, then stood waiting for the pallbearers to join them. The applause slowly died away and Gareth began to speak.

His words were lost on Maria; inside she was dead. She felt shrivelled, lost in a world totally alien to her. Matt's arm supported her throughout and she vaguely heard, somewhere in the background, the sound of raised voices singing hymns she must have chosen at some point, but now had no recollection of doing so.

Gareth moved into the part of the service he knew would be the hardest for the family to bear. He spoke glowingly of Tim's popularity at school, evidenced by the huge crowds inside and outside the church, and mentioned the standing ovation afforded to the much-loved thirteen-year-old.

Rose briefly let her mind drift back to Diana's funeral, the standing ovation she had received at the funeral that Tim had watched with them...

Gareth's eulogy lasted for quite some time as he outlined Tim's achievements, his support of his mother after his father's death and his recent duties as best man at his brother's wedding.

The church fell silent as Craig Middleton walked to the front. He carried notes which he placed on the lectern, and coughed before beginning to speak.

'My name is Craig Middleton and I am captain of Castleton under 14s football club.' He paused briefly. 'But more than that, I am a friend of Tim.'

He looked across at the coffin, at Tim's photograph standing on it, at the white flowers covering it, and visibly swallowed.

'We, as a team, are all finding it difficult to come to terms with what has happened and I asked if I could say something on behalf of the team, to try and let you know what a star he was.'

'Tim was our centre-forward. He was a leader and was always the one to be handed the captain's armband if I couldn't play. We asked him to be our captain; he was so much better than me at the job, but he wouldn't do it. He said there would be times when he would need to be at home with his mum.'

Maria's head dropped and she sobbed.

'That was the sort of person Tim was, totally selfless and a brilliant kid who would have grown up to be an awesome and caring man. We played our last game together the day before he died. One of our players got a bit over-enthusiastic and brought one of the opposition's players down. That lad was injured enough to go off and be replaced, but it was Tim who was the first one to go to him and recognise that he needed help. He stayed with him until that help came. After the game, he went straight to that boy to check he was okay. I've seen Adam here today; he's come to pay his respects.'

Craig took the top sheet and placed it below the remaining two sheets. He noticed the smoke first and then suddenly, with an audible swoosh, the rest of his notes erupted into flames.

He ducked out of the way and Gareth ran across to the bewildered Craig, pulling him away from the lectern. Several people in the congregation stood and looked around in consternation, unsure what to do. They had attended Matt and Beth's wedding and once again, in their eyes, strange things were happening in this church.

The glass of water placed beneath the lectern by Gareth, concerned that Craig might need it to get through the ordeal of talking about his dead friend, was used to put out the fire. He slapped at the remaining few flickers with his bare hands and the congregation fell silent once more. The mourners who had stood at the appearance of the flames sat down, and waited for Gareth to speak.

'I know Craig had more to say about the remarkable young man we are burying today, but I think we will now move on to the next part of our service. We all have our own memories of Tim and what an amazing person he was. Maria has asked that we sit for a while and listen to Tim's favourite piece of music from the last few weeks, Boyzone's Picture of You, while remembering how he impacted on all our lives.'

There was a moment of complete silence and then the opening bars of the Boyzone single filled the air, the sounds mingling with the smell of charred paper and lavender. Noise started to drift in through the doors and then was taken up by the people in the church as everyone joined in with the song. It was a glorious three minutes and Gareth couldn't help but reflect, wryly, that hymns were never quite so enthusiastically sung.

He brought the service to an end as quickly as he could and once more the men lifted Tim onto their shoulders. They began the walk, carefully and slowly, up to the grave of Tim's father, newly opened to take the remains of his son. The line of people following the coffin to the graveside seemed never-ending and Gareth deliberately led everyone away from the site of Lavender Paulson's grave, a grave that should have been her final resting place, and clearly wasn't. Lavender was most definitely not at rest.

It was with a sigh of relief that he recognised the excavated grave was still the same as it had been earlier in the day. He had half expected the sides to be caved in, or the excavation area to be full of water; it looked surprisingly normal.

The artificial grass covering the excavated earth was piled high with floral tributes; in all Gareth's years of conducting funerals, he had never seen so many as there were for this young man.

He waited until the coffin had been lowered into the ground, then spoke the final words of the funeral ceremony. The box of earth was passed around to Tim's close family and friends, and then everyone began to drop roses. It was a beautiful sight, a moving tribute. Maria was heartbroken; she couldn't take comfort from the outpouring of grief from his friends. She wanted to hold her son again, just one last time. This funeral was so final. Until today, Tim had still been with her, now he was with his father. And his Father. 'Dear Lord, keep him in your loving arms, surround him with your angels and let him know of my love always. In the name of the Lord, Amen.' And she knew she had kept her faith.

Through her tears and her almost silent prayer, she watched as Craig Middleton walked up to the edge of the grave. He leaned forward, said, '*Bye, pal*' and dropped the captain's armband onto the rose-strewn coffin. It landed exactly on the brass plate.

That small action finished Maria. She was distraught. Rose moved to her side and held her tightly.

People began to slowly drift away, Gareth having said during the service there would be no wake at Maria's request. It felt anti-climactic almost, but with Maria in complete meltdown, Rose knew it had been a wise decision to simply go straight home. She was in no fit state to mingle with people and make small talk.

The small group of ten people headed back to Maria's and everyone sank gratefully onto assorted chairs. Rose waited a couple of minutes then moved into the kitchen to switch on the kettles. She began to remove the cling film from the sandwiches and slowly the tears leaked from her eyes.

She hadn't felt as low as this, even back in 1991, when she had lost her grandparents and sister all at once. This death was different; this death was unforgivable; totally unforgivable. The events of today, combined with her husband lying unmoving and unconscious in his hospital bed, were making her realise she wasn't coping. Decisions would have to be made, and made today. She would talk to Flora and Alan when they were home in Winterscroft.

She dried her eyes, and then poured the water into the teapots. In the lounge, no one was speaking. They were just sitting, staring into space.

'Okay,' Rose said as she placed the heavy tray carefully on the coffee table, 'the food is laid out in the kitchen and this tea will be ready in a couple of minutes. Help yourself when you feel ready. Let's keep Tim alive in our memories. Let's talk about him, laugh about the things that he did that were just a little bit crazy.'

Maria gave a small flicker of a smile, and stood. 'Thank you, Rose, you're a good friend. Please, come and get some food and thank you for understanding why I couldn't cope with being in a big crowd.'

Matt also stood and moved to his mother's side. 'Of course we understand. Come on, folks, eat. And thank you, Mrs. Paulson and Rose, for doing this for us. I hope there are scones...'

Rose smiled. 'Would I dare feed you without providing scones?'

'Scones?' Bill stood and moved towards the kitchen. 'Oh, well, maybe I might just try a small one...'

And the ice was broken, the tears withheld for a short time.

***

Gareth heard the tap on the office window and looked up to see the face of Andy Lupton, his grave digger. He waved his hand in a cup of tea drinking motion and Andy nodded before moving around to the side door.

'Tea or coffee, Andy?' Gareth asked.

'Tea, please, boss.' The gruff voice always came as something of a shock to Gareth, but he was getting used to it now.

Andy sat in the chair at the desk, opposite where Gareth had been sitting staring into space when Andy had knocked on the window.

'You okay, boss?' Andy asked.

'I'm fine, and I'm not your boss.'

'Who tells me where to dig my holes?'

'Well, me, I suppose.'

'Then you're my boss. Been a bit of a strange one today, hasn't it?'

'He was so young, Andy. It was always going to be huge; a much-loved young man of this village, dead at thirteen. I had to rig speakers up outside, as I knew we wouldn't get everybody in.'

'I was there. Decided to stay for this one, know Maria from school, and I dug the grave for Carl, her man, less than a year ago. To be digging it again...'

'I know.' Gareth handed him his mug of tea.

'Well, the little lad is all covered up now, and the flowers are like mountains. I've put the big one from Maria, Matt and Beth at his head and the one from the Paulson family at his feet. The rest are just placed where I could get them.'

'Thank you. If they want to change them, I'm sure they'll be down tomorrow to look at them, and they can do it then.'

'Something's puzzling though.' Andy pursed his lips as if deciding whether to carry on with the conversation or not.

'Oh?' Gareth knew as he spoke that he should have simply waited, and maybe Andy wouldn't bother carrying on with his thought.

'Yeah... something a bit odd. When all them kiddies from his school threw flowers down, I could have sworn they were all roses. In fact, I saw their teacher handing them out to them, so I know they was roses. Aye, they was roses, all right.' He paused as if wondering whether to continue.

'They were – very pretty, all different colours.'

'Well, they're not now.'

'What? They're dead?' Gareth felt sick – he thought back to the list of information Rose had given Tony March, the one that spoke of the first unexplained thing to happen; the dead flowers that Matt had brought to Winterscroft.

'No, they're not dead. About half are still roses, but the rest is lavender. I didn't see no lavender thrown down, but there's nay mistaking it. Smells strong an' all.'

'You've left it in there?'

'Well, of course I have. I'd no reason to take it out. Left that captain's armband as well. That was a lovely touch.'

'Yes, it was,' Gareth agreed. He took a drink from his cup, trying to process what Andy was telling him.

'It still smells of lavender,' Andy continued, oblivious to the pallor of his vicar.

'What?'

'Aye, well it would, wouldn't it? There's a piece of it in every wreath, every spray. I tell you, I like lavender as a smell that you just catch a whiff of sometimes, when you walk past a lavender bush and just brush it, but this is something else. It's strong. Nearly knocks you over. Hope it's faded for when his family come down, or else they'll allus associate lavender with young Tim, instead of his smile, his football... know what I mean?'

'Yes, I do, and thank you for telling me.'

'No problem, and thanks for the drink. Do you need anything else?'

'No, you're all right, Andy. Get off home now and thank you for everything you've done today.'

'You're very welcome, boss. I prefer it when they're eighty and not thirteen, though.'

'Me too, Andy, me too.'

Gareth watched as Andy walked up the path and arrived at the heaped flowers on Tim's grave. He saw him pause for a moment, and then continued out of the top gate, heading towards home.

Gareth sat for a moment, feeling vulnerable. The events at Winterscroft had scared him, and with John now in hospital as a result of further activity in the house, he knew he had every right to be scared.

He stood and went through into the church where he spent fifteen minutes on his knees in front of the altar. He prayed for help; not just for himself, for the entire village. Who knew where her vindictiveness would take her next?

32

'Maria, we'd like to stay, just until Monday. Will that be okay?'

Maria looked at her sister. 'Stay, Sue? I'd be happy for you to stay, but I won't be good company. And you haven't come prepared to stay...'

'James, do you want to bring the luggage in now, love?'

James nodded. 'Right away, my love. Is that okay, Maria?'

Maria smiled at them both. 'You've planned this then?'

'Yes. I don't want you being on your own, not yet, big sis.'

'Then thank you. The bed is newly made up. Matt and Beth have stayed a couple of times over the past two or three weeks, so I stripped it off yesterday. I must have known...'

James went out to the car and returned trundling two suitcases behind him; two large suitcases.

Maria looked at them. 'How long are you here for?'

Sue kissed her cheek. 'As long as it takes.'

***

John looked no different, Saturday morning. Rose hadn't seen him for a day, and nothing had changed. He still had a greyness about his skin, still had his eyes closed, was still hooked up to a multitude of machines and drugs and she sat by his bed, feeling full of despair. She took hold of his left hand and squeezed it, but felt no answering squeeze.

'Okay, John Broadbent. This has got to stop. I need you at home with me. We have things to sort out because I'm about to become a kept woman.'

Not a flicker. No hand movements. Nothing.

'I haven't discussed this with anyone yet, but I'm stopping work. It's not fair on the school, as they're having to bring in supply teachers to cover for me, so I'm going in Monday morning to tell them I've left. I am then going to Paris to bring our children home. Our family is fragmenting, and worrying about letting the school down isn't helping. So, you'll have to keep me. I need you to wake up though, so you can do that.'

No response.

She told him of her planned trip to Paris; it would take two days because the children wanted to take her to see the Mona Lisa. They assumed she had never seen it before, and so she went on to share again with him the joy of their first trip to Paris before they were married, and said she would tell the children she had been to Paris before, but had never been to the Louvre. He had to keep the secret. Would he promise to keep the secret?

Still no response.

'Am I right, John? Am I right to give up teaching? It will mean I can take over the admin side of your business, which I know you hate, and it will mean we can grow the business. I don't think we'll even notice a lowering of income. Everything is running smoothly at work. You don't need to worry.'

John very clearly wasn't worrying.

'While I am in Paris, Mum and Dad will be here to sit with you. I'm sorry no one was here yesterday, but it was Tim's funeral. It went well, all his school friends were there, and...'

She paused. The new mobile phone her father had bought her was ringing for the first time. She fished it out of her bag and looked at it with something approaching shock. The name on the screen said Maria.

She pressed the answer button. 'Maria?'

She heard a sob, and then Sue's voice came on.

'What's going on, Rose? Why is my sister babbling on about Lavender being the cause of all the trouble?'

Rose could hear background noise. 'Where are you, Sue?'

'In the church yard. At the grave. All the flowers are dead, except bloody sprigs of lavender, standing in the middle of each wreath, each spray. They can't have died as fast as this, and now I've got Maria in bits all over again.'

'Take her home, Sue. I'll be there in half an hour and we'll have a chat.'

She pressed the end call button, wished she'd never agreed to have a mobile phone, and bent down to kiss John.

'I have to go home for a bit, my love. Try to open your eyes, or something. I'll be back later.'

As she walked towards the nurses' station she realised they didn't have this new telephone number, and that had been the whole point of Alan buying them one each. She wrote it down and handed it to Lucy.

'Just in case,' she said, 'just in case.'

She drove away from the hospital at speed, wondering how to tell Sue and James what was happening. It sounded far-fetched and surreal, but Tim, Tony March – that wasn't far-fetched and surreal. They were facts.

She headed straight for Maria's house, still not knowing how to start the conversation. She pulled up outside and instantly the front door was opened. Sue looked angry.

Rose locked the car and walked towards her. 'We need to talk.'

'Too bloody right we need to talk. I can accept the part that Maria has told me, but what I can't accept is that I'm only just finding out.'

'Maria doesn't know everything,' Rose said quietly. 'We've tried very hard to protect her, to cushion her almost. Let's go inside and you'd better prepare yourself. It's not a good story.'

They moved into the lounge, and Maria stood. She had clearly been crying, and she turned to face her friend. 'Rose, I'm sorry...'

'Maria, there's no need to be sorry. I'm going to tell Sue and James the whole story. It won't do any good, but it concerns you and yours, so I will tell them.'

The anger was still evident on Sue's face and she pulled Maria towards her. 'My sister is a mess,' she said. 'Apparently, we have some supernatural stuff going on that's getting worse. What about that vicar? Can't he help?'

'Sit down, Sue, James. I'll tell you everything you need to know, but get rid of the aggression, please – I can do without it. My husband is in a hospital bed in a coma because of this "supernatural stuff" as you called it, and I've left his bedside to come here and talk to you. You threaten in any way, and I'm heading back to Sheffield. Is that understood? Because, believe it or not, I'm reaching the end of my tether, too. Now sit down and listen.'

There was a stunned silence in the room, and all three of them sat down and waited for Rose to begin talking.

She spoke for half an hour and nobody responded. When she finished, she sat back and waited for the fallout. Sue stood and walked over to her, leaned down and hugged her. 'Rose, I am so sorry, and I apologise unreservedly for the way I was with you. I want to say, "can we help?" but it would be just words, because I know we can't.'

'So, you believe me?' Rose felt exhausted.

'Of course I believe you! It's all very well people saying *I don't believe in ghosts* but this isn't about ghosts. It's about malevolent spirits, and they're out there. When we first married, we moved into a house that felt wrong, but we took it anyway because we had nowhere else to live. All sorts of things happened; our toilet door opened out onto the landing, not inwards into the toilet. I had left the door open while I nipped downstairs for a new bottle of bleach, and as I walked back up the stairs I watched the toilet roll, which was fixed to the door, unroll itself completely. We used to go to bed at night and all the bedding would be in a big pile on the floor. We heard a woman's voice on more than one occasion. We stayed there for six months and then couldn't stand it any longer. Things would move around in the kitchen cupboards... oh, all manner of stuff happened. So yes, I do believe in restless spirits. It just seems that this restless spirit is a murderous one. And you believe it's Matt she's after? How on earth...?' Sue finished speaking with a look of perplexity on her face.

'I have no idea.' Rose felt and looked weary. 'She can't have him, she doesn't exist. But does she know she doesn't exist? We don't know where to turn, Sue. I've tried to keep a lot of it from Maria, as she's gone through enough this last year, but you've forced my hand now.' She stood.

'I have to go back to John. I need to keep talking to him, trying to get through whatever this fog is that is keeping him from us.'

'Thank you. And please – I really am sorry. It was worry for Maria that turned me into a bolshie cow.'

'Look after her,' Rose said, as she walked to the door. 'She needs someone with her. If there's anything else, I'll contact you.'

She closed the door quietly behind her, not knowing whether she had helped or not. It seemed more and more people were finding out, and still nobody knew what to do.

Before heading back to Sheffield, she called home. She needed to have a conversation with Alan and Flora now that she had spoken to John. She hoped that somewhere in the darkness of his mind he had heard her.

Flora was at the door as Rose parked the car.

'What's wrong?'

'Nothing. Don't worry, Mum. I had a phone call on this little phone and I had to come back...'

The relief was written on Flora's face.

She held the door open for her daughter. 'That's okay then. Are you going back? Do you want a drink before you do?'

'No thanks, Mum. I'm all tea'd out from being at Maria's. I do need to speak to both of you, though. Is Dad here?'

'I'll get him. He's in the greenhouse.'

Rose sat at the kitchen table, letting the warmth of the room comfort her. She felt exhausted, and it wasn't even lunchtime yet.

Alan stood in the doorway in his stockinged feet and looked at her. 'What's up, love? Is it John?'

She shook her head. 'No, it's me, Dad. Come and sit down, you two, I need to tell you about decisions I've been making for the past week, really.'

They looked at each other and Flora moved to switch on the kettle. 'Mother's instinct tells me we might need a drink,' she said.

'Okay,' Rose said with a laugh, 'we'll have a cuppa, and maybe a sandwich in a bit, but let me tell you my news first. Sit down, Mum.'

Flora followed instructions and Rose began to tell them of her decision.

'I'm finishing work. I'm going into school on Monday, and telling Richard I won't be back. I owe him that much, and he'll be able to sort out a permanent replacement for me.'

'But you love teaching!' Flora looked shocked.

'I know I do, but I love my family more, and when John does come home he's going to need looking after. And I'm bringing Holly and Jacob home next Thursday. Under present circumstances I want to be here for them. I'm going to take on the admin side of John's business; I think it's ready to grow anyway. We've had to turn down some of the smaller jobs because we need more men out there working, so it's time I stepped up to the plate. I can work from home; it fits in with everybody then.'

There was a moment of silence while her words were digested, and then Flora stood. 'I said we'd need a drink.'

Rose winked at her father. 'Stop looking so worried, Dad, it's what I want to do, and I think it's the right time now to do it. I'll miss all my children at school, but I'll still see them when I go to pick up Jacob every afternoon.'

He smiled back at her. 'Rose, love, I'm not worrying. In fact... I actually think this is a good decision. You're right about the business. I went out to see the lads the other day. Thought I ought to tell them how John is going on, give them a bit of a boost that they've not been forgotten, and all of them were working like beavers, and all of them had a next job to go to. Tom's doing a grand job, but wages need sorting properly, and we need to stop turning down work. I'll help, of course I will, but paperwork is your forte, not mine.'

'I've given it a lot of thought, Dad, and I know I'm right. So, although Richard doesn't know it yet, I've retired. I'll see him first thing Monday morning, and put the wheels in motion for making it official. It will be such a relief. I've felt so guilty...'

Flora placed a cup in front of her. 'Drink this. I'll make us some lunch – ring the hospital, make sure everything's okay there, and have a rest for a couple of hours. If there's any change in John they'll ring you anyway.'

'The doctor said this morning there's absolutely no change; they're completely baffled why he's not responding. It's heartbreaking to see him lying there so still, so grey. He's always looked healthy because of working outside, but now he doesn't.'

She stood and moved towards the hall. 'I'll ring the hospital, check everything's okay while you're making a sandwich, Mum, and then go back to Sheffield later.'

They could hear her talking, but couldn't make out the conversation. When she returned to them she looked unhappy. 'They've talked me into not going back in today. He's no different, and Lucy has promised to ring me even if he sneezes. We've left it that I'll see him tomorrow. I'll go straight to the hospital after church.'

'Then have a rest. You don't need to be ill yourself. Ring the children, have a chat with them and then maybe have a nap. It won't hurt you.'

She shook her head. 'No, I'm going to give Matt and Beth a ring, see if they're in. I need to tell them about this morning. I can't help but feel...'

'What?' Alan looked closely at his daughter.

'You'll think I'm stupid, but because I had to tell the whole sorry story to Sue and James earlier, it kind of made me look at everything from a distance, I mean really think. We've been seeing isolated incidents from Lavender, each one getting bigger. She started with killing flowers, now she's killing people. I think Tony, Violet's baby, Tim and John, who I assume she tried to kill, not just injure, were all practice people. She's been building up strength, and I think she is going to go for Matt next. As soon as she has the strength, she will take Matt and that will be the end. Once Matt is dead, he is with her and that's what she wants. Our problems will be over; Lavender will be at peace. But Maria and Beth will be out of their minds. Tell me I'm wrong, Mum, Dad.'

They both looked at her, horror written on their faces.

'Don't look like that,' she said. 'We've known from the start that it was the wedding that triggered all this activity off. And then we really upset her by helping Matt and Beth. She's paid us back for that and I think she's reached her endgame.'

'What can we do?' There was a crack in Flora's voice.

'I have absolutely no idea. I hope I'm wrong. I have to speak with Matt – and Beth, of course. If they pooh-pooh what I tell them, then it's all out of my hands. If they see I'm talking sense, then we have a much bigger problem because I don't have any answers. James and Sue did me a favour because they forced me to look at everything all together instead of individual odd happenings, but I can see her growth now. And I believe she meant to kill in

Holly's bedroom. I don't think it was about destruction. I think she maybe went for John then. You know I have a strong faith, Mum, Dad, but it's being sorely tested.'

***

Matt opened the door to Rose with a smile on his face. 'Welcome, fair Rose. You're my first official cup of tea visitor. Sorry Beth is out in Sheffield, you might have got scones as well if she'd been here. Now all I can offer is ginger biscuits.'

Rose smiled back at him. 'Make it coffee, Matt, and put a brandy in it.'

He hesitated. 'Will I need a brandy?'

She nodded without speaking.

She followed him through to the kitchen and waited for the coffee. He handed her the brandy bottle and she poured some into her cup.

'You meant it then,' he said, and took the bottle from her, adding some to his own drink.

'Oh, I meant it all right.'

He stared at her; she sounded strong, angry even. 'Rose... Is it John?'

'It's all of us, Matt. But most of all I think it's you.'

There was a moment of silence while he digested her words and then she saw him shiver.

'Tell me what you mean, Rose.'

'I mean that by Tuesday, the anniversary of her death, she will be so strong that it's possible you won't survive. Probable.'

He stared at her. 'I'm going nowhere, Rose.'

'And I imagine Tony March and Tim thought that, if they'd been given time to think. Listen to me, and don't go all macho on me, because that will seriously cut no ice. I have been sitting at John's bedside with nothing to do but think, think and analyse. Listen to what I have to say, and if at the end you decide I'm wrong, then give me the way you see it.'

He nodded.

'She has grown steadily in power. Remember the dead flowers? Then the binful of bugs? Then I believe she tested herself with Tony March. I don't think she would have been successful if he had been away from her grave, but he was right by her. Then, of course, we had the fiasco with the tree branch breaking; come on, Matt, even you can see that wouldn't have happened under normal circumstances. That branch was massive; no way should it have broken off the main trunk.'

She paused. 'And her appearances, mainly to Holly, but John felt her by his side. There have been lots of little incidences of supernatural activity, all adding to her strength. She has been growing week on week; the baby, Tim, all dead because of Lavender and her fixation. Then we come to the biggest issue of all, the attack in Holly's bedroom. I firmly believe she intended to kill that day, make the biggest statement she could. *This is me going up against your God, I am the strongest.* But it didn't work. She did go up against God, and we do know who was the strongest.'

Matt was quiet. He was listening intently, adding things up just as she had done, day after day. And Rose knew she had him.

'John was her ultimate aim. I think he was her target in that bedroom, and when that didn't work she moved that shoe. John wouldn't have even thought about anything being on the stairs, we just don't do that. Nothing is ever left on the stairs; if we have something that needs taking up to a bedroom, it's put on the hall stand until someone claims it as theirs, and takes it up. He stood on that shoe and catapulted all the way down to the bottom. She was there, I could smell her.'

'John would have been the last part of the jigsaw for her, would have shown her just how strong she was, strong enough to go for the biggest prize on the coconut shy, you. But first she closed my husband down. I don't know if he'll ever come out of it, Matt, but I don't want your death to follow on from this bloody awful nightmare I'm going through.'

'How do I stop her?'

Rose was so relieved to hear the words, to know that he finally understood and agreed. 'I have absolutely no idea. She was weakened by prayer, by "For where two or three gather in my name, there am I with them", but I don't know what the answer is. I came to you hoping Beth would be here as well, because we need to brainstorm this through.'

'No!'

'But talking might help...'

'I meant no to Beth being involved. She's frightened, Rose; she's not strong enough to stand up to this evil... thing! I loved her so much, you know, the real Lavender, but whatever this is, it bears no resemblance to my Lavender. My girl wouldn't have killed a bug even; she was the gentlest person I have ever known. It's six years on Tuesday...'

'Exactly. That's what I was leading you towards. I firmly believe she will be at maximum strength on that day, and there will be no hiding from her. She'll come for you. What do we do? Surround you with everybody? Keep you safe for the entire day? Without John, we are depleted. There's the three of us, you, your mum and now Sue and James. They know the full story and I'm sure could be relied upon to help. I will talk to Gareth on Sunday but I don't know how he will feel about it. If Beth is scared, she needs to be out of the way, she would be a weakness in our ranks that we can't afford.'

'She's working Tuesday, we're both due back at our jobs on Monday.'

'You can't go to work...'

'I know. I'll have to ring in sick. I'll play-act on Monday so it doesn't come as a surprise when I ring Tuesday.'

'We'll all meet here. Yours is the smallest lounge. We need to be confined, so that we're closer together. It will be physical, I think. You have to end up dead so that you are with her forever, Matt. I think that's always been the plan.'

'And I think you're right.'

He looked completely disheartened; unbelieving that this could be happening. He had been so happy when Beth had said yes...

'What time does Beth leave for work?'

'Around eight o'clock.'

'Then we have to be here as soon as she has left. Ring me the second she walks out of the door. I don't want you left alone.'

'Rose... I'm a man. Lavender was a mere slip of a girl.'

'And did you not see that power she has in Holly's bedroom? The utter destruction she caused? Don't tell me you're stronger, Matt, because you're bloody well not. I'm more worried that the eight or nine of us won't be strong enough come Tuesday. Tuesday is her day and it will be bad.'

***

Gareth was deep in thought when he heard the doorbell, followed by Lorna's footsteps as she went to open the door.

His study door opened and Lorna popped her head around. 'It's Rose.'

He stood. 'Rose, come in,' he called, and reached behind him for the coffee pot.

Rose smiled. 'I can always rely on the coffee being already made here. Milk, no sugar, please, Gareth.'

He indicated the chair across from him. 'We'll sit at the desk, if you don't mind, Rose. I'm waiting for a phone call.'

'If you're busy...'

'I'm not. Now sit down, do as you're told. How is John?'

'No different. Still in the coma and they've still no idea why. I go to see him most days and I talk to him constantly, but then I think, what if he can hear me and he can't tell me to shut up? What if it's a kind of stroke where he is fully aware but he's locked into himself? It's torture to me, Gareth, so what must it be like for him?'

'Be patient, Rose. He'll come back one day, keep the faith.'

'That's what I want to talk to you about really,' Rose said. 'Keeping the faith. Tuesday is the anniversary of Lavender's death. I've had a chat with Matt and we've decided to meet the issue head on, and not wait for her to catch us unawares. I think she is so strong now, that she is going to attempt to take Matt.'

Gareth nodded. 'Tell me what you want me to do.'

***

Before heading back home, Rose stopped by Lavender's grave. In the late afternoon sunshine, it looked a peaceful place; the white marble reflected the sun's rays. She stared around at the other graves, many centuries old, and allowed her eyes to roam beyond them to where Tim had been buried. All the wreaths had been removed, as far as she could tell, and been replaced by a solitary vase, crammed with chrysanthemums.

She laid a hand on the headstone and felt nothing. 'Lavender,' she began, and then took her hand away. What could she say? The grave they had visited for over five years had been a peaceful place, a place to feel close to the lovely person they had lost; this wasn't the same place now.

Rose glanced up at the tree, the jagged scar where the branch had broken still clearly evident. She felt angry. And scared.

She turned and walked away and the sun disappeared behind a cloud. The white marble turned to grey and became icy cold. Lavender had heard her sister speak.

Rose passed by Tim's grave, pressed a kiss to her fingers and bent down and touched the mounded earth. 'Sleep tight, lovely boy,' she whispered, and headed home.

The drive into Sheffield passed in a blur and she walked into the ward, praying for a miracle. There wasn't one.

John looked no different; his face still bore the same grey tinge, his eyes tightly closed.

She pulled her chair close to him, kissed him and sat down. Today she had decided not to waffle on, just in case he could hear and he found it aggravating. She took out her book and began to read. The door opened and she turned to see who had entered.

Beth stood in the doorway. 'Okay to come in?' she whispered.

'Of course it is. Is Matt here?'

'No, I've been to see a friend in Jessop's. She's just had a baby, a little girl, so I thought I'd have five minutes with John before going back to the car.'

She moved to the other side of the bed and pulled a chair forward.

'No change?'

Rose shook her head. 'None at all. He's having physio to keep his muscles working, but even through that there's no response. You ready for going back to work?'

'I am, but I wish I could say the same for Matt. He's not getting over Tim's death; he's worrying about his mum, worrying about me, worrying about you... and I can't help him. I think I'll get over everything quicker by being back at work, but that's because I work with people – a library is always busy. But Matt, he works in such a quiet environment in that office, it will give him too much time to think. I believe firmly that he needs counselling, but he's far too much of a man for that. In his eyes, it would be a sign of weakness.'

They sat in silence for a few moments, each lost in their own thoughts, each fearful for the man in the bed.

'Would you like two minutes alone with him and I'll go and get us a coffee?' Rose asked quietly.

Beth shook her head. 'No, I'm fine thanks. I never drink coffee anyway, can't stand the smell or the taste. I can't wean Matt off it, though,' she finished with a laugh. 'How are you coping?'

'I'm leaving the school.'

'What? But why?'

'Because I can't split myself into five or six people; I need to be a mum, I need to be a daughter, I need to be a wife, I need to be a friend – do I need to go on? And what we've gone through during the last six months was worse than when we first lost Nan and Grandpops and Lavender. I need to stop worrying about going back to work, about letting Richard down, because I can't do my job at the moment. I'm going in tomorrow to tell him, and Thursday I'm bringing the children home. I'm sick and tired of running scared. We need normality.'

Beth stood. 'You're such a strong woman, Rose Broadbent. If you need anything, and I mean anything, you just shout. I'm heading back now. You need a lift or did you drive here?'

'I drove, thanks, Beth. I'll be going home soon. Take care driving, and good luck tomorrow at work.'

Rose sat back in the armchair and closed her eyes. She reached out to hold John's hand, and was comforted. Slowly sleep overtook her and she was startled awake by a nurse coming through the door to take John's blood pressure.

She could smell the lavender immediately. The nurse moved to John's side and wrapped the cuff around his upper arm. She looked at the reading and then repeated the actions.

'What's wrong?' Rose asked. 'You did it twice?'

'Y – e – s – s – s...' the young nurse said. She made an entry on his notes and turned to go. 'I'll check it again in ten minutes. It's a bit high.'

Rose glanced around her. The perfume was sickly, and she could almost taste it in the back of her throat. There was a flicker of white, mist-like, on the periphery of her vision, and she spun round to look.

Nothing. There had definitely been something, but now nothing. The smell began to disperse and she knew her sister had gone.

The nurse returned, along with Dr Bailey. He picked up the chart and looked at the figures. 'Let's check him again. This is the highest it's been.'

She wrapped the cuff around his arm once more and they waited. Perfectly normal. Bailey looked at the readout and said 'Do it again.'

The second time gave the same result, and he shook his head. 'Well, Rose, I've no idea why that happened, but I've also no idea why he's in this coma. Your husband is a bit of a conundrum as far as I'm concerned.'

Rose smiled at his comments. 'You're sure he's okay? Can I safely go home?'

'Yes. There's no sign of him coming out of this, and we would ring if any changes were spotted.'

She stood and picked up her coat. 'I could do with an early night. I'll be here tomorrow, but Tuesday I have things to do.'

She kissed John, walked slowly down to the car park and sat for a while in the car. Lavender had been there. Checking up on John? And had John been aware? His blood pressure said he had.

She started the engine and drove slowly home, occasionally brushing a tear away from her cheek. She needed John home.

33

Beth left at eight o'clock for the drive into Buxton. She felt quite excited by her return to work; it meant freedom from worrying about a ghost.

She pulled into the car park. Miss Chambers, the head librarian, was already there, and it caused mild amusement in Beth that she had never managed to be there first. Miss Chambers probably slept there, she was so bound to the job.

Beth locked the car door and crossed the car park. She waved through the doors and Miss Chambers crossed to let her in.

'Come in, Beth, come in. Is everything all right now?'

'Not exactly, Miss Chambers,' Beth replied, quite taken aback by her assumption that it would be. 'We buried my thirteen-year-old brother-in-law on Friday, so it's not all right at all.'

'Oh!' The older woman looked startled. 'Well... if you need more time...'

'No, I'll be fine, thank you. I need to be in work. It will help me get over it much faster, I'm sure,' Beth said, and walked across to the staffroom.

Miss Chambers jaw dropped. Just who was this strange, confident young woman who used to be Beth Barnes in a previous life?

She began to tidy her already tidy desk and looked up as Beth approached her.

'What do you want me to do first, Miss Chambers?' Beth asked; it still irritated her that all the staff members still had to use such an archaic form of address to the woman, when everyone else used first names.

'We've had a delivery of new books. I'd like you to get them logged on to the system, stick date sheets in the front and get them out onto the shelves. The shelves could all do with a good clean, but now that you're back I think we can make that a job for tomorrow.'

Beth nodded. She loved all aspects of her job, even the dusting and polishing, so while Miss Chambers might think she was giving her a mini-punishment duty for daring to take extra time off after her holiday, in actual fact she was looking forward to it.

She went back into the staffroom and dragged out the box with the new books in it. By the time she had finished it was lunchtime, and she walked outside to buy a sandwich from the bakery next door. She walked up to the Pavilion Gardens, found an empty bench and sat down to eat her lunch. She huddled inside her coat, keeping out the chill as best she could. Her mind drifted back to the funeral and she felt a tear escape and trickle down her cheek. She missed Tim so much; it was like having a second Matt around the place, they were so alike.

Her anger towards Lavender was ferocious; this... malevolence... had been the cause of all the problems, the deaths, everything. She finished her sandwich, screwed up the paper and aimed it at the waste bin. She missed and walked over to pick it up. Dropping it into the bin, she caught the slight fragrance of lavender and looked around her. Nothing. But the fragrance was still there, and getting stronger. She looked in the bin and saw the sprig of lavender.

Spinning to her right she looked all around, but could see nothing. The perfume was now really strong and she knew that one sprig, without being really crushed, could not be causing this depth of fragrance.

She paused for a moment. 'Lavender, fuck off,' she said, and walked away, heading down the hill and back to the library.

***

'You're leaving?' Richard was shocked. 'But why? Rose, have you really thought this through? This school has been your life...'

She nodded. 'Yes, it has, but now my life has changed. I know you only half believed me when I told you why Jacob wouldn't be here for the start of the school year, and that's fine. Believe what you want. But I know without any shadow of doubt what's happening. I have John to consider – one day he will come out of the coma and he's going to need some care. I now have children in different schools which brings its own awkward logistics; and I have parents who are not getting any younger. I can't be in school day after day, Richard, and not have a breakdown. I just can't. So, the sensible thing for both of us is that I step aside and allow you to get a permanent replacement for me. It will be better for the children as well. They need stability, and my leaving will give them that.'

Richard reached across the desk and took her hand. 'Rose, I believed you. Please don't think I didn't. There's sc much out there that we don't understand, so why would I dismiss the issues you have? And the circumstances of Lavender's death were so horrific that I find it very easy to accept that she isn't at rest. I just don't want to lose you. I'm quite happy to put you on extended leave, so take as long as you like...'

He could hear the plea in his voice and hoped she could as well. She was a valued member of his team and the children clearly adored her; her face was expressionless.

'I'm leaving, Richard. I've made my decision, and it hasn't been easy. I also have a business to sort out, with John in hospital. So this is the only option I have, really.'

He knew when he was beaten, and he nodded. 'I'll ease the way for you. I give in; I can see that nothing is going to change your mind. And Jacob? Have you given any thought to his return?'

'Constantly.' Her laugh was shaky. 'I'm going to Paris on Thursday and bringing both of them home. They'll both be in school next Monday.'

'Is it safe? Have things improved?'

She shook her head. 'Not in the slightest, if anything they've got worse. But my children need their education, and wonderful though Paris is, they need to be here in little old Castleton.'

She stood and moved to the door. 'I really am sorry to be leaving, Richard, but I think you understand.'

'I do, Rose, I do. My door is always open, whether you're a teacher or a parent.'

She smiled, and walked away. She held on to her tears until she turned into the gates of Winterscroft, and then she leaned against the massive oak tree at the bottom of the drive and sobbed until she could cry no more. She was paying dearly for having had a sister called Lavender.

Flora watched from the kitchen window, her heart breaking. She knew how difficult the decision had been for Rose, and she hated to see such sorrow in her first-born daughter. But equally she knew Rose would handle it, even if it meant tears first.

Rose dried her eyes and began the walk up to her home. She went through the front door and into the wing that had felt so comfortable until Lavender had begun to wreak such havoc. She wandered around, noting how cold it now felt without John and the children there to bring it to life. She peeked into Holly's bedroom and a smile crossed her face. The new furniture and the brightness of the paintwork made it a dream place ready for Holly's return. They had changed the layout and now her bed faced the window; she would have a view of the back garden while in her favourite position, reading on her bed.

She wandered around the house and then returned to be with Flora and Alan. Flora was baking bread, and the smell was delicious.

She slipped her arms around her mother's waist and leaned her head against Flora's.

'Smell's gorgeous,' she said.

'Keeping busy,' Flora responded. 'Is it done?'

Rose sighed. 'It's done. I don't think Richard was thrilled about it, but I don't think it was totally unexpected either. I feel strange. The sooner I get into the admin for the business the happier I'll be.'

'Your dad is out doing the rounds of the jobs right now. We had a couple of phone calls over the weekend, tentative enquiries, so he's gone out to look at them. I just hope he doesn't underquote – he's only helped John out in the past, never had the responsibility of pricing a job.'

'Mum, if he does, he does. It won't bankrupt us, whatever he does. He's been a brilliant help these past couple of weeks, but it's time I pulled my weight. I'm going in to see John later, in view of what we think will be coming tomorrow.'

Flora paused. 'You scared?'

'More angry than scared. This is ridiculous that we're having to surround Matt to keep him safe.'

'Well, I'm scared.' Flora spoke quietly. 'This is supernatural activity, Rose, something I've always pooh-poohed in the past, but suddenly it's very real. My God, even my vicar says it like it is, and I bet he's feeling out of his depth. Is he coming to Matt's tomorrow?'

Rose nodded. 'He is. I believe that his prayers saved all of us from death last time, so I'm trusting that will happen again if things turn nasty. Am I right, Mum? Do you think she's waiting for tomorrow to get Matt? Will she be at her strongest on the anniversary of her death?'

Flora bent down and opened the oven door, then took out the batch of bread cakes. She placed them on the cooling rack before turning to answer her daughter.

'I'm absolutely certain she's going to gather dark forces tomorrow. If I didn't think that, I wouldn't be going to Matt's house at some dreadful time in the morning. But you know the strength of my faith, Rose. He will keep us from harm.'

'She isn't here anymore, is she?'

'No,' Flora replied. 'I don't think she is, and I find that a bit disconcerting. Where is she? Already at Matt's house? In the vicarage? Quietly building her strength to maximum? She needs Matt dead so that he can be with her and not Beth, so I am in total agreement with what we're going to do tomorrow, but that's why we can't feel her here anymore. She has other places to be.'

They both turned as the sound of an engine drifted through the open window. Alan climbed out of the cab of the small truck and wandered across to the kitchen door. He took off his wellington boots and sniffed as he came into the kitchen.

'Smells good, lass. They for lunch?'

'Well, they're really to keep me busy, but they'll taste okay with some roast ham on them, I reckon,' she said, smiling at him. Things never seemed quite so dark and in turmoil when he was around, and she sensed Rose felt the same.

Rose grinned. 'So, can we have lunch early, while they're still warm?'

Alan looked at her. 'Tha's been brought up reight, lass, brought up dead reight,' and he went to wash his hands while his two favourite ladies prepared lunch, early lunch.

34

Beth went a little earlier to work on the Tuesday morning, keen to get on with cleaning the shelves. She had discussed where to start on the mammoth job the previous day, so was eager to get going.

She pulled into the car park and saw Miss Chambers' car already there. She grinned to herself and decided to give up – she would never be the first into work. She pulled an overall out of the boot, picked up her bag and walked across to the main doors, where she waved just as she did every day, seeking entrance into Miss Chambers' sanctum.

She made them both a cup of tea before heading off to the first aisle. They dusted the shelves every week, but every six months or so the books were actually taken off the shelves and a thorough cleaning was undertaken. Beth enjoyed this part of her job; she loved the feel of the books, and usually came across some little gem that she wanted to read.

With no members of the public in the library until ten o'clock, she felt safe singing along as she sprayed the lemon verbena scented polish, removing it and buffing the shelf with a fluffy yellow duster.

She sensed Miss Chambers' presence and then heard her speak. 'That lavender polish smells beautiful, Beth, simply beautiful.'

***

As soon as Beth left the house, Matt made three phone calls, simply saying *she's gone* each time the line connected.

Within two minutes the small house began to receive its visitors. Maria, Sue and James were the first to arrive, followed a minute later by Flora, Alan and Rose. They were all very subdued, uneasily waiting for Gareth to arrive; when he did, there was a collective exhalation of breath.

He took charge, leading them immediately in prayer. The chorus of *Amens* was heartfelt and they began to find seats, slowly beginning to speak to each other.

Matt asked how many wanted tea and Gareth said he would prefer if they just drank water, and nobody could go and get the water on their own. They nodded their agreement and James and Sue went into the kitchen, returning with an assortment of glasses and cups, and two jugs of water.

Matt apologised for the shortage of glasses – they didn't get any for wedding presents, was his explanation.

Gareth began to speak, asking them all to have their Bibles within touching distance, to remain close by each other, and to ignore the outside world. No telephone calls, no music, no television; he wanted them to focus purely on driving this entity away, and giving it rest.

The conversation didn't flow easily, and it was clear everyone was nervous, waiting for the unexpected to happen. The rattle of the letter box as post was delivered caused momentary panic, as did the knock on the door that later proved to be a meter reader promising to come back the following day.

There was unease; Matt's usual sense of humour was not in evidence and even Sue, known for her chatter, was abnormally silent. Flora was deep in thought; whatever else might happen on this difficult day, this was the anniversary of the death of her much-loved daughter, a girl who had been the light and the love of everyone surrounding her world. And she missed her, missed her so much.

She reached forward to get her glass of water and took a sip. As she did so she noticed the very first hint of the fragrance they had been dreading. She reached for Alan's hand and he looked at her and nodded. He too had noticed it.

And so had Gareth. 'Our Father, who art in Heaven, hallowed be thy name...'

The others joined in as the prayer progressed and the perfume began to drift lazily around the room.

'...for ever and ever, Amen.' All their heads remained bowed and every one of them heard the phrase *que sera sera* followed by a brief burst of manic laughter. The smell slowly dissipated and gradually they released each other's hands.

'Que sera sera?' Gareth queried.

Matt nodded. 'It was a phrase that Lavender used a lot. We watched a film called *The man who knew too much* one night; it had Doris Day and Stewart Granger in it. She heard Doris sing the song and it became her thing, her phrase. If I queried anything she would follow up with *que sera sera*.'

'James Stewart,' Alan said. 'It was James Stewart, not Stewart Granger.'

They all looked at him, and burst out laughing.

'You're absolutely right, Alan,' Matt said. 'I haven't thought about that film for some years now, and I got a bit mixed up. But that's taking us away from the issue.'

Flora nodded. 'It is. She was here, and now she isn't. She isn't in this room. The smell has gone. Did the Lord's Prayer drive her away? Or was she just showing us that we're powerless against her?'

'Don't let your guard down, any of you. Next time she could be here to show us just how destructive she can be. I need to keep reminding you that this isn't the Lavender you all knew and loved, this is some evil... thing... that is attacking all of us.' Gareth paused. 'And I believe that was just a taster to show us she can touch us whenever she wants, and she wants Matt dead and with her.'

***

By ten o'clock Beth had completely cleaned the first two sets of shelves. Any books out of order had been put back in the right place, and she had seen a couple of novels that had taken her fancy and been placed to one side ready for checking out before going home with her.

She put down her polish and duster in the small staffroom and switched on the kettle. She knew Miss Chambers would want a drink and she filled the teapot with boiling water. Today it was just the two of them; Tuesday was the slowest day of the week in their library and only required three members of staff. Rosalind, the other librarian, was taking a week's holiday, so Beth poured out just two cups of tea before carrying one through to Miss Chambers.

'You don't need me?'

Miss Chambers shook her head. 'No, you're fine to carry on, Beth. It's been very slow. Do you need a hand with the big one?'

She was referring to the large bookcase in the oldest section of the library that held reference books. It had its own sliding ladder for reaching the top three shelves and was tricky to clean.

'I'll see how I go. With only the two of us working it will be difficult for you to leave the desk. If I'm struggling with it, I'll leave it till Rosalind is back next week, and we can do it together.'

Miss Chambers nodded. 'That might be the best idea anyway. Thank you, Beth, you're a good worker.'

Beth was amazed. This was so out of character... she gave a small smile and carried her cup of tea back towards the huge book stand. She actually wanted to clean it herself. She loved it, loved the way the ladder moved with ease, the feel of the old books, the appearance of it after a coat of polish had been applied. She set her cup down on the table, slipped the polish and the duster into her pocket and climbed the ladder. She managed to clean the very top shelf by sliding books backwards and forwards, but the second shelf down had acquired some new books and she knew she would actually have to move some of them in order to create a space, so the rest could be moved around for her to dust underneath them. She figured if she carried a dozen or so down to the table, that should do it.

She carried six down on the first trip, and then went back up the ladder for the second half dozen. She was laying them carefully on the table when she heard the creak. She turned around and was aware of the bookcase beginning to move. The top began to lean and she heard herself shout. Within seconds it had crashed to the floor, stifling any sounds from Beth, burying her completely.

There was pandemonium as Miss Chambers and two library users tried to lift the heavy item of furniture. They managed to manoeuvre some books underneath it, slowly lifting it away from Beth's inert form, and then they heard the blessed sound of emergency vehicles. The professionals took over and within minutes the bookshelves had been moved away.

'Is she...?' Miss Chambers' voice was muted, as if she didn't really want an answer. The words almost stuck in her throat as she tried to get rid of the cloying sickly smell of lavender.

'Unconscious,' the paramedic said, as he slipped an oxygen mask over Beth's face. 'We'll get her moved into the ambulance, and then we can have a look and see if we need to do anything before transporting her. Does she have family?'

Erica Chambers' hand went to her mouth. 'Oh my God! She's newly married. I'd better ring her husband...' She hesitated, hoping someone else would say they were going to do it. Nobody did.

She watched as they lifted Beth's slight form and placed her in the back of the ambulance. Erica blinked several times, trying to clear her vision; it almost looked as if a silver haze was surrounding Beth, enveloping her completely. She shrugged and decided it was a trick of the light inside the ambulance; she turned and went back inside to make a very difficult telephone call. She hoped Matthew would still be on bereavement leave, because if he wasn't, she didn't know where he worked.

She picked up the receiver and dialled the number given to her only the day before by a happy and newly confident Beth. She waited and prayed someone would answer.

***

It was just after ten thirty when the sound of the telephone interrupted their thoughts and quiet chat.

They looked at each other and Gareth held out his hand, palm down.

'Don't move, don't answer it,' he said. 'Focus. We are protecting Matt, focus.'

The ringing tone seemed to go on forever, then stopped abruptly. One minute later it began again and they all just stared at the instrument.

Silence fell again until Matt spoke.

'This is ridiculous. We can't just sit around all day. What if she doesn't show? What if we're still all here when Beth gets home? How will I explain this, explain keeping it from her?'

'Tell her the truth, Matt,' Gareth said. 'Tell her that you protected her by having her away from the house on what we perceive to be the most dangerous day of all. She will understand.'

Matt stood and paced over towards the window, then turned and faced them all. 'I wish she'd come, let's face her head on, this Lavender thing. Let her try to take me, because one thing's for sure, I can't live the rest of my life like this.'

'Move away from the window, Matt, and come back into our circle, please. Don't make anyone else vulnerable because you're having a strop.'

Matt opened his mouth to argue, but then closed it again. Gareth was right; it wouldn't help to cause trouble. He moved back to join everyone else; the silence was uncomfortable.

They all heard the car pull up outside around midday but nobody moved. The knock on the door startled everyone.

Matt once again moved towards the window and peered through the lacy curtains.

He stepped backwards, clearly shocked.

'It's a police car,' he said, turning to face the others.

''I'll go,' Gareth said. 'Everybody, surround Matt. We don't know what this is.' He made the sign of the cross into the room and hurried down the hallway. He used caution in opening the door.

'Mr. Peterson?'

'No, sorry. Gareth Bruce, vicar at St. Edmund's. Can I help?'

'Is Mr. Peterson here?'

'Err... yes. You'd better come in.' Gareth stepped aside and led them through to the kitchen. 'I'll just get him.'

He went back to the lounge and spoke to Matt, saying they wanted to speak to him. 'Rose, come with me, will you? He can't go in there on his own, so if the two of us go in with him, it's a small amount of protection.'

Matt looked bewildered. 'Did they say what they want?'

'Just that they wanted to speak to you. Come on, we're with you,' and Gareth stepped aside for Matt to lead the way.

'Mr. Peterson?'

Matt confirmed with a nod, and then said 'What can I do for you?'

'There's been an accident, Mr. Peterson. Your wife...'

'What? Beth? Where is she? Is she hurt?'

'Please – sit down.' The younger of the two officers gestured towards a kitchen chair.

'I'll stand, thank you. What's happened?'

'It happened at work, at the library. I believe a Miss Chambers tried to contact you by telephone, but there was no answer. One of the large bookcases has collapsed on top of her. She has been taken to Buxton hospital. I can't give you any further details, but we can take you there now.'

Matt stared at them. 'Is she alive? What are you telling me?'

'When they took her in the ambulance her pulse was weak, but she was alive. She was unconscious. Do you need us to take you, sir?'

Gareth stepped in. 'No, officer, I'll take him. Thank you for coming out to tell Matt, but Rose and I will look after him and make sure he gets there within the hour.' He escorted the two men to the front door while Matt was putting on his jacket.

Rose was explaining to the others while putting on her own coat and within two minutes Rose, Gareth and Matt had left Castleton and were heading for the hospital.

The others tidied the cups and glasses away and went back to Maria's home to wait for news. They hardly spoke; they had nothing to say.

Matt jumped out of the car and began to run towards the main entrance. Gareth shouted, 'Matt!' and he stopped in his tracks, looking back towards his vicar.

'Wait,' he called. 'You're in danger. Wait for us.'

His head dropped and he knew Gareth was right. He would be no good to an injured Beth if he was dead at Lavender's hands.

All three of them entered the hospital together, Rose and Gareth flanking Matt at every step. They were directed to a waiting room and told a doctor would be with them as soon as he had finished examining Beth.

Their wait seemed interminable. Eventually the door opened and a doctor who looked much too young to bear the title walked in to meet them.

'Well, she's a very lucky lady in that she had sensible people who lodged books under the shelves to try and lift it off her. If they hadn't done that... Anyway, she's stable, but still unconscious. She's going for a scan and we'll know more after that, but she is breathing on her own. You can see her now, but she'll be taken to the scan room in about ten minutes.'

They followed him through to the small room where they were monitoring Beth, and Matt gave a small cry. She looked so fragile, so petite, and he leaned over to give her a kiss.

'Love you, Beth,' he whispered.

Rose walked around to the other side of the bed and she too bent over the still form and kissed her forehead. 'God bless you, Beth,' she said. There was no response and they looked at each other, knowing that they had got it so wrong.

The door opened and two porters came in, then disappeared with Beth. They looked at each other and Gareth said, 'Coffee?'

Rose went to get the drinks and they sat in the relatives' room waiting for news and talking quietly, skirting around what they should be talking about.

'There was no smell.' Matt sounded thoughtful.

Rose nodded. 'I know. And I expected that there would be. So, she's not here. I bet it reeked of lavender in the library though.'

'I'll speak to Miss Chambers tomorrow, assuming the library will be open. See if she mentions it. I can hardly ask her outright, as she'll think I'm an idiot. It sounds as though I owe her a huge thank you, as well.'

Rose smiled, 'Erica Chambers is one of the most sensible people I know, and it doesn't surprise me in the slightest that she saved Beth's life. I've known her for years – we were at school together – and I've always had a lot of time for her. Matt, I'm going to ring your mum, let her know what's going on, and I'll tell her you'll be staying with her tonight, yes?'

He shook his head. 'No. I'm staying here.'

'Oh, no.' Gareth was firm. 'If you stay here you're away from our protection, and vulnerable. We can't leave you here. You need to come back with us and at least one of us will come back to the hospital with you tomorrow. This may be Lavender's strongest day, but it doesn't mean she's weak once this day is finished. Far from it. I can't force you, Matt, but please do as I ask.'

Matt acknowledged defeat by resting his elbows on his knees and dropping his head. Whichever way he turned he couldn't win.

'If she's still unconscious when they bring her back to her room, I'll go home with you. If she's awake, I'm staying.'

They finished their drinks as the nurse called them back into the side room. Beth was back and still oblivious to everything.

'There's no major damage. She'll be bruised, badly bruised, but she will come out of this. We're keeping her in here until she does wake up, because we can monitor her more closely. I suggest you all go home, get some rest tonight and be back for visiting at ten o'clock. I'm sure she will have come round by then.'

'You'll ring me if she wakes during the night?' Matt looked anxious.

The nurse smiled at him. 'If that's what you want me to do, but we can take care of her, you know.'

'I know. It's just...'

'Go home, Matt. Sleep. Come back for ten o'clock. Beth will be fine.'

She ushered them out of the door.

35

Matt was waiting outside the ward doors ten minutes before they opened. The telephone call at just after nine had been to tell him that Beth had woken up and within five minutes he had been in the car and on his way to Buxton.

He was first in the queue as the doors were opened and moved to the bedside to give Beth a kiss.

Then he stepped back and looked at her. 'You've got a black eye.'

'And a bit of a crushed chest,' she said. Her voice was slightly husky.

'Are you in pain?'

'Not really. The morphine's seeing to that. Now stop worrying. I'll be home in a couple of days, as good as I ever was.'

He nodded. 'I thought I'd lost you, Beth. Don't scare me like this again! So how are you feeling, and tell me the truth...'

'Oh, you know me... que—'

'You're not okay! Stop being brave. A bloody great book case fell on you, to say nothing of hundreds of books.'

Beth smiled.

***

There was no change in John. Rose kissed him gently and then sat down and told him everything that had happened.

'So now we have two of our merry band in hospital and no end to the nightmare. I'm going to Paris on Saturday to bring home the children. Everything seems to have gone quiet at home, no smell of lavender, no activity – I know I'm taking a massive risk, but the children need to be in school, they need to be at home with me. Or preferably, with us.'

There was nothing; no reaction of any sort.

'It seems that this thing, this spirit, can travel at will, so what's to stop her attacking the children in France? She almost killed Beth in Buxton, so we know that she can move around to wherever she wants.'

She stared at her husband for a long moment. 'God, John, I'm missing you so much. If you can hear me, just move a finger, or blink, or something. Give me hope, my love.'

She waited a few minutes then left the room, returning five minutes later with a coffee. She sat and chatted quietly, telling him of Richard's unhappiness at her leaving her job, filling him in on his own work, the company he had painstakingly built up, and confirmed she was taking over the administration side. There was still no response; she knew there wouldn't be.

She finished her coffee, threw away the cardboard cup and put on her coat.

'I'm going home,' she said, 'but if you feel like a chat later, give me a ring.' She smiled to herself and left the room. She met Gary Bailey as she walked down the corridor and stopped to speak with him, but he had nothing new to tell her.

'We have absolutely no idea why he won't wake up. He's breathing on his own; nothing is showing on any tests, he's simply asleep. As you've seen, we've removed all his plaster casts, so he could be at home with you now, if he was awake. Something in his brain is saying it's better to be asleep, and so that's what's happened.'

She thanked him and walked away from the hospital and towards the car park, feeling thoroughly down-hearted and miserable.

***

Rose was startled to hear the ringing of her mobile phone. She fished it out from the bottom of her bag and answered with some trepidation.

'Hello?'

'Hi, Rose, it's Matt.'

She breathed a sigh of relief. 'Thank goodness for that. I was afraid it was the hospital...'

'Oh, sorry. I rang you on this one because I need a chat and I didn't want you to have to sit in the hall and talk to me.'

She laughed. 'You're always so thoughtful, Matt Peterson. Is everything okay? Mum said Beth might be coming home tomorrow.'

'Hopefully she will be. I've had a chat with work, and they've told me not to worry, to take the rest of the week off. I told them what had happened, of course, and they were full of sympathy.' He felt as though he was babbling. 'What do you think happened, Rose?'

'Matt, I don't think it takes a genius to work out that we underestimated Lavender's power. We knew she would be at her strongest yesterday but we thought it would be you she would attack. We thought we were doing the right thing by sending Beth off to work and not telling her anything, protecting her. Never in a million years did I suspect she would attack Beth, and she obviously intended to kill her. If it hadn't been for Erica Chambers...'

'I know,' Matt responded. Rose heard him sigh. 'She's always one step in front, isn't she? We think we can outwit her, and we damn well can't. Is this it for the rest of our lives? Is she going to keep wanting me until eventually she causes my death? Because believe me, Rose, I'd rather die right this minute than have anyone else in our circle die.'

'Matthew Peterson, don't you ever make stupid statements like that again. Gareth will have the answer, I'm sure. He was starting to tell us something yesterday when the police arrived. Trust him, keep the faith.'

'Don't worry, I'm not going to kill myself, I'm just telling you how I feel. It was when I heard Beth's voice, heard the deeper tones in it, that I realised just how near I had come to losing her. Her voice was like that, she said, because her chest was crushed.'

'Look, go to bed and try to sleep. If you're bringing your lovely Beth home tomorrow, you'll be busy all day, so sleep well tonight and for heaven's sake, ring me if you need me. Okay?'

'Okay,' he laughed. 'You always cheer me up, Rose Broadbent. I love you.'

'And I love you. Now go to bed. Night, God bless.'

She smiled as she switched off the call. He would have been a lovely brother-in-law, and if only the clock could be turned back...

36

Thursday morning was a bright, autumnal morning and Beth drew in a deep breath as she stood on the hospital steps.

'That feels good,' she said. 'It was so hot all the time in there. Come on, let's call round at the library.'

'What?'

'It's only a couple of minutes away and I want to say thank you to Miss Chambers. And let her see I'm alive,' she said with a smile. 'I can't imagine how it must have been for her...'

Matt looked at her for a moment. 'Okay, five minutes and no longer. They said you need to rest. Now get in the car, woman. I want you home by lunchtime, no arguments.'

'I know, but it's important to me.'

He kissed her. 'Come on then, and hold on to my arm.'

She limped across the car park, and sank gratefully into the passenger seat. 'I'm a bit stiff,' she said.

'A bit stiff? Slight understatement. Remember – five minutes to say thank you, then we're going home.'

She nodded. 'I hear you, oh master,' and she laid her head back and closed her eyes.

As they walked through the door of the library five minutes later, Miss Chambers hurried across to them.

'Oh, it's so good to see you, Beth. I was going to pop round to the hospital later...'

'No need, Miss Chambers. Really, I'm fine. Just a bit stiff and sore, but that will go and they've given me plenty of painkillers. I just came round to thank you, because I know you saved my life. If you hadn't thought to stack books to hold that unit off me, I could have died.' Beth leaned forward and kissed Erica Chambers on the cheek.

'Oh, don't be silly, girl, I don't need thanks.'

'Yes, you do. And I need to go and look where it happened.' She held up a hand. 'No, Matt, on my own.'

'But...'

'On my own.'

She walked away from them and round the first two shelving units. Then she arrived at the space that had ruined her day. The unit had been righted and all the books replaced, but it was now fixed firmly to the wall. She stood looking at it for a minute, then smiled and walked back round to join Matt.

'I'm okay now. Can we go home, Matt?'

'We can. Thank you again, Miss Chambers. I don't know what I would have done...'

Erica Chambers touched his hand. 'That's absolutely fine, Matthew. Now take her home. And you, young Beth, take as long as you need to get better.'

She watched them walk to the car and offered up a small thank you to a God she wasn't sure she believed in. It never hurt to say thank you, she figured.

She took a couple of books back in and then went to replace them on the shelves. As she passed the unit that had fallen she was aware of the strange smell again, the one that she had put down to the furniture polish Beth had been using. It clearly wasn't from that. She doubted Beth would be doing polishing of any sort for a while! Then she spotted the small sprigs of lavender, one on each shelf, and she shivered.

She had no idea who had put them there – she was as sure as anything that it hadn't been Beth, she had carried nothing in her hands – but she swept them all into her own hands and dumped them unceremoniously into a waste bin. If anybody was going to put flowers in her library, it would be her.

Maria was waiting at their home when they arrived. Sue and James had gone into Sheffield, she explained, and she wanted to see for herself that Beth was okay. Besides, she'd made some soup for lunch.

Matt smiled at her. 'Thank you. Soup it is then. I'll settle Beth into the lounge and we'll have it on trays in there.'

Beth limped through to the armchair and sank down with a sigh. 'It's so good to be back. I'm ready for some painkillers and maybe later I'll have a bath.'

'Just say when, and I'll run it for you.' He kissed her gently and went into the kitchen.

Maria heard Beth giggle as she carried the first of three trays through. She placed it on Beth's lap and smiled. 'You sound happy. That's a corker of a black eye you have – suppose it's too late to slap some steak on it.'

'There's no steak going on my eye,' she laughed. 'If there's steak going anywhere, it's in the freezer.'

'Well, I have to admire you, Beth. You sound really happy – bit hoarse so it's not quite the voice we know – but happy.'

'That's because I am. I didn't die so I'm clearly meant to live; que sera sera!'

Matt froze. He hadn't heard that phrase since Lavender's death, but he had certainly heard it many times before that. It had been her favourite sing-along song. He experienced a brief flashback to the day he had asked her to marry him and she had asked for time to think. She had explained it wasn't because she didn't love him; it was because she was starting at university and then she had sung Que Sera Sera to him. What will be, will be.

So why had Beth said it?

He was quiet throughout the meal and he left Beth alone for a few minutes while he walked Maria back to her own cottage.

'Do you think Beth is... different?'

Maria tilted her head to one side. 'Why do you ask?'

'Oh, nothing. I just think she doesn't seem the same. Maybe it's the drugs they've pumped into her to help with the pain.'

'Mmmm, maybe. We've had six months and more of nothing being right, Matt. All I will say is, be careful. You're absolutely right, there is something different, but strong painkillers do change people. She'll be fine when she's just managing with paracetamol. But be careful, sweetheart. I can't lose either of you two.'

He kissed her cheek. 'I know, Mum. I'll head off back when I see you inside your house. Love you.'

'Love you, too,' she said, before going through the front door. He waited for a moment until he saw her wave through the net curtain, and then he walked back home, deep in thought. Que sera sera. Coincidence? Maybe, if taken as a single incident, but in view of the terror of the last few months he ruled that out.

So just what did it mean?

Why had Beth been allowed to live?

He pushed it to the back of his mind because Beth asked him to run a bath when he got home.

'I'll have a soak then go and have a lie down for an hour. Is that okay?'

'Of course,' he said. 'I'll run it now.'

She followed him upstairs a few minutes later and he helped her undress.

'Wow! Your back is a mess. Bruised all over!'

'Yes, when Lavender does something, she really gets it right, doesn't she?'

Her back and thighs were purple and he realised anew just how lucky she had been. Or was it luck?

He shook the thought from his head, helped her into the bath and left her to soak. 'Give me a shout when you're ready to get out,' he said. 'Don't hurt yourself by trying to get out on your own.'

'Thank you, sweetheart. This is so good.'

She rested her head on the bath pillow and closed her eyes. Matt looked at her and went downstairs. He heard her begin to sing, something he had found totally endearing at the beginning of their relationship, and he smiled. It was only as he heard which song she was singing that he felt the unease start to settle on him again. "Back for Good", a Take That song; he heard her pretty voice singing *I just want you back for good.*

He pulled out a notepad and began to write things down while they were still fresh in his mind, still listening to the words coming out of Beth's mouth. Back for Good.

1. Que sera sera.
2. Not Dead. Why not?
3. Smiling and happy. Who is? Lavender or Beth?
4. Remarkably fast recovery? Is Beth there at all?
5. Voice is different.

6. Am I now married to Lavender?
7. Was this the plan all along? Did we read her wrong?
8. Played right into her hands on Tuesday.

He sat with his head in his hands for a while, just trying to rearrange his points into some sort of logical order. It was then he heard the song she was singing become even more familiar to him; que sera sera, whatever will be, will be.

He heard Beth call for him and he put the notepad away; she couldn't see it.

After helping her from the bath, he dried her back very gently, and then assisted her into her pyjamas. She closed her eyes immediately and he moved to the door.

'You haven't kissed me.' He stopped. Did he want to kiss her? He returned to her bedside and leaned down, brushing her lips gently with his.

'Sleep tight,' he whispered.

'Love you,' she said.

'Love you, too.'

He headed back downstairs and took out the notepad once more. He stared at the words he had written; he struggled to accept the conclusions he was drawing.

It was driving him mad and he put the notepad away. It was all in his imagination, he couldn't destroy his newly married relationship just because his head was being played with.

He heard Beth get up and go to the bathroom, then head back to the bedroom, so he went upstairs to see if she needed anything.

'No thank you, I'm fine. I'm going to stay in bed because the painkillers make me drowsy and I can just nod off whenever I feel like it. You can join me if you want.'

'No, I'm fine. I'm going to make something to eat, a sandwich or something. What about you?'

She shook her head. 'No, not bothered, thanks, maybe a hot chocolate later, but I don't want anything at the moment. I'm going to read for a bit.'

He nodded and went back downstairs. His evening passed quietly and when he went upstairs to go to bed, Beth was fast asleep, her hot chocolate left to congeal on the bedside table.

He slid into bed by her side and lay awake until just after two o'clock, then he got out of bed and went back downstairs.

He took out the notepad and wrote two letters, one to his mother and one to Rose. He placed them carefully in a cupboard and then went back to bed.

37

Matt was up an hour before he heard Beth stir. He heard her go into the bathroom and then she came downstairs, her hair tousled, and with a smile on her face.

'Can we do something?'

'I was going to suggest the same thing. It's a lovely day, bit cool. Shall we go into Sheffield, have a walk round and maybe a spot of lunch?' he responded.

'That would be lovely. 'I'll have a quick shower and if you can make me a slice of toast...?'

'No problem. I'll bring the car round.'

She nodded and went back upstairs, still favouring her left leg. He walked around to the garage and drove the car round to their front door.

She was coming down the stairs as he walked back through the door. 'I'll put a slice of toast in for you.'

'Thank you. Have I done something wrong?'

'No, of course not,' he replied. 'Why would you think that?'

'You're quiet, and I haven't had my good morning kiss.'

'That can soon be arranged,' he said, and laughed. A forced laugh. He kissed her and moved into the kitchen.

The toast took a couple of minutes and he made her a cup of coffee to go with it. He watched her drink it, and knew he was right. Beth never drank coffee, hated even the smell of it.

He took her cup and plate away and washed them, then dried them and put them away. She stood in the kitchen doorway.

'Do I look okay?'

He smiled. 'Better than okay. Slightly marred by the black eye, but you always did look beautiful.'

He helped ease her into the passenger seat then walked around to his own side.

'Damn. I haven't picked up my wallet. Give me a minute.'

He went back inside, took out the two letters, kissed both of them before placing them on the table and went back out to the car.

'All set?'

She nodded. 'It's certainly a lovely day for an illicit jaunt,' she joked. 'We should both really be in work.'

'Let's just enjoy it.'

He drove out of the village, through Hope and on to Bamford. He stopped at the traffic lights momentarily and then began to pick up speed on the long straight stretch heading towards Hathersage. He had reached 65 miles an hour when he turned to his wife.

'Lavender?'

'Yes, my love?'

He put his foot down further and heard her gasp as his left hand clicked open the seat belts. He approached the bridge at something approaching 80 miles an hour, closed his eyes and kept the car going in a straight line.

They hit the bridge and life was extinct within seconds.

Blackness.

38

'Mrs. Broadbent? Rose? It's the Hallamshire Hospital.'

'Yes?' She trembled. She always rang them, they didn't ring her.

'It's John. Your husband. He's awake and asking for you.'

Her shout of laughter echoed down the phone. 'I'll be there in half an hour or so. Is he okay?'

'He's absolutely fine. Wants to know what's been going on in the world.'

'I'm on my way.'

She called through to Flora and Alan to tell them the news and ran out to get in her car.

She negotiated the bad bends through her home village, then the curvy road through Hope before hitting the traffic lights at Bamford. She was faced with a diversion sign sending her up into the village of Bamford because two police cars were blocking the straight stretch of road leading to Hathersage.

She shook her head in annoyance. This would add an extra ten minutes or so on to her journey. As usual, it would be a road traffic accident, probably caused by speed.

Would people never learn about this dangerous stretch of road; never learn that speed kills?

She put on her left indicator to follow the diversion signs and saw the policeman controlling the traffic was Adam Morton. She lowered her driver window and waved at him. He looked startled and walked over towards her.

'Mrs. Broadbent... Rose.'

'Is it another accident?'

'Mrs. Broadbent, you might want to pull in over there...'

THE END

Acknowledgements

My first thank you has to go to Dave, my husband of fifty years, who patiently waits for me to finish a writing session so that we can do non-literary things like shopping! He is also my biggest publicist, telling everyone he meets that his wife is an author and they should buy her books.

Secondly, I have to thank my publishers, Betsy and Fred Freeman of Bloodhound Books for continuing to support me and believe in me. You're amazing.

I also have three people to thank for making an appearance in Winterscroft – Val Spencer, Karen Aristocleous and Gary Bailey. Karen Aristocleous also deserves a second thank you; in a competition launched by me she came up with the name Winterscroft for the house in the book, a worthy winner.

My book publicist Helen Claire deserves a special mention; she puts in lots of hours for all the Bloodhound authors, a lovely lady.

And special thanks go to Sarah Kenny, who listens to me when I need to have a rant, and calms me down. She will be organising the online book launch party for Winterscroft so a good night will be had by all!

My final thank you is to three ladies who join me as Wordsmiths, a small but select group of four who chat constantly, but more importantly give invaluable encouragement, feedback and love. A massive thank you to Donna Maria McCarthy, Audrina Lane and Rita McDermott Ames; stars, all of you. Wordsmiths united!